PRAISE FOR THE NOVELS OF
#1 NEW YORK TIMES BESTSELLING AUTHOR
BARBARA FREETHY

"I love *The Callaways*! Heartw~~~~~ ~~~~ ~~~~ pense
and sexy alpha heroes. What ~ ~~~~~~~~~~~~~~~~~~~~~~~~~~~ ***Andre***

"I adore *The Callaways*, a fami ~~~~~~~~~~~~~~~~~~~ ..ew
book is a deft combination of ei ~~~~~~~~~~~ ..c..se and family
dynamics. A remarkable, compelling series!"
-- *USA Today Bestselling Author **Barbara O'Neal***

"Once I start reading a Callaway novel, I can't put it down. Fast-
paced action, a poignant love story and a tantalizing mystery in every
book!"
-- *USA Today Bestselling Author **Christie Ridgway***

"Barbara manages to weave a perfect romance filled with laughter,
love, a lot of heat, and just the right amount of suspense. I highly
recommend *SO THIS IS LOVE* to anyone looking for a sexy romance
with characters you will love!"
-- ***Harlequin Junkie***

"*BETWEEN NOW AND FOREVER* is a beautifully written story.
Fans of Barbara's Angel's Bay series will be happy to know the
search leads them to Angel's Bay where we get to check in with
some old friends."
-- ***The Book Momster Blog***

"In the tradition of LaVyrle Spencer, gifted author Barbara Freethy
creates an irresistible tale of family secrets, riveting adventure and
heart-touching romance."
-- *NYT Bestselling Author **Susan Wiggs**
on Summer Secrets*

Also By Barbara Freethy

To my amazing and brilliant daughter Kristen!

ALL A HEART NEEDS

The Callaways

BARBARA FREETHY

HYDE STREET PRESS
Published by Hyde Street Press
1819 Polk Street, Suite 113, San Francisco, California 94109

© Copyright 2015 by Hyde Street Press

All A Heart Needs, is a work of fiction. All incidents, dialogue and all characters are products of the author's imagination and are not to be construed as real. Any resemblance to persons living or dead is entirely coincidental.

Printed in the United States of America

Cover design by Damonza.com
Interior book design by KLF Publishing

ISBN: 978-0-9906951-4-1

One

⟶⟫⟪⟵

She was beginning a new adventure, Jessica Schilling thought as she walked through the doors of Drake's, a nightclub in San Francisco's North Beach neighborhood, with her friends, Nicole and Emma. She was on the verge of something exciting; she just didn't know what that something was yet. But it had to be better than what had come before.

At twenty-seven, she'd lived through a lot in the past three years, the death of her husband, the kidnapping of her stepson, and a move to San Francisco after her son had been reunited with his twin brother, Brandon. It had been a crazy couple of months. She was definitely not living the life she'd ever imagined for herself, but she was going to try to keep rolling with the punches.

But tonight wasn't about the past; it was about fun and letting loose a little. She hadn't been to a club like this in four years, not since she'd gone from Vegas dancer to wife and stepmother. She hadn't ventured out on a Friday night to do something other than pick up pizza or take her kid to a movie in months, and she was looking forward to a night out with the girls.

She'd traded in her usual jeans and a t-shirt for a red mini-skirt, high-heeled black boots, and a lacy top under a short black jacket. She wore her long brown hair down, and it now danced around her shoulders in thick waves. She'd put on more make-up than she'd worn in years, and for the first time in a long time she felt young again, hopeful, maybe even a little reckless.

"It's packed in here," Emma Callaway shouted, as they walked through the crowded room.

Emma was a slender woman with short, silky blonde hair that angled off her face and highlighted her bright blue eyes. Emma wore skinny jeans with high heels and a silky sheer blouse over a black camisole. On the other side of Emma was Emma's older sister, Nicole, who had blond hair that was a little longer than Emma's and eyes that were a lighter shade of blue. Nicole had upped her look tonight by trading in her usual conservative mom clothes for a short, clingy dress that showed off her legs and curves.

"I told you we should have come earlier," Nicole said with a frown. "Drake's is always packed on a Friday night."

"I couldn't get off work," Emma replied.

"You always use that excuse, Em."

"Because it's always true."

Jessica let their argument go on without her. She'd gotten to know Emma and Nicole pretty well the last few months, and she was used to their friendly bickering. She'd been an only child, so she was often fascinated by their sisterly interaction and wished she had a sibling to not only spar with but also share her life with. And Emma and Nicole didn't just have each other. They were part of the big Callaway family and had six other siblings, one of whom they'd come to see perform tonight. Her heart fluttered at that thought, knowing that the invitation of a night out with the girls had become much more exciting when Emma had told her they were going to see Sean's band perform.

She'd met Emma and Nicole's brother, Sean, three months

ago during the kidnapping ordeal. Nicole's son, Brandon, had also been taken, and it was then that they'd discovered the six-year-old boys were identical twins that had been separated at birth.

During that terrible time, Jessica had found an instant connection with Sean, and she'd often wondered since then if they'd met under different circumstances or at a different time, if they would have acted on the attraction between them. But on the few occasions she'd seen Sean since she'd moved to San Francisco, he'd been stand-offish, making her wonder if she'd imagined the sparks, or if they'd only been on her side.

Not that it mattered. She wasn't looking to get involved with anyone, much less a musician. She had her hands full raising her son and sharing co-parenting duties with Nicole and her husband, Ryan. Since the boys had been reunited, they'd all agreed that it was important to keep them together as much as possible.

But she wasn't going to think about all that tonight. She was excited to see Sean perform, and there was a small, slightly vain, part of herself that thought it would be nice for him to see her at her best and not at her worst. Maybe it wouldn't be so easy for him to ignore her.

She should probably be careful what she wished for, because while Sean's disinterest bothered her, she didn't know what she would do if he were interested. Love had always scared her, and having lost her husband in an accident sixteen months earlier, she was all too aware that pain was often the flip side of love.

"I'm going to get drinks," Emma announced. "Find a spot by the stage, and I'll catch up with you."

"I feel old with all these twenty-somethings," Nicole muttered as they weaved their way through the crowd. Then she added quickly, "Sorry, Jessica. I sometimes forget that you're six years younger than me. You're so mature, and I mean that in a good way."

She'd always been mature, forced to grow up early. "No worries. I actually feel kind of old, too. I don't exactly have a *clubbing* kind of life anymore."

"Do you miss that life?" Nicole asked, a curious gleam in her blue eyes. "I can see why you would. You're only twenty-seven. Most people your age are leading a *clubbing* kind of life."

"I don't really miss it. I wouldn't trade my life as Kyle's mom for anything, but lately I've been feeling a little..." She tried to come up with the right word to describe her mood. "Restless. I needed a night out."

"I know that feeling well. Let's make the most of it."

"The most of what?" Emma asked as she rejoined them.

"Our night," Nicole said.

"That's the right attitude," Emma said with an approving smile as she handed them their drinks.

"What's this?" Jessica gave the glass of amber-colored liquid a wary look.

"Fireball whiskey. It's not as dangerous as it sounds."

Jessica took a sip and immediately liked the cinnamon flavor. She had no idea how strong it was, but she didn't have to take care of anyone tonight. Kyle was spending the night at Nicole's house, under the supervision of Nicole's husband, Ryan, so she was a free woman, and she was going to enjoy herself.

"They're starting," Nicole said.

Jessica turned toward the stage as Sean and his band walked out. Sean wore faded jeans that hung low on his hips and a button-down light blue shirt that emphasized his broad shoulders. His brown hair was thick and a little on the longish side, curling around his collar. His deep blue eyes showed anticipation and excitement as he grabbed his guitar and stepped up to the microphone.

The rest of the band took their places, but Jessica didn't see any of the other guys. Her gaze was solely on Sean, her heart beating way too fast, her stomach fluttering with a desire she thought had gone dormant after the death of her husband. It was back now and in full force.

She tried to tell herself that it was the whisky sending a shiver down her spine, but when Sean looked into the crowd, directly at her, she knew her nervous tension had nothing to do with the Fireball and everything to do with him.

Sean held her gaze for a long moment and then his lips slowly curved into a smile.

She smiled back, at the same time feeling a little foolish for even considering that he was actually looking at her. There were lots of women in the crowd, and who knew what he could see beyond the bright lights?

With a *one-two-three*, the band began to play, a lively beat with a rock and roll edge. Sean was the lead singer, his deep baritone voice raising the hairs on the back of her neck. As he sang, he brought the crowd into the music. He made the words mean something. He was in complete and absolute control on that stage, and they were all just along for the ride.

It was an amazing thing to watch. Sean had been born to do this. He was truly living out his dream. How many people could say they were doing that? Certainly not her. She wasn't even sure what her dream was anymore.

She reminded herself that Sean's dream was a solo journey. Musicians were notorious for failed relationships, unable to commit to one person, which was completely understandable considering the love affair they could have every night on the stage surrounded by beautiful women. She'd lived through her mom's fascination with musicians, watching her date one guitar player after another. Her mom always thought she was the one being sung to, that the lyrics of love and longing had been written just for her. But that was almost never the case.

Jessica had criticized her mother for being foolish, telling her to look at reality, stop making decisions based on her heart. Now she felt guilty at how harsh she'd been, because she could feel the magic of Sean's music wrapping itself around her like a warm pair of arms, drawing her in, whispering in her ear, making her feel like she was the only woman in the room.

She blew out a breath and downed the rest of her drink in one long swallow. She wouldn't make the same mistake her mom had made so many times. But she didn't have to leave. She was just here to have fun, and that's what she intended to do.

At some point in the set, Emma handed her another drink.

"Thanks," she said, enjoying the warming slide of liquid down her throat. She began to sway with the beat, thinking how long it had been since she'd wanted to dance. She'd given up dancing when she got married, but now she was starting to miss it.

The crowd burst into applause as Sean's band finished their encore. Despite shouts for more, they finally made their way off the stage, and the lights came up.

"That was awesome," Emma said, her face lit up with excitement and pride. "I can't believe my brother is that good."

"I never thought Sean would be this talented when we were kids," Nicole agreed. "He used to drive us crazy practicing his guitar every other second. I guess it paid off."

"Should we get another drink?" Emma asked. "Do we want to stay for the next act? I think it starts in about fifteen minutes."

"Not me," Nicole said with a shake of her head. "I have to get up early tomorrow and be a mom."

Nicole's words made Jessica feel guilty. "I should go, too."

"No, you should stay," Nicole said firmly. "Kyle is already asleep at my house. Relax and enjoy yourself."

"What do you think, Jess?" Emma asked.

"I'll stay." It was an easy decision. She wasn't at all ready to leave yet.

"I'll walk Nicole out and make sure she gets a cab," Emma said. "Do you want to get us another drink, Jessica?"

"Sure." She made her way to the bar as Emma and Nicole left. There was a long line, so she was in for a wait. As she glanced around, she saw Sean coming out of the hallway, heading in her direction.

Her pulse began to race, and her mouth went dry. He was even sexier up close, and she couldn't stop the tingle that ran through her body. It was silly. She felt like a teenage girl with a crush on a rock star. She needed to get a grip. Despite the mental reprimand, she couldn't help feeling pleased that Sean passed by a lot of other women on his way to her.

"Jessica," he said, a husky note in his voice. "I was surprised to see you in the crowd."

So he had seen her. He had smiled at her. She wasn't completely crazy.

"Ryan offered to watch the boys so Nicole and I could come. Emma is here, too."

"Yeah, I saw them. Where are they now?"

"Nicole is on her way home. Emma went to help her get a cab. She'll be right back." Jessica was rambling, but Sean's gaze was so deep and intense that she felt more than a little rattled. She tucked her hair behind her ear, feeling self-conscious under his close scrutiny. "You're staring. Do I have something in my teeth?"

"No. But you look—different."

Her cheeks warmed under his smile. "I hope in a good way."

"In a beautiful way. It's great to see you out enjoying yourself."

"It's nice to be out. It's been a while."

The crowd jostled her from behind, and she found herself suddenly pushed against Sean's broad chest. She grabbed his strong arms as his hands settled on her waist. His touch was firm, almost possessive, and he didn't seem in a hurry to let go.

She didn't want to let go, either. In fact, she was fighting back the urge to pull him even closer. Her brain screamed at her to step back, move away, say something, but she couldn't seem to do anything but look at him.

His deep blue eyes darkened as he gazed down at her. His lips parted, his breath hitting her mouth like a kiss—a kiss she very much wanted.

"Jess," he murmured. "Beautiful Jess. What am I going to do about you?"

The tender, caressing words washed through her like a hot silky breeze. Everything else faded away. The only person she could see was Sean. The only voice she could hear was his.

The crowd swelled around them, and Sean pulled her closer. It was her undoing. With his hard body against hers, she felt an incredible, reckless yearning.

She didn't know who moved first—it was probably her. All she knew was that she felt an imperative need to kiss him, and when their lips came together, it felt absolutely right. She sank into the kiss, loving the taste of his warm mouth, the pressure of his firm lips, and the way he held her against him, as if he never wanted to let her go.

Another jostling move from the crowd broke them apart. Sean's hands dropped from her waist. He stared at her with an unreadable gaze. She wanted to say something, but she was having trouble catching her breath. What the hell had she just done?

"Jess," he began.

She waited for him to say more, but he couldn't seem to find words.

Then Emma appeared at her side. Jessica was more than

grateful for the interruption. She was also relieved that Emma hadn't arrived a minute earlier and seen them kissing.

"Sean, what a great show." Emma gave her brother a hug. "Your best yet, I think."

"Thanks." He cleared his throat. "Glad you could make it, Em."

"How's this next group?"

"They're good. I'm going to get a drink. Do you two want one?"

"I'll take another Fireball," Emma said.

"Jess?"

"Nothing for me." Another drink was not a good idea. She'd already made one bad decision.

As Sean made his way to the bar, Emma gave her a curious smile. "Everything okay?"

"Uh, sure." At the sound of a female squeal, her gaze moved from Emma to the tall blonde woman who had just launched herself into Sean's arms. "Who's that?"

"Never seen her before, but she looks like Sean's type."

"Which is what?"

"Tall, skinny, blonde, big boobs. You know, every man's type."

"She is attractive." Jessica felt a twinge of jealousy as the woman put her arm around Sean's waist and leaned in close to whisper something in his ear.

Jessica deliberately turned her back on Sean and faced the stage as the next group came on. Their first song was more loud than good, and her ears were ringing when it finished. Emma tipped her head toward the back of the room, and they found a quieter space away from the speakers.

"Better," Emma said.

"Yes. I'm not sure how much I can take of this group though. Not my favorite."

"They're definitely not as entertaining as Sean's band."

At the end of the next song, Sean found them. He handed Emma her drink and then took a swig of his beer. For a few moments they just watched the band.

Jessica felt more than a little uncomfortable. She didn't know if she should apologize to Sean or pretend the kiss had never happened.

When the next song ended, Emma turned to her brother. "So who was the blonde you were talking to?"

"Laura. She's a friend of Trevor's fiancée."

"Are you seeing her?" Emma asked. "Is she your girlfriend?"

Jessica shifted her feet, waiting for his answer but trying to act like it didn't matter in the slightest, because it shouldn't matter. She might have kissed him, but she wasn't stupid enough to think it meant anything.

"I don't have time to see anyone," he said. "I'm too busy for a girlfriend."

Sean wasn't looking in her direction, but Jessica still wondered if his comment was directed at her.

"That's just another way of saying you haven't met someone you want to make time for," Emma said, sipping her drink.

He shrugged and turned back to the stage as the band played on.

After two more songs and five more minutes of awkwardness, Jessica was more than ready to call it a night. Noting Emma's now empty glass, she decided to make a break for it. "Are you ready to go, Emma? I have a lot to do tomorrow with the move, and I should probably get home. Or I can go on my own if you want to stay."

"I'm fine to leave."

"The move?" Sean interrupted, speaking directly to her for the first time since their kiss. "Are you going somewhere, Jessica?"

"Yes, to a house around the corner from your parents. My apartment building went condo, so I had to find a new place to live."

"That sucks."

"I'm not thrilled having to move again so soon, but I'm looking forward to getting back into a house with a yard."

"She's moving into the Emery house," Emma interjected.

Sean's jaw dropped, and something dark and unreadable flashed through his eyes. "What? What did you say?"

"She's moving into the Emery house," Emma repeated, her gaze filling with concern. "Sean? Are you all right?"

It was a good question Jessica thought. Sean had gone white at the mention of her house.

"I can't believe it," he muttered. His gaze swung from Emma to her. "How could you be moving into that house?"

"Nicole heard that Mrs. Emery was moving into an assisted living facility and wanted to rent out her house," Jessica explained, wondering why Sean was so disturbed by her news. "In exchange for a discount on the rent, I'm going to clear out her attic. Apparently, she's built up a ton of stuff over the years and has never been able to throw anything out." She paused, frowning. "Is there something wrong with the house?"

"There was a fire. Two people died. One was a little girl," he said shortly.

Jessica was taken aback by his words and by what now appeared to be anger in his eyes. "No one told me about a fire."

"I told Nicole that she should mention it to you," Emma said. "But she didn't think it was a big deal. I'm surprised Helen didn't tell you."

Jessica wondered the same thing. "When did it happen? Was it recently?"

"No, it was a long time ago," Emma replied. "Twenty years, right, Sean?"

He gave a tight nod.

"That's why Nicole didn't think it was important, and I'm sure Helen doesn't like to talk about it since it was her son and granddaughter died in the fire," Emma added.

"I didn't know," Jessica said again, trying to catch Sean's gaze, but he wasn't looking at her anymore. In fact, he wasn't looking at anyone. He seemed to be completely lost in thought. "Sean—"

"I have to go," he said, cutting her off. "Thanks for coming tonight."

As Sean took off, Jessica frowned and said, "What am I missing, Emma?"

"Sean and Stacy, the little girl who died, were best friends. In fact, she was playing at our house earlier that day. I guess the memory hit him really hard. It's kind of strange. Sean rarely gets worked up over anything. He's always super chill, sometimes annoyingly so."

"It's disturbing."

"Don't let his attitude bother you, Jessica. Every house has a past, right?"

"Not always a past tragedy."

"If it makes you feel any better, the house was remodeled after the fire. I'm sure there aren't any ghosts left. It's going to be a good place for you and Kyle to live."

"I hope so," she said, trying to shake off the uneasy feeling that Sean's behavior and Emma's mention of *ghosts* had created.

Maybe it was a good thing Sean didn't like the idea of her moving into the Emery house. She'd just given him another reason to stay away from her. And if he didn't come around, it would be easier to forget him.

But the taste of Sean's mouth still lingered on her lips, and the voice inside her head called her a liar.

Two

Sean struggled to wake up, but the nightmare had him in its grip.

Orange flames licked the night sky like a monster. The smoke made his eyes water. Small pops turned into loud bangs, the fire leaping higher in the sky with each one. He heard sirens in the distance.

Someone was screaming. It was Stacy!

Did she see him?

He heard her voice. "Sean, look in the light, look in the light."

He squinted but he couldn't see anything. He tried harder. Still nothing.

"It's right there in front of you," she said.

The light was so bright it was blinding. He couldn't look anymore. He turned away, relieved when the pressing brightness turned to darkness.

His lids fluttered open. He stared at the room in confusion. He wasn't outside. He was in bed, and he'd been dreaming. The nightmare had come once again.

He rolled over onto his back, realizing that the light he'd been trying to avoid was coming through the blinds he'd forgotten to close the night before. He drew in a deep breath, trying to slow his pulse. It had been at least ten years since he'd dreamed of Stacy and that night. And he knew why she'd come back now, because Jessica was moving into her house.

He pressed his fingers to his temple. His head pounded, not just from the dream, but also from the drinks he'd consumed the night before. He didn't usually drink much when he played, at least not anymore, but last night he'd been thrown off of his game. First, by Jessica's surprising kiss—what the hell was that—and second, by the news of her move. He hadn't been able to wrap his brain around either event, so he'd had a few drinks after Jessica left and had definitely made things worse. Now, he had a hell of hangover.

Glancing at the clock, he realized it was almost noon. He sat up in bed and ran a hand over his jaw. He needed to shave and take a shower—a cold one. Then maybe he'd be able to get the fog out of his head so he could think clearly and figure out what he was going to do.

No, that was wrong. He didn't need to figure anything out. He knew exactly what he needed to do—stay away from Jessica, especially now that she was moving into the house of his nightmares. Actually, that should make it easier to stay away from her.

Leaving her alone was a goal he'd set for himself three months earlier when an unexpected and unwelcome attraction had sparked between them at the worst possible time. Jessica's son had been kidnapped, and she was terrified. Despite the horrendous circumstances, he'd found her incredibly likeable and sweetly gorgeous, even without a speck of makeup on. When Kyle had come home and all was well, he'd gotten to see her happy and relieved, and he'd liked her even more.

But he'd figured nothing would come of it. She lived in Angel's Bay. And she was a widow, and a mother. Their lives were practically on different planets. Unfortunately, those planets had come a little closer when she moved to San

Francisco, but he'd still managed to keep his distance. It hadn't been that difficult. His band had been touring most of the past three months.

Now the tour was over. He and Jessica were in the same place. And damn if she hadn't been sexy as hell last night in the short skirt that showed off her beautiful dancer's legs. He'd never seen her looking so hot. And she'd been happy, swaying to the music—his music. He hadn't been able to take his eyes off of her.

Still he hadn't expected her to end up in his arms. He hadn't anticipated seeing desire in her big brown eyes, and then that kiss—that reckless, impulsive and electrically charged kiss had sent him over the edge. He'd thought about having her mouth on his a dozen times, but now he knew that his imagination had not been nearly as good as reality.

He drew in a breath, feeling his body harden at the memory. He wanted Jessica. But he couldn't have her. She was not for him.

A knock came at his door, followed by his father's booming voice. "Sean?"

He groaned in dismay. He'd never wanted to move back home, and even though the garage studio was detached from the main house, it was still too close to his parents for his taste. But he'd sublet his condo when he'd gone on tour and that lease wouldn't run out for another three weeks. So, he'd accepted his mother's offer to stay here. He had a feeling he was about to regret that decision.

Another impatient knock came at the door, which didn't surprise him at all. Jack Callaway was a determined man with strong opinions, and he usually got what he wanted when he wanted it. Success was always his goal and failure was never an option. Jack had high expectations for himself and everyone in his family, and Sean had never managed to meet those expectations. He and his father had been butting heads since he was a kid. He had a feeling that would never change.

Rolling out of bed, he stumbled to the door, knowing Jack would no doubt have something to say about the fact that it was almost noon, and he was just getting out of bed. He might be twenty-eight years old, but his father had yet to see him as anything but the kid who'd always disappointed him.

He opened the door, his gaze narrowing on the sight of his father dressed in a black suit. "Where are you going?"

"The same place you are." Jack gave his wrinkled t-shirt and sweats a look of disapproval. "Why aren't you dressed? We're leaving in ten minutes."

"What are you talking about?" He rubbed his temple again, the pain in his head getting worse now that he was talking to his dad.

"Your cousin Camille's wedding. It starts in an hour."

He vaguely remembered his mother mentioning something about a wedding, but he hadn't realized it was today or that he was supposed to go. "I thought just the two of you were going."

"When have we ever had a family wedding where everyone wasn't invited? Not that you would know, since you rarely show up to anything."

He had no reply to that. It was the truth.

"Well, are you coming or not?" Jack demanded.

"No, I can't come. I have to work today."

Irritation flashed through his father's eyes. "Can you get out of it? It would make your mother happy if you'd come with us."

"I can't imagine that she'll miss me. There will be dozens of Callaways in attendance."

"That's what you always think, but it's not true, Sean. When you're not there, you are missed. You're part of this family whether you want to be or not. You take family for granted. Someday you may regret that." Jack paused. "Since you're not going to the wedding, you can do your mother a favor."

"What's that?"

"She promised to send a stepladder over to Jessica. She's moving into the Emery's old house today. You can take the one in the backyard."

His stomach turned over. That was the last thing he wanted to do, but he could hardly turn down such a simple request. "Fine. Is that it?"

His father stared back at him and then shrugged. "That's it."

Sean closed the door and let out a sigh, bothered not only by the conversation with his father but also by yet another mention of the Emery house. His feelings were completely irrational, but that didn't make them any easier to shake.

Another knock came at his door, and he jumped. Damn he was on edge.

It was his stepmother, Lynda, this time. Although stepmother wasn't really a label that made any sense, since Lynda was the only mother he could remember. His biological mother had died when he was a toddler.

Lynda, an attractive blonde with blue eyes and a warm, loving smile, wore a short maroon dress with black heels. In her hands she held a plastic container.

"Jack said you're not going with us to the wedding," she said.

"I'm sorry. I didn't realize it was today, and I have some things to do."

"Well, I'm disappointed, and I think Camille will be as well, but I'll give her your best. Your dad says you'll take the ladder over to Jessica. I want you to take this, too. I made Jessica some sandwiches. She's going to be too busy unpacking to worry about food. Keep it in the fridge until you go."

He took the container out of his mom's hands with a sinking heart. "All right. So is anyone else around today?

Shayla or Colton?" he asked, referring to his two youngest siblings, who still lived at home. Maybe once his parents left, he could rope one of them into going over to the Emery house.

"Shayla is coming to the wedding with us, and Colton is working. Give my best to Jessica."

"Yeah, all right," he said, knowing he was out of luck.

After his mother left, he put the food into the refrigerator, then headed for a shower.

A half hour later he was headed down the street with the sandwiches and the ladder. As he traced the steps of his childhood, he felt like he was going back in time. While he'd visited his parents' house over the years, those visits had usually been quick hits, and he'd never taken any time to walk around the old neighborhood. Now he was assailed with memories.

All the houses in this part of the city had yards, an unusual sight in San Francisco, but the blocks around his parents' house felt like a suburban slice in an urban environment. He and his brothers and sisters had taken full advantage of the wide streets and grassy lawns, playing baseball, football, kickball and hide-and-seek with the other neighborhood kids. They'd played late into the night, especially on long summer evenings.

Good times, he thought, feeling a slight pang for the past. But as he turned the corner, the wistful longing turned into a racing pulse of fear. There in the middle of the block was the Emery house.

It was a two-story structure with three wide brick steps leading up to the front door. After the fire devastated the garage and first floor, the house has been remodeled. Despite the cosmetic changes, it still felt like Stacy's house. He could almost see her sitting on the steps, tossing a baseball into a mitt while she waited for him, or she might have been on her skateboard speeding along the sidewalk, or turning cartwheels on the front lawn.

The memories made his gut clench, and as he drew closer, his steps slowed. He couldn't remember when he'd last been on this street. He'd avoided it after the fire. Even when he'd gotten his driver's license he'd managed to never go down the block. A desperate desire to flee grabbed hold, and it was all he could do not to run.

He reminded himself that he wasn't eight years old anymore, and the fire was ancient history. That drove him another fifteen yards down the sidewalk. He paused under the tall, shady trees across the street from the house. It was where he'd been standing when Stacy had come running out of the fire.

His heart thumped against his chest. He had the shocking thought that he wasn't going to be able to do this. He wasn't going to be able to walk across the street and go inside that house.

What the hell was wrong with him?

The front door opened, and Jessica came out. She wore faded jeans and a clingy knit top, her hair pulled back in a ponytail. She set a potted plant on the top step. As she straightened, she saw him, and instantly stiffened. After a second, she gave him a wary wave. She was probably wondering why he was just standing there, staring at her house.

Knowing he couldn't take off now, he forced himself to cross the street, thinking it would have been a lot simpler to just go to his cousin's wedding.

"I didn't expect to see you, Sean," she said as he reached the bottom step.

"My mother said you needed a ladder."

"I do, but I'm sorry she bothered you with it."

"It's no big deal. She also sent sandwiches."

Jessica came down the steps and took the container. "That was nice of her."

"She likes to feed people."

An awkward silence fell between them.

"So you're moved in?" he asked.

"The house came mostly furnished, but I had our bedroom sets delivered and some other personal items. I still have to unpack clothes, linens, all that stuff." She cleared her throat as she met his gaze. "Sean, I feel like I should apologize."

"Why? You can move into any house you want to."

"I'm not talking about the house. I shouldn't have kissed you last night. I guess I had a little too much Fireball whiskey."

He didn't know what to say. He couldn't remember a time when a woman had apologized for kissing him. Was he now supposed to say he was sorry for kissing her back?

He wasn't at all sorry. He'd thought about kissing her for months. And the fact that she'd taken the decision out of his hands was just fine with him. But the kiss was over. And it shouldn't—make that *couldn't*—happen again.

"I hadn't been out in a while," Jessica added. "I loved your music so much. I got caught up in the moment."

"Don't worry about it. It's not a big deal."

"Right. No big deal."

They stared at each other for another long minute. Finally, he said, "So what do you need the ladder for?"

"The switch for the trapdoor leading into the attic isn't working, so I need the ladder to reach the latch on the ceiling. I tried a chair but I wasn't tall enough. I need to get into the attic so I can see what Mrs. Emery has stored up there. Then I'll know how much work is ahead of me."

"What are you going to do with all her stuff?"

"First I'm going to organize it, then talk to her about what she wants to keep and what items need to go to charity or in the trash. Apparently, she doesn't have any relatives who can help." She paused as she gave him a long look. "Emma told me you were good friends with the girl who died. I'm sorry about what happened. You must have been devastated."

"It was rough."

"I know what it feels like to lose someone without any warning. It's hard to take it in. You keep thinking it's a mistake."

As Jessica spoke, he could see the lingering pain in her eyes. She'd lost her husband in an accident less than two years ago. But she had it together. Here he was, shaken up over a girl who'd died two decades ago. He needed to get over it. "Where do you want the ladder?" he asked.

"You can leave it out here. I'll take it inside later."

He liked her answer, because it meant he wouldn't have to go into the house, but he knew she was just making things easier for him and harder for herself, and that he didn't like. "I'll bring it in." He hoped he wouldn't regret the impulsive decision.

She gave him a doubtful look. "Really? This house seems to bother you a great deal."

"I can handle it."

"Okay. Then follow me."

After they entered the house, Jessica paused just inside the entry. "I'm going to put the sandwiches in the refrigerator. Then I'll show you where the attic door is."

As she disappeared down the hall, he propped the ladder against the wall and walked into the living room.

Aside from the original fireplace, everything was different. When Stacy had lived here, the room had been filled with dark blue couches and fluffy pillows. There had always been toys or books lying around. There had been a television in the corner with video games and they'd played those for hours on the weekends. But there was no real sign of life in this room now. The furniture was elegant but old and appeared to be very uncomfortable. The cream-colored walls had been painted gray, making the room look dark and unappealing. It might have suited Helen Emery, but it sure didn't look like Jessica.

"Does the house look the same to you?" Jessica asked, coming up next to him.

"The living room sure doesn't. It's kind of drab, don't you think?"

"Yeah. I'm going to get rid of that furniture eventually, but it's going to take some time to sort things out. Are you ready for the upstairs?"

"Lead the way." He grabbed the ladder and followed her up the steps.

As they reached the landing, he saw the door to the master bedroom was open, but the doors going down the hall to the right were closed. Relief ran through him. He wasn't ready to walk into Stacy's bedroom just yet.

"The trapdoor is there." She walked past the closed doors and the bathroom, stopping at the end of the hall. She walked over to the wall switch and flipped it. "See, nothing happens. I need to pull the steps down manually. It looks like there's a latch on the ceiling."

He gazed overhead and saw what she was talking about. He opened the ladder, then climbed up and unhooked the latch. Then he pulled on a cord to lower the collapsible staircase. Those stairs brought another memory into his head. He and Stacy used to go up to the attic to play with all the costumes in her grandmother's chest. He wondered if they were still there.

"I'm going up," Jessica said as he moved the stepladder out of the way.

"I'll go with you."

"Really?"

"Stop asking me that," he grumbled. He'd come this far. He might as well go the rest of the way.

He followed Jessica up the steps. The attic was exactly like he remembered, which wasn't surprising. The fire had been contained to the first floor.

What he was surprised at was how much junk had been

crammed into the space. There were steamer trunks, dressers, suitcases, boxes, old furniture, skis and poles, tennis rackets, even a bunch of camping equipment. The only light came from a bulb hanging on a wire overhead, and a small window that looked out over the street.

"Well," Jessica said, planting her hands on her hips as she surveyed the room. "This is going to be a big job."

He nodded, his attention moving to the easel in the corner. The chalkboard had magnetic letters on it, and Stacy's name was still spelled out across the top. His stomach turned over, and despite his resolve to face his fear, he felt a little sick.

"Sean?" Jessica questioned. "Oh. Her name is still there."

"As if she stopped playing a second ago," he muttered, finally dragging his gaze away from the easel and back to Jessica.

Concern showed in her eyes. "Maybe you should go, Sean. This is obviously hard on you."

"It is hard, because there's something you don't know."

"What is it?"

He really shouldn't say anything. Getting Jessica involved in his past was only going to bring her deeper into his life when what he needed to do was keep her out. But there was something about her open, honest gaze that made him want to confess a terrible secret.

He swallowed hard, and then said, "It's my fault that Stacy died. If it weren't for me, she'd still be alive."

Three

---⇒≫≪⇐---

Jessica's eyes widened as Sean's unexpected words ran around in her head. "What are you talking about? Wasn't the fire an accident?"

"It was, but Stacy shouldn't have been here in the house." Tension tightened his jaw. The easygoing, free-spirited musician she'd seen on the stage last night had disappeared. This house, and all the memories that went with it, had taken Sean to a very deep and intense space, and she was almost afraid to go there with him. But how could she not? The fact that he wanted to tell her something personal touched her deeply.

"Tell me what happened," she said quietly.

His chest heaved with the stress of taking another breath. Then he said, "We were playing together at my house that day. Stacy's mom had taken her brother, Blake, on a field trip, and Stacy was supposed to stay with me until her mom picked her up, but we had a fight. It was a stupid eight-year-old fight. I wanted to build a fort in my room, and Stacy wanted to play catch in the backyard. She got mad, and I told her to get out."

Jessica nervously licked her lips. She had a feeling she knew where this was going, and it wasn't to a good place.

"I didn't know right away that she actually left the house," he continued. "I thought she just went downstairs to find someone else to play with. There were always a lot of kids around, not just my siblings, but also half the neighborhood. I think it was about an hour later that I looked out my bedroom window, and I saw smoke coming over the trees and a weird light in the sky. I knew there was a fire close by, and I wanted to see it."

"So I left the house," he continued. "I ran down the street and around the corner. I wasn't supposed to go that far by myself, especially after dark, but I had to see what was going on. I was fascinated by fire. My father was a firefighter, and he was working that night. I thought I might see him charging to the rescue on his big red fire engine. I was excited at first. And then I got closer." Sean walked over to the small attic window. "I was over there."

She joined him at the window, following his pointed finger to the house across the street.

"When I got to that tree I realized it was Stacy's house that was on fire. I couldn't believe it. I just stopped and stared. The fire was huge, much bigger than what I'd seen from my window. And then Stacy came running through the front door." He turned to Jessica, his eyes bleak and filled with pain. "Stacy's clothes and her long blonde hair were on fire," he said, his voice rough with emotion. "There were orange-red flames surrounding her. It was the strangest sight. It didn't seem real. But she was screaming in terror and running around in a crazy circle."

"Oh, God," she whispered, putting her hand to her mouth, his words painting a very vivid picture.

"The fire engine pulled up in front of her house. I saw my dad run to Stacy. He wrapped her in a blanket and rolled her on the ground. Someone else beat at the flames shooting off of her. And then she wasn't screaming anymore."

She put a hand on his arm. "You don't have to do this,

Sean."

"I do. I have to say it all. I can't stop now."

"Okay. What happened next?"

"I watched them put her on a stretcher. She was quiet, really quiet. I knew it was bad, because Stacy talked more than anyone I knew. That's when I ran. I don't remember how I got back to the house or what I did when I got there. I think I went up to my bedroom and hid under the covers. Some time passed. Then my mom came to my room. My dad was with her. He smelled like smoke. His face was black with soot. They told me there was a fire, and Stacy was hurt. They didn't tell me then that she was dead. Maybe they didn't know yet." He let out a breath, then added, "My mom put her arms around me. She was kind and sympathetic, but my dad was furious. He wanted to know why Stacy was at her house when she was supposed to be playing with me."

"Oh, Sean." She felt a wave of anger at Jack's callousness. She understood why he'd be angry, but Sean had been eight years old, barely older than Kyle was now. She searched for comforting words that would make him feel better, but there were none. Sean had witnessed something no one should see. He'd clearly been traumatized. No wonder he'd been so shaken to come into this house, to relive that night.

"I told my father that I didn't know she'd left, but he didn't care about my excuses."

"He was upset. I'm sure it hurt him to see Stacy in that condition, too. He took it out on you, and he shouldn't have done that. Did you tell your parents that you saw Stacy?"

"No. I was already in enough trouble. And I can't say I didn't deserve everything my father dished out. It was my fault that Stacy was at home. If I had told someone, maybe my mom would have come over here and seen the fire before it became too big. Maybe Stacy would be alive now. Maybe her dad would be, too."

"That's a lot of maybes."

He ran a hand through his hair. "I have more of them running through my head. You don't know how often I've relived that night. I had nightmares for months. I'd see monsters in the shadows of the trees. I'd hear voices whispering that it was my fault. I'd see lights flashing in my head. And Stacy always showed up at the end, screaming in terror."

"I'm so sorry, Sean," she said, feeling his pain. "I know you blame yourself, but you were a child. The fight you had with Stacy is one I have witnessed with Kyle and his friends a dozen times. It's normal for kids to tell each other to go home or go away. You couldn't know what would happen to Stacy when she ran out of your room. You certainly couldn't have predicted that she'd go home and get caught in a fire."

"Logically, I know what you're saying is true, but I can't shake the guilt, Jess. I thought I had gotten the dreams out of my head. But when I heard you were moving in here, all the memories came rushing back. It's like it happened yesterday and not two decades ago."

"Now, I know why you looked like you'd seen a ghost last night."

"I did see a ghost—I saw Stacy." He blew out a breath. "But I will get over it. The shock is already starting to wear off. Thanks for listening."

"Thanks for sharing."

He moved away from the window, walking back toward the center of the room. "It looks like Mrs. Emery kept some of Stacy's things. I wonder what she'll want you to do with them."

"I have no idea. I'll know more what's here once I start going through the boxes. Then Helen and I will have to have a long talk." She paused, watching as he poked around some of the boxes. "How did the fire start, Sean?"

"I don't really know. All I ever heard was that it was an accident."

She nodded, thinking about what he'd told her. "So, you said Stacy got out of the house but didn't survive her injuries. What about her father? What happened to him?"

"They couldn't get to him until the fire was out. He was trapped in the garage. By the time they got in there, it was too late."

"It must have been a fast-burning fire if he couldn't get out of the house."

"It looked like a monster to me, but I was eight years old. Everything seemed bigger then."

She sighed. "I had no idea that I was moving into your nightmare."

He gave her a tight smile. "That pretty much describes it."

"I wish I could tell you that I'd move out, but I signed a lease."

"I understand. This isn't your problem, Jessica, and there's no reason you shouldn't live here. It's just a house. I'm seeing that more clearly now that I'm inside."

She didn't know if she entirely believed him but hoped what he'd said was at least partly true. "I'm glad that being here is helping you come to terms with the past. I think you should also tell your parents what you saw that night. Your dad might be able to help you deal with the images in your head. As a firefighter he's seen people get burned. He's had to find a way to live with those kinds of memories."

"I don't know how he does it. After what I saw that night, I lost all interest in being a firefighter and I couldn't understand why anyone would want to run into a burning building. I refused to go down to the station or go out for junior firefighter in school. My father was so angry with me. Firefighting is the family business. Generations of Callaways have been firefighters, including four of my siblings. It's in the Callaway blood, but not in mine."

"If you'd told your dad why you couldn't be a firefighter,

don't you think he would have understood?"

Doubt flashed in Sean's eyes. "I think he would have told me to suck it up and get over it."

"Really? Your dad has high expectations for his kids, I know that, but he loves you. Would he be that harsh?"

"Yes. And my father's love comes with strings. If you do what he wants and you honor him, he'll have your back until the day you die. If you go against him, he'll never let you forget it. And it's not just about firefighting, it's also about serving the community, choosing a noble profession. That's the Callaway way. Nicole isn't a firefighter, but she's a teacher. Shayla is going to be a doctor. Those are acceptable careers in his mind. But me, I play guitar at nightclubs. I'm not changing the world for the better, and I'm fine with that, but my father is not."

"I still think you should tell him what you saw."

"My problems with my dad are not based on that single event. There's a lifetime of crap between us. And it would take forever for me to explain it all to you. While my dad might love me, because he's my father and he feels he has to, he doesn't respect me. He doesn't listen to me. He has no interest in my interests. That's why we can't have a relationship."

"It doesn't sound like you respect him either," she couldn't help pointing out. "Or that you have an interest in his interests. Maybe your relationship isn't about that one event, but you can't deny that that event wasn't hugely important in framing your opinions about firefighting as a career choice." As she finished speaking, she saw angry thunderclouds gathering in Sean's eyes and realized she was getting far too deep into his life. "I'm probably overstepping here," she added quickly. "But I don't think I'm wrong." She let out a breath, a little shocked that she'd been so blunt. She was usually better at keeping her opinions to herself, but she hated seeing Sean in pain or turmoil, and he was clearly in both.

"You're right, you are overstepping. You've known my

family for about five minutes, so don't presume to think you know everything about us."

She slowly nodded. "Okay. That's a fair point. I never had a father who cared a speck about me, so maybe I don't know what I'm talking about."

He let out a frustrated breath. "Look, I'm sorry, Jess. This house has been making me crazy for years. And now I'm taking that crazy out on you."

"I did stick my nose into your business," she conceded.

"Only because I put my business right in your face."

"How about we call a truce?" She held out her hand.

He hesitated, then took her hand, squeezing his warm fingers around hers.

The truce had been a good idea, but not the handshake, because neither one of them could seem to let go. The sparks that had flared the night before were back, heightened by the emotion of the last few minutes.

"What am I going to do about you?" he murmured.

It was the same question he'd asked last night.

A few possibilities ran through her mind, but thankfully she didn't say any of them out loud, because all of them were bad ideas.

"I like you, Jess. You're beautiful and smart, a little more outspoken than I thought, but pretty damn amazing."

Her nerves tingled at his words. "I feel the same way about you. Although, I'd substitute handsome for beautiful," she said lightly.

He gave her a smile, but as the seconds ticked by his smile faded. "You and me—we don't go together, Jess. You're tied to my family forever through your son and my nephew. If we started something, and it didn't work out, it would be awkward and uncomfortable for a lot of people. And I don't want to ruin what you have going with Nicole and Ryan, this little family unit you have set up. It's good for the boys. We can all see that."

"I understand." Nothing he'd said was a surprise. And he was right, any relationship between them would be complicated, but that wasn't the only reason they wouldn't work. "It would be best if we just remained friends. And not just because of the family ties."

"What do you mean?"

"While you're very attractive and there's a connection between us, I could never have a relationship with a musician. I know what loving a musician looks like. My dad took off before I was born, and my mom fell in love every other year after that. Her favorite guys were guitar players with long hair and soulful voices. She always thought they were singing to her and about her. But they weren't. They were singing for themselves. I saw her get her heart broken a lot. And to be honest, my heart got broken, too. There was one guy I really wanted to stick around. He was the closest thing I'd ever had to a dad, but he couldn't stay, because the road called to him, just as it calls to you. So while you might be a good time, Sean, I can't be with a man who's always leaving. I've watched too many doors slam in my face, and I don't just have myself to think about now. I'd never put Kyle through what I went through."

"Are you done?"

"Yes."

"Okay," he said, an odd expression in his eyes. "It sounds like we're on the same page."

"Then you should let go of my hand."

Instead of loosening his grip, his fingers tightened around hers. "Just for the record, I wouldn't be a *good* time, I'd be a *fantastic* time."

"So cocky," she murmured, refusing to admit that his words had sent a thrill down her spine. "That's another strike against you."

"How many is that?"

"At least two."

"Then I might as well go for broke." He pulled her up against his chest, his other arm going around her waist. He lowered his head and pressed his mouth against hers.

She felt both hot and shivery as his passionate and demanding kiss set off a dizzying wave of desire. This kiss was nothing like the night before. He wasn't just meeting her tentative lips with his; he was taking control. When she opened her mouth to breathe, he slipped his tongue inside, taking the kiss deeper, making her feel as if she was a part of him, and he was a part of her. It was heady, exhilarating and terrifying. Her hands roamed his back, reveling in his male form, the tight muscles in his back, the broad shoulders, the strong arms that held her so close.

What was she doing? She couldn't do this. She couldn't have him. And he couldn't have her.

With her brain finally re-engaging, she managed to pull away.

He stared back at her, his gaze filled with desire, his ragged breathing telling her he'd been on the same wild ride with her.

"What was that?" she asked.

"Apparently strike three."

Actually, he'd come close to hitting a home run, but she wasn't going to tell him that. Instead, she said, "So we're done now?"

He gave her a long look. "I wish we were, but somehow I don't think so."

And with that troubling comment, he turned and left the attic.

She sank down on a nearby chest, her legs feeling suddenly weak. She felt like she'd just been through a tornado of emotions, dealing with Sean's sadness and anger about his friend, and then fighting the passion that had been brewing between them for months. She was exhausted and charged up at the same time, and she had no idea what was coming next. The only thing she knew for sure was that friends or not, Sean was going to be a problem.

Four

Sean jogged down the stairs and out the front door, feeling a desperate need to get out of the house before he did something stupid—make that *something else* that was stupid. Kissing Jessica had certainly not been a good idea. But he'd been revved up after spilling his guts about Stacy. When Jessica told him she had no interest in musicians, he'd wanted to prove to her that she couldn't dismiss him so easily, but all he'd really proved was that he liked her even more. He should be happy she didn't want to date a musician, because he didn't want to date a woman who was tied to his family and had a kid. He also didn't like the way he felt like spilling his guts when he was around her. He'd never told anyone about being at Stacy's house, so why had he told her?

Shaking his head in bewilderment, he walked briskly back home, but once there he found the idea of going inside unappealing. He needed to clear his head and get some perspective, so he dug his keys out of his pocket and got into his van.

He drove across town toward the beach, leaving his car in a spot off the Great Highway. Then he crossed the street to the wide sandy beach and stared out at the water glistening in the sunlight. The waves were high today, crashing down with an angry force that matched his mood. He felt restless, unsettled, and he didn't know if it was memories of the fire or kissing Jessica that had him in such turmoil. But one way or the other, he needed to get back on an even keel.

He walked along the beach for a while and then sat down on the sand. As he watched a little girl and her father walk along the water's edge, he was reminded of Stacy and her dad. He hadn't really thought much about the fact that Stacy had been with her father when the fire broke out. Why hadn't her father been able to get out of the house? Why had Stacy been alone when she'd come through that front door?

The fire had to have exploded, taken them both by surprise. But what would cause such an explosion? His father could probably tell him, but the last person he wanted to ask was Jack. Emma was an arson investigator. She might be able to pull up the old case file. He took out his phone and called her.

"What's up, Sean?"

"I need your help."

"Seriously? You never need anyone's help. What's wrong?"

"Nothing's wrong. I just have a question. Are you at home?"

"On my way. I should be there in about ten minutes."

"I'll meet you there."

"See you then."

He hung up the phone and walked quickly back to his car. It might be smarter to leave the Emery fire in the past. On the other hand, he'd already tried that, and his emotional reaction today had only reminded him that he'd never completely gotten over what he'd seen that night.

But how Stacy had ended up in the middle of that inferno was something he'd never really questioned. Was there more to know?

Jessica spent a half hour in the attic and soon realized that the job was going to be long and tedious. She'd only looked in a couple of boxes, but it became quickly apparent that Mrs. Emery had dumped piles of papers into boxes without any attempt at organization. Jessica would need to pace herself. Twenty years worth of junk wasn't going to get cleared out in a day.

Grabbing one of the smaller boxes, she headed downstairs. She'd peruse the contents while having a glass of iced tea and one of Lynda's sandwiches. After that, she would focus on getting her own life settled before digging any further into the past.

She had just reached the first floor entryway when the doorbell rang. Her pulse quickened. Had Sean come back? She couldn't imagine who else would be calling on her.

She set the box down and opened the door. It wasn't Sean on the porch, but an attractive middle-aged woman with dark red hair and bright green eyes. Despite being dressed in workout clothes, she had on a thick layer of make-up, and a pair of diamond earrings sparkled in the sunlight.

"Hello," Jessica said. "Can I help you?"

"I'm Sally Watson. I live next door." She tipped her head to the white two-story house on the other side of Jessica's driveway. "Are you Helen's new tenant?"

"Yes. I'm Jessica Schilling."

"It's nice to meet you, Jessica."

"You, too."

"I'm so sad that Helen had to move out. I'm going to miss her so much. We've been neighbors for twenty years. She's such a sweetheart, practically a grandmother to my children. Anyway, I wanted to come by and say hello. This is a nice neighborhood, and we try to watch out for each other. Helen told me that you have a child?"

"A six-year-old son. His name is Kyle."

"That's such a cute age. I miss having little kids around. My husband and I have had an empty nest for two years now. Our three girls are in their twenties. You'll probably see Christie at some point. She's our middle child and only lives a few miles away. She's about your age—twenty-five?"

"I'm twenty-seven," Jessica said.

"You had your little boy young."

She shrugged, not really wanting to get into the whole story of how she'd come to be Kyle's stepmother. Instead, she said, "Are there any other children in the neighborhood?"

"There are a couple of kids. Not as many as when my children were small. Times have changed."

"I thought I saw a boy across the street."

"That's Grayson. He's eight. He's Brett's stepson."

"Brett?" she queried.

"Brett Murphy, our local hero, at least that's what he thinks," she added, an edge of bitterness in her voice. "He's lived here for years, mostly alone. His first wife, Natasha, left him a long time ago. Adrienne and Grayson are his second family. Of course Adrienne is young and beautiful. Brett always goes for the trophy." Sally's gaze drifted across the street, and for a moment she seemed lost in thought. Then she gathered herself together and said, "Anyway, there are a couple of other children at the end of the block. I'm sure your boy will find some friends to play with."

"I'm sure he will." She didn't know what to make of Sally. The woman's friendly smile didn't quite ring true. "Thanks for stopping by."

"No problem. So, Helen told me you're going to clean out her house. That will be a big job. Helen was always a pack rat. She hated to throw anything away. I offered to help her more than once, but she always put it off. She must finally be ready to let go."

"I guess."

"Did she tell you about the fire?"

"I've heard about it. Did you live next door then?"

"I did. I wasn't home though. By the time I arrived, it was over. It was very sad."

"What happened to Helen's daughter-in-law and grandson?" She might as well participate in the conversation since Sally seemed eager to gossip.

"They left right after the funeral. Lana took Blake and went to live with one of her sisters. After she moved away, Helen and her husband, Tom, moved back in to oversee the remodel. It had originally been their home, you know. They'd raised Robert in the house, but after he got married to Lana, Helen and Tom retired to San Diego. After the fire, they came back. Tom died last year and Helen has lived like a hermit since then. Anyway, I'm rambling on. My husband always says I talk too much. I'm sure he's right."

Jessica liked Sally a little more for admitting her flaws.

"I should go. I have a Pilates class," Sally said. "Please let me know if you need anything."

"I will. Thanks for stopping by."

As she closed the door, Jessica wondered why Sally had found the need to bring up the fire. Was she just a nosy neighbor or had she been trying to get some information out of Jessica? But what information could Jessica possibly have that Sally wouldn't already know? And then there were her odd comments about the man across the street. What was that about?

Frowning, she walked down the hall to the kitchen and decided to focus on lunch and unpacking her kitchenware. It was time she concentrated on her own life.

-→➤➤◀◀←-

"I just realized you're not at Camille's wedding," Emma said, as she let Sean into her apartment. "Why didn't you go?"

"I had some things to take care of."

She gave him a knowing look. "Funny how busy you get when there's a family event."

"Hey you're not there, either."

"I was going to go, but I had to walk through a fire scene this morning."

Her words reminded him that Emma, like so many other Callaways, lived in the world of fire, the world he had wanted nothing to do with until now.

"Do you want some tea?" she asked.

"I definitely don't want tea," he said following her into the small kitchen "Do you have anything else?"

She opened the refrigerator. "Beer, soda, orange juice."

"I'll take the juice."

As she poured him a glass of juice, he sat down on a stool at the counter. "Where's your husband today?"

"Max is working a homicide. It happened last weekend, and he's having trouble finding a lead. He's been working overtime all week."

"Sorry to hear that."

She shrugged. "It's the job." Emma filled the teapot with water and turned on the stove. "So what's this favor you want?"

He took a sip of juice, as he thought about what he wanted to say. Getting Emma involved in any part of his life was asking for trouble. His sister was a great person, but she also loved to meddle. Once he let her in, he'd never get her out. On the other hand, he had questions he wanted answered.

"Come on, spit it out," she ordered. "Does this have something to do with Jessica?"

He frowned. "Why would you ask that?"

"Because I've noticed a little spark between you two. But it seems like you go out of your way to avoid her. That makes

Nicole very happy by the way. She does not want you and Jessica to get involved with each other. She's afraid you'll break Jessica's heart and drive her away and ruin everything."

Exactly what he'd told Jessica. "Nicole doesn't have to worry. Jessica and I are just—friends." He stumbled over the word, knowing that their last kiss had been anything but friendly. He cleared his throat. "I didn't come by to talk about Jessica."

"So why are you here?"

"It's the Emery house. I've been thinking about that fire. I have some questions, Emma."

"Like what?"

"Do you know how the fire started?"

She thought for a moment. "I don't think so, but I was eleven when it happened, so all I remember is everyone at school crying. And then there was that huge funeral. There must have been four hundred people there."

"I remember." He hadn't wanted to go to that funeral. He'd had some crazy idea that if he didn't go to the mass, Stacy would still be alive, but his parents had insisted they all attend. So he'd sat in the pew with his family and tried not to look at the small white casket next to the big dark one. He pushed that thought out of his mind. "Would you be able to access the records regarding that fire?"

Emma gave him a speculative look. "What do you want to know?"

"I want to know how the fire started, why Stacy's father couldn't get out."

"Why does it matter now?"

"Because it does."

"That's not an answer."

"It's all I've got. Can you help me?"

"I could look into it, but you might be able to get a quicker and more direct answer if you talk to Dad. He was on that fire, and I'm sure the department conducted a thorough investigation. Dad and Mom were good friends with Stacy's parents."

"I don't want to talk to Dad about it."

"Why not?"

"I want the official version, not his version."

She frowned. "What does that mean? You think he'd lie to you?"

"I don't know."

"Sean, he wouldn't lie. Jack Callaway is the most honest person I know."

"How long will it take you to find the report?" he asked, changing the subject.

"It will take a little digging. It was twenty years ago."

"But you'll do it?"

She nodded. "Yes, because I'm your sister, and you've made me a little curious."

"That's always dangerous," he said with a smile. "But thanks, I appreciate it."

"I still don't know what you're hoping to find."

"I don't know either, but being in Stacy's house again brought back a lot of memories."

"Whoa! When were you in Stacy's house?"

He realized his mistake a second too late. "An hour ago," he admitted. "Mom asked me to take a ladder over to Jessica." He didn't like the sudden gleam in his sister's eyes. "It was a favor to Mom. That's all it was."

"Sure, whatever you say."

"Anyway, when I stepped into that house, it was like I stepped into the past."

"Isn't the inside different now?"

"It was different, but also the same. And the memories were still there. I spent a lot of time in that house with Stacy."

The teapot began to sing, and Emma took it off the stove.

She poured the hot water over a teabag and then brought it back to the counter. "If you don't want to talk to Dad, you could talk to Mom. I'm sure Dad spoke to her about the findings."

"I'd rather just look at the report and not get them involved." He finished his juice and set the glass down. "I have to get to practice."

"You guys were great last night."

"It was a good show. Glad you enjoyed it."

"You're playing in Russian Hill tonight, right?"

"Yeah. Are you coming?"

"No, tonight is for my husband. We're going to spend some quality naked time together."

He rolled his eyes. "You're over-sharing again, Emma."

She laughed. "I'm just being honest."

"You look happy. You're really in love, aren't you?"

"So much I can barely believe it. And to think I almost lost Max. I don't know how I would have survived."

He nodded, thinking back to Emma's wedding day, when just before the ceremony, Max and his brother, Spencer, had been caught in a bank robbery. Max had been shot, and he'd come very close to dying, but luckily he'd survived. Two weeks later was able to exchange vows with Emma. "Is Max completely back to normal now?"

"He's a hundred percent, thank goodness."

"How's his brother doing?"

"Spencer is in culinary school. He's going to be a chef."

"Good for him."

"And he has a girlfriend."

"Wait, let me guess, the beautiful redhead from the bank?"

"Yes, the woman who helped Spencer save Max's life—Hallie Cooper."

He shook his head in amazement. "Talk about an unlikely place to fall in love."

"You never know when you're going to meet the right person. And sometimes they don't seem like the right person at first. I didn't like Max at all in the beginning. He was arrogant and territorial about his cases."

"And you're not?" he challenged.

"I might be territorial, but I am not arrogant. Of course, I soon found out that Max was just being a jerk because he was trying not to fall in love with me. Why do guys do that?"

He could not begin to answer that question, especially since he'd been guilty of it himself, and recently, too. But he was not falling in love with Jessica. No way. That wasn't going to happen. He slid off the stool and stood up. "Thanks again for the help."

"I haven't helped you yet."

"You'll call me when you find out anything?"

"Yes, but it won't be until Monday."

"That's fine."

"I'll see you tomorrow though."

He sighed. "What's tomorrow?"

"Wow. You really don't listen to anything that includes the word family and event, do you?"

"Just tell me."

"Tomorrow Ryan is throwing Nicole a birthday dinner at their house. It starts at six. Everyone will be there." She gave him a mischievous smile. "Including Jessica. But since you're just friends, that won't be a problem, will it?"

Five

Jessica spent the rest of Saturday setting up Kyle's bedroom and then her own. Despite the headache of having to move again, she was happy to have a house in a good neighborhood with a yard for Kyle to play in. Even though the house had been touched by tragedy, it had all happened a long time ago, and she couldn't let herself get caught up in that. She was determined to make a good home for Kyle and for herself.

It was close to midnight when she was finally done unpacking her clothes. She grabbed two empty boxes and took them downstairs. There was a side door off the kitchen that led to the driveway and the recycle and garbage bins. As she put the boxes in the plastic container, she heard a voice on the other side of the fence. She couldn't see through the shrubbery, but it sounded like Sally was talking to someone.

She moved a little closer, hearing only Sally's voice and no one else's. Maybe she was on the phone.

"I don't know if there's anything to be found," Sally said.

The odd tense words caught Jessica's interest. What was Sally talking about?

There was silence for another moment. Then Sally said, "I know it's been years, and nothing has ever come to light, but I can't help but worry now that someone else is in the house and going through Helen's things. Maybe Helen never really looked through Robert's belongings." She paused again. "Yes, I asked Helen a bunch of times if I could help her, but she always said no."

Jessica frowned. What on earth was Sally talking about? And why was she having a conversation on the phone while standing in her driveway a little before midnight? The only answer was that she didn't want her husband to hear.

"I thought this was over," Sally said, frustration in her voice. "I am not crazy to worry. Maybe you should be a little worried. I'm not the only one with secrets." She paused again. "Okay, I'll talk to you later."

A moment later, Jessica heard footsteps, then a door closing. Sally had gone into the house.

She let out the breath she'd been holding, not sure what to make of what she'd heard. Sally was worried that she was in Helen's house, going through Helen's things? Why? What was there to be found?

And to whom had Sally been speaking? Because according to Sally, she wasn't the only one who had a secret or who should be worried.

A shiver ran down Jessica's spine. What on earth had she landed in the middle of? Was this about the fire? But it was so long ago, and Sally had had years to get into Helen's house, to find whatever she was worried about being found. Still, what else could Sally have been talking about? She'd mentioned Robert's name. If it had to do with him, then it had to do with the fire.

Did Sally know something about that fire that Sean didn't? Or was Jessica just letting her imagination run wild after a few whispers on a dark night?

A cold breeze blew through the trees, lifting the hair off the back of her neck. She shivered, the shadows from the tall trees suddenly giving her charming neighborhood a more eerie atmosphere. She hurried into the house and locked the door behind her.

She reminded herself that Helen had lived in the house without incident for two decades. There was no reason anything should be different now.

Or was there?

Helen was no longer living in the house; she was.

Jessica woke up Sunday morning feeling just as tired as when she'd gone to bed. After getting herself worked up the night before, she hadn't been able to fall asleep for hours. Every little creak seemed as loud as a gunshot. Her dreams were filled with whispering voices and fiery flames. She'd felt the heat of a fire, and thick smoke had seared her lungs as she'd run for her life, probably much the way Stacy had done. Poor Stacy! How terrified she must have been. And how terrified Sean must have been when he saw his friend on fire.

As her thoughts turned to Sean, she felt a mix of emotions. Putting her hand to her lips, she remembered the firm pressure of his mouth, the heat between them, the passion. They needed to stay away from each other, but so far they were not doing a very good job of that. She'd started things off on the wrong note with her impulsive kiss on Friday night, and he'd taken it to another level yesterday, but today they needed to put the brakes on.

They were going to be a part of each other's lives forever. It would be smarter to keep their relationship at the friend level. And she was a mom; she couldn't afford to be driven by passion. If she was going to be with someone, it had to be the right someone, a man who would stick around, who would be good for her and for Kyle.

Getting out of bed, she took a long shower and then made

herself breakfast. She was just finishing up her oatmeal and blueberries when she heard a car pull into the driveway. She went out the side door and smiled as Kyle jumped out of the passenger seat of Nicole's car and ran towards her, a huge joyous grin on his face. She wasn't surprised. Her six-year-old, blond, blue-eyed boy was almost always smiling.

Kyle loved life. He was curious about everything, always had a million questions, and thrived on meeting new people. She was lucky that he was such a resilient child, because he'd certainly been through some pain in his young life. His teenaged birth mother had been forced to give him away. Then his adoptive mother had died of cancer, and his adoptive father had died in an accident a few years later. Now he was living with her, and despite the fact that there was no blood between them, it was as if they'd been mother and son forever.

"Mom, I'm going to play on a baseball team," Kyle announced. "Look, I already got a mitt."

She looked at the weathered leather mitt in his hand. "Where did you get that?"

"Brandon's dad gave it to me. He said it used to be his when he was a kid. I told him I'd share it with Brandon," Kyle added, glancing over his shoulder at his brother. Brandon stood next to the car, not looking at all sure about coming any closer.

Brandon was the mirror image of Kyle, but he was a faded version, a little paler, less energetic, and there was rarely any light in his eyes. On occasion, there was a spark, usually when he was doing something with Kyle. Nicole had told her that the sparks came more often now than they had before, but Jessica had no frame of reference.

"Brandon isn't sure he wants to play," Kyle said, turning back to Jessica. "But I think he'll like it once we start practicing. Ryan is going to coach us."

"That's exciting." She glanced at Nicole, who had encouraged Brandon to walk down the driveway with her. "So a baseball team, huh?"

"It was all Ryan's idea," Nicole said, a smile in her eyes. "He took Brandon and Kyle to the park by the recreation center yesterday, and they were having signups for T-Ball. I know he should have asked you first. But you can get Kyle out of it if you want to."

"It's fine. I'm sure Kyle wanted to sign up."

"Can I show Brandon my new room?" Kyle interrupted.

"Of course. It's all ready for you." Kyle had seen the house once but not with his own bedroom furniture in it. She hoped he was going to like it.

"Come on, Brandon," Kyle said. "I still have the bunk beds. We can make a fort like we did in the last place."

Brandon didn't say anything, but when Kyle grabbed his hand he went along with him into the house.

Nicole let out a sigh, relief in her blue eyes. "One hurdle down. I wasn't sure how Brandon would handle your new house. He doesn't like change."

Jessica nodded. In the past three months, she'd come to understand the challenges that Nicole faced every day in dealing with Brandon's autism. There were few easy moments, and Jessica felt so much admiration for Nicole and Ryan, too. They'd had some bumps in their marriage dealing with the stress of a special needs child, but they'd come through those hard times together.

"I thank God every day that we found Kyle," Nicole added. "For three years, I searched for a way to link Brandon to the world. I just couldn't connect with him. No one could. But Kyle is the link. Through his twin brother, Brandon can communicate in a way that he can't do with anyone else."

"It is kind of amazing how in tune they are."

"I wonder sometimes if Brandon would have slipped into autism if he'd had his brother with him all along, because he was perfect until he was two years old. Then the lights in his head went out."

"Hopefully, they're coming back on."

"I think they might be, and it's because of you and Kyle."

She shook her head. "You have to stop thanking me, Nicole. We're in this together. Kyle may not be autistic, but he needs Brandon, too. And he also gets to have you and Ryan, which is also wonderful."

"Ryan is in heaven that he's going to get to coach Kyle in baseball. He's wanted to do those kinds of dad things all along, but with Brandon, he couldn't. With Kyle around, it's like we're real parents again." She frowned. "That didn't come out exactly right. I don't want you to think that we're trying to steal Kyle from you, or that I don't love Brandon, because I love him more than anything. He's my son, no matter what condition he's in."

"You don't have to watch your words with me. I understand. When the boys are together, it feels right, because it is right. They're brothers. They were always supposed to be with each other. And we all get something out of our extended family."

Relief flashed in Nicole's eyes. "I'm so glad you feel that way. I'm going to head out now. I'll see you at the party. Come whenever you want. And if Brandon wants to leave sooner, just give a call, and either Ryan or I will come by and get him."

"I will, but I think we'll be fine."

As Nicole left, Jessica walked down the driveway to pick up the Sunday newspaper. Apparently, Helen hadn't stopped the paper when she moved out. As Jessica reached the sidewalk, she saw the curtain fall in the front window of the house across the street, as if someone had been watching her. A shiver shot down her spine, reminding her of how unsettled she'd felt the night before when she'd heard Sally's conversation.

She was about to turn away when the front door of that

house opened and a man stepped out. He was in his late forties or early fifties she thought. He was attractive with dark hair and a deep tan. He wore tan slacks and a cream-colored polo shirt and moved with a quick step. He was halfway across the street before she realized he was coming to talk to her.

"Hello," he said with a friendly smile. "You must be my new neighbor. I'm Brett Murphy."

"Jessica Schilling," she said, shaking his hand. He had a firm confident grip.

"Did I see twin boys run into the house a moment ago?"

"Uh, yes," she said, deciding the twins separated at birth story could wait for another time. "Kyle and Brandon. They're six. You have a son, too, don't you?"

"Grayson is my stepson. He's eight. We should get the kids together one day."

"That sounds good."

His smile faded. "I'm sorry Helen had to move, but I hear you're going to help clean out her house."

"That's the plan," she said, a little surprised that her neighbors seemed to know so much about her arrangement with Helen.

"If you need assistance, let me know. I'm happy to move boxes or whatever you need."

"Thanks for the offer. I haven't really gotten started yet."

As she finished speaking, Sally pulled out of her driveway in her BMW. She gave Jessica and Brett a long look as she drove by.

"Have you met Sally yet?" Brett asked.

"Yesterday."

"She's a nice woman, but she loves to gossip. Count on whatever you tell her going around the neighborhood."

"Thanks for the tip. Have you lived here a long time?"

"Going on twenty-six years."

"So you were here during the fire?"

His expression sobered. "Yes. That was a terrible night."

A beautiful blonde stepped out on his porch, calling his name. The woman couldn't have been more than thirty, but Jessica was the last person to judge. She'd married a man fifteen years older than herself and had been incredibly happy.

"That's my wife, Adrienne," Brett said, a proud note in his voice. "We've been married almost a year. Still newlyweds. Coming!" he yelled back. "Don't forget, we're just across the street if you need anything."

"Thanks."

As Brett jogged back to his house, she took the newspaper inside. Setting it down on the kitchen counter, she went upstairs to check on the boys. It was then she realized that she'd left the ladder to the attic down, and, of course, that's where her curious little boy would go.

When she reached the attic, she saw her son pulling costumes out of a big trunk. Brandon was kneeling next to him, playing with a pile of loose beads.

"Look at all this stuff," Kyle said, amazement in his eyes. "Where did we get it?"

"It's not ours. It belongs to the woman who used to live here. I'm going to help her organize and clean things up."

"Can we have the costumes?"

"No. We're just going to see what she has here and then find out what she wants us to do with it."

"Maybe she wants us to keep everything."

She smiled at the hopeful look in his eyes. "I don't think so. You need to put that stuff back."

"Can we just play for a few minutes?" he pleaded.

"Fine, a few minutes. But stick to that trunk."

While Kyle went digging for more costumes, she pulled a box off a shelf and found herself looking at a stack of photo albums. She sat down on the floor and opened the first one. The only person in the Emery family she'd met was Helen, so she doubted she'd recognize anyone, but she was curious to see what the rest of the family looked like, especially the little girl who had been Sean's best friend.

Unfortunately, the first album went back too far in time. She flipped through black and white photos that appeared to have been taken in the nineteen forties and fifties. She set it down and went quickly through the next album, which was more of the same. Digging a little deeper into the box, she pulled out a bright pink album, and her nerves tightened. It was a child's photo album, and she had a feeling that child was Stacy.

She was right. Pictures of a baby girl, proud parents and grandparents filled the first few pages. Helen was in many of the shots, holding Stacy. And then a little brother arrived, and there were more pictures. It was the first time Jessica had seen the entire Emery family: Helen's husband, Tom, her son Robert, his wife, Lana, and their kids, Blake and Stacy.

While Helen, Tom and Robert all had dark hair, Lana and the two kids were blondes. Jessica flipped through several more pages, eager to see if there were any pictures of Stacy with the kids in the neighborhood, particularly one kid.

She found Sean a few pages later, an adorable picture of him and Stacy holding hands in front of a Catholic elementary school. The caption read, *First Day of Kindergarten.*

Stacy wore her long blonde hair in a single braid. Sean's brown hair was tousled as if he'd just gotten out of bed. They both wore versions of the school uniform: Stacy in a blue plaid skirt, white blouse and navy sweater and Sean in navy blue pants and a white shirt.

She smiled at the five-year-old version of Sean. His blue eyes were bright and filled with energy. He looked happy, eager to start school. She wondered what kind of student he'd been. He seemed more creative than academic, or maybe the passion for music had come later.

Turning the page, she found more shots of Stacy and Sean as they got older—a birthday party, a Halloween carnival, a soccer game—even a shot of Stacy holding a lizard while Sean looked on. Stacy was obviously not a girly girl. She liked sports, bugs and getting dirty. She also liked Sean. It was easy to see their love for each other. It was so innocent and pure.

She'd never had a male friend like that. She couldn't even remember any of the kids she'd gone to school with, but then she'd changed schools every couple of years. Her mother had always told her that they had to go where the jobs were and to look at it as an adventure. It hadn't taken her long to realize that the adventure was for her mom and the challenges and problems were all hers.

Shrugging off that thought, she turned to the last page in the album and saw a candid shot of Stacy on a swing, her gaze on the horizon, a light of excitement in her eyes. Jessica suddenly realized that this wasn't just the last page of photos, but the end of Stacy's short life.

Her stomach turned over. It had been one thing to hear about a long-ago fire, but to see the girl that had died, to know that that little girl had lived in this house and probably played in this attic made it all too real. And if it felt real to her, it was no wonder Sean had been so shaken up to come back in here.

Her heart broke as she thought of the pain he must have suffered—the pain that had never really gone away. She closed the book and wished she'd never opened it, because she didn't just feel more connected to Stacy, but also to Sean. She wanted to put her arms around him, to tell him that she understood his guilt and his sorrow, but what good would her understanding do him? He was going to have to make his own peace with what had happened. And putting her arms around him would be another bad idea, although the thought of it sent her heart racing.

She shook her head, annoyed with her reaction. She was

going to have to find a way to be close to Sean without wanting him. And she was going to have to do it fast, because she only had a few hours before Nicole's birthday party.

Six

—➤ ➤➤ ◄◄ ◄—

Sean got to Nicole's birthday party a little after seven. As he stepped out of the car, he threw back his shoulders and lifted his chin, feeling as if he was going into battle. He could see the crowd of people through the living room windows, and there were probably at least thirty Callaways inside Nicole's house. Many of those Callaways had big personalities, and at parties like this, there always seemed to be a competition for attention. He'd always preferred to stay out of that competition. It had been easier when he was a kid. His older siblings had usually been happy to steal the spotlight. But now that he was an adult, everyone seemed a lot more interested in his life.

Emma wanted to find him a girlfriend, and Nicole wanted to keep him away from the one woman he was actually interested in, the one woman who was no doubt at the party.

With a sigh, he told himself to stop stalling. The sooner he went in, the sooner he could leave.

As he stepped through the front door, he was greeted with a chorus of "*Sean*" by three of his younger, giggling teenage cousins who were in high school. Since his music career had started to take off, these girls had apparently decided he was cooler than he used to be.

After fending off a series of questions about which hot

musician he'd met recently, he made his way down the hall and into the big country-style kitchen. He came to an abrupt halt, his pulse jumping as he saw Jessica standing by the doors leading out to the back deck. She was talking to his brother, Drew, and Drew's girlfriend, Ria. Jessica laughed at something Drew said, her face lighting up with amusement.

Jessica was happy in San Francisco, he thought. And it wasn't just the city making her smile, but also his family. She'd been through hard times in her life, and she'd often felt alone. But she wasn't alone now. She'd landed in the middle of his crazy, loving family. And while he didn't always see the value of being one of so many, for Jessica it appeared to be a good thing.

Jessica looked away from Drew, her gaze meeting his. Her smile made his heart beat faster, and as much as he wanted to look away, he couldn't seem to look anywhere else but at her.

"Really, Sean?"

"What?" he asked, turning to see Emma at his side. She had a very smug smile on her face.

"If you're going to pull off this *just friends* thing with Jessica, you're really going to have to stop looking at her like she's your favorite flavor of ice cream."

"You're imagining things."

"I don't think I am."

"Where's Nicole?" he asked, changing the subject. "I want to wish her a happy birthday."

"Last time I saw her, she was out on the deck with Mom and Dad."

"Then maybe I'll get some food first."

"Chicken," she teased.

"Actually, that chicken looks good," he retorted, heading to the buffet on the kitchen table. A plate of chicken wings was calling his name.

Emma followed him across the room. She grabbed a carrot

and munched on it as she said, "Why were you so late?"

"I was working."

"On what? Are you writing a new song?"

"That was part of it," he said as he loaded up his plate.

"Part of what?"

"Why do you have so many questions?" he asked, taking a bite out of a spicy chicken wing.

"Why do you have so few answers? Sometimes I think your musician gig is just a cover. Maybe you're in the CIA and that's why you're so mysterious."

He grinned. "That would be something. And, wow, do you still have a big imagination."

"Are you criticizing my wife?" Max interrupted, putting an arm around Emma's shoulders. "Do I need to defend her?" he added with a grin.

"Sean thinks my imagination is too big," Emma said.

Max smiled. "I think it's just perfect." He finished his words with a kiss on her cheek. And then he whispered something into her ear.

Emma's cheeks turned pink. "Max, stop it."

"Yeah, stop it," Sean echoed. "You two should get a room."

"We have one," Max said. "Unfortunately, we're not going to be in it for a while. I have to go down to the station, Em. We just located our witness."

"Well, that's good news."

"Can you get a ride home from someone?"

"Absolutely. I'll walk you out."

As Max and Emma left, Jessica walked over.

"Hi," she said softly, a sparkle in her brown eyes.

"Hey." He set his half-empty plate down on the table, his appetite deserting him.

Silence fell between them, as he searched for something to say, but when Jessica was near, he couldn't seem to find words.

He got too caught up in her big, brown eyes, her soft, sexy mouth, and lips that were way too inviting. But he wasn't going to kiss her. Not here. Not in front of his family. Not anywhere, he added firmly, giving himself a mental kick. Jessica was off limits. He had to stop thinking of her in a sexual way. He had to stop now.

"Sean?" she queried, her voice a little rough, her eyes questioning. "Everything okay?"

"Yeah. Did you get moved in?" he asked, proud that he'd managed to string a couple of words together.

"I got our bedrooms set up, and the kitchen, too. That was a big job."

"You look tired," he said, noting the shadows under her eyes.

"I didn't sleep very well last night. Too many odd little noises."

"Really?" he asked, feeling tense at her words. "What kind of noises?"

"It was nothing, just the house settling, I'm sure. I'll get used to the creaks." She paused and gave a self-deprecating smile. "I think I scared myself a little."

"How did you do that?"

"Last night, I took some boxes outside to the recycle bin around midnight, and I heard my next door neighbor talking on the phone to someone."

"Mrs. Watson?"

"Yes. Sally had come over and introduced herself to me yesterday afternoon. She was friendly to me then, but when she was on the phone, she was definitely on edge. And she said some weird stuff."

"Like what?"

"She was worried that someone new was living in Helen's house, obviously referring to me. She said something about secrets and not sure what might be found in Robert's belongings."

"That's strange."

"It is. Right?" she asked, meeting his gaze. "Also, when I spoke to her earlier in the day she offered to help me clear out Helen's stuff. She was very curious as to what might be in the attic. When I put that offer to help with what I overheard later, I have to think that she didn't come over to be neighborly but to see what I was doing."

"She's lived next door to Helen forever. I'm sure she's been in the house on many occasions."

"That's true, although she did say she'd offered to help Helen on numerous occasions, but Helen always refused. She wasn't ready to let go of anything."

"Some people like to hang on to the past," he murmured.

"It's possible I misunderstood Sally's conversation. It was dark and I was tired. Maybe I imagined her tension."

He doubted that, but he couldn't come up with a logical reason for why Sally should care that Jessica was clearing out Helen's things.

"On another note," Jessica continued. "I found some photo albums in the attic. One of them belonged to Stacy. There were pictures of you and her together at kindergarten, soccer games, birthday parties. She was holding a large lizard in one shot."

He nodded, remembering that lizard all too well. "She named him Henry. She loved to name bugs and animals." He shook his head at the nostalgic sadness that ran through him. "It's funny the stuff I remember. I wonder why Lana left that album behind."

"It looks to me like she left a lot of things behind. Oh, and Sally isn't the only one interested in my cleanup. I also met Brett Murphy. He lives across the street. He offered to help move boxes, and he told me not to trust Sally with any information I didn't want going around the neighborhood. What do you think about that?"

"You're certainly drawing a lot of interest," he said, not quite sure what to make of the overly friendly neighbors.

"I guess I should be happy everyone is being so nice. But for some reason, they both rubbed me the wrong way. I don't know why."

"You should trust your instincts." He stopping talking as a crowd of people came into the kitchen. Kyle and Brandon and some of the younger kids made a beeline for the kitchen counter where Ryan was setting up an enormous triple layer chocolate cake.

"I guess it's time for cake," Jessica murmured. "Chocolate is my favorite."

"Yeah? Vanilla is more my flavor."

"That surprises me, because there is nothing vanilla about you," she said with a smile.

"Well, I do like a tart filling," he admitted.

More people entered the kitchen, and Sean and Jessica backed toward the wall to make room for everyone. As he inhaled the sweet scent of her perfume or maybe it was her shampoo, his heart began to race. She was too damn close to him. She smelled sexy and pretty, and he wanted to wrap himself up in that scent, wrap himself up in her. It would be so easy to put his arm around her, to pull her up against him, to bury his face in the curve of her neck.

He began to sweat. He couldn't remember when he'd felt so attracted to a woman. What the hell was wrong with him, and why did it have to be her? Why did Jessica have to be the one to get under his skin and into his head? She was all wrong in so many ways and yet very much right in others.

Jessica gave him a smile as more Callaways squeezed into the space and moved even closer to him. "We always seem to be in the middle of a crowd," she said.

He nodded, his jaw tightening, as he gazed down at her. The last time they'd been in the middle of a crowd she'd kissed him.

Her eyes darkened as she read his mind. "You don't have to worry. I can behave myself,"

"I wish I could say the same," he muttered. "I have to get out of here."

"Sean—"

"You don't want to stop me, Jess."

She stared back at him and then shifted so he could get past her. As he hit the hallway, he heard the group in the kitchen burst into an off-key but noisy rendition of *Happy Birthday.*

—→→◄◄←—

After escaping the kitchen, Sean thought about leaving the party entirely, but apparently not everyone was in the kitchen. His father was standing by the front door talking to his Uncle Kevin, and he wasn't in the mood to deal with either of them. He slipped into the guest room looking for some quiet and found his older brother, Aiden, changing his baby daughter's diaper.

His tension evaporated as he watched Aiden wrestle with his squirming and very happy three-month-old daughter, Chloe. Chloe was taking great delight in kicking her father's hands away as he tried to wipe down her bottom.

"Well, isn't this a picture," Sean drawled. "How the mighty have fallen. From rebel smokejumper to poop scooper."

Aiden had his sleeves rolled up to his forearms, a towel over one shoulder and a bottle of baby powder in his hand. He shot Sean a dark look, but when he turned back to his daughter, he was nothing but sweet. Aiden fastened the diaper and pulled up his daughter's leggings. "There you go, princess, all done," he said to the baby, then swung her up into his arms. As he turned to Sean, he added, "Just for the record, dealing with this kid is far more difficult and also far more exciting than jumping into a raging forest fire."

"Really?" he asked doubtfully.

"Trust me, one day you'll know."

"Yeah, we'll see about that. So fatherhood is going well?"

"Better every day," Aiden said with a nod. "I'm finally feeling like I know what I'm doing, at least some of the time."

"Chloe is getting big," Sean said.

"And more fun. She smiles and laughs, and her eyes light up when she sees me."

"She's a good looking kid."

"All Sara," Aiden said, referring to his wife.

As Aiden cradled the baby in his arms, Sean was touched by the tender protectiveness he saw on his brother's face. "You really are different now, Aiden. You look happy, content, a family man. Quite a change from the guy who used to like to walk on the wild side."

Aiden tipped his head. "I had to grow up some time. I wasn't sure I'd be a good husband or father, but falling in love with Sara, and now this little girl, has changed all that. I'd kill for them. The love I feel is overwhelming. I never imagined that it could be like this. I was the guy who had to jump out of planes to get his heart pumping, who had to break rules in order to know he was pushing the limits. Now all it takes is for Chloe to smile at me, and I am over the moon."

"I can see that. I kind of miss you as a troublemaker though. I liked it when you and Dad were fighting; it took the heat off of me." Second in the line-up of siblings, Aiden had been the first one to really test their father. He'd been a hell-raiser. And while he'd gone into firefighting, Aiden had left the city fire department to become a smokejumper, which hadn't pleased Jack. But Aiden hadn't let anyone stop him from doing what he wanted to do. In many ways, Aiden had been his role model. But his brother had definitely changed.

Aiden grinned. "Sorry, but I'm a responsible husband and

father now. You're on your own. What's going on with you and Dad?"

"The usual."

"He's disappointed and you're pissed off," Aiden said with a knowing nod. "I remember those days well. You're never going to win, you know. Jack Callaway won't ever change."

"I'm not trying to win or expecting him to change. I just wish he'd leave me alone."

"Aren't you living in the garage apartment?" Aiden asked dryly.

"For three weeks. Trust me, I'm counting the days."

"Well, try not to let Dad get to you."

"That's not easy. He hates everything I do."

"I've been there," Aiden said. "But try to remember that just because Dad doesn't like your choices doesn't mean he hates you. He just worries and wants the best for you." Aiden patted his sleepy daughter's back. "Now that I'm a father myself, I'm starting to understand him better."

"Hello, what's going on in here?" Sara asked as she came into the room. Aiden's pretty dark-haired wife gave them a smile. "How are you Sean? I didn't see you come in."

"I'm good. And you?"

"I'm tired. Chloe doesn't let us get much sleep. I think my daughter is going to be a night owl like her father."

"Hey, if I could go to bed right now, I would," Aiden cut in.

She laughed. "And I'd be right there with you."

As Aiden and Sara exchanged a loving look, Sean found himself yearning for that same kind of shared connection. Unfortunately, that kind of connection came with a lot of strings, so he shoved that idea out of his head.

Sara turned back to him. "Jessica told me that she moved into the Emery house. I couldn't believe it. I know it's been a long time since the fire, but I always felt like that house was kind of spooky after that."

He wasn't surprised that Sara would have the same reaction he'd had. Sara had grown up next door to his parents' house, and she'd known the Emery family, too.

"I remember when Stacy died," Sara added. "Her mom came over to talk to my mom after the fire. She was crying so hard. She said it was all her fault that Stacy was dead. My mom tried to convince her it was just an accident, but she was hysterical. Two days later, she was gone. My mom tried to get in touch with her, but she never called back. I guess she couldn't bear to talk to anyone from the neighborhood."

"Why would Stacy's mom think she was to blame for the fire? She wasn't even home," Sean asked.

Sara shrugged. "Maybe Mrs. Emery felt guilty because she wasn't there. She probably thought she could have gotten Stacy out if she'd been at home. But I don't know why she'd think that, because her husband couldn't save Stacy. If Mrs. Emery and Blake had been there, they probably would have died, too."

And if he hadn't let Stacy run away from his house, she wouldn't have been there at all.

"Maybe it's good that Jessica and Kyle are living there now," Sara continued. "We'll all be able to look at that house in a different, happier way."

"Yeah, maybe," he said, not at all sure about that possibility.

"It's just a house, guys," Aiden said. "It was rebuilt after the fire, and Helen Emery has lived there for years without any problems. It's not like it's haunted or anything."

"How do you know? You haven't been in the house, have you?" Sara challenged her husband.

"No, I haven't. But I don't believe in ghosts, and I've seen plenty of structures come back to life after a fire."

"You're being logical," Sara said, with a dismissive wave of her hand.

Aiden smiled. "Well, someone in this room has to be, don't you think?"

"I'm sticking with my opinion," Sara said. "Are you about ready to go, Aiden?"

"Any time."

"I'll say goodbye to Nicole and get my bag. Then we'll go. Nice to see you, Sean. Don't be a stranger. Come by and visit us sometime."

"I will," he promised.

After Sara left, Aiden gave him a speculative look. "Are you really bothered by Jessica moving into that house?"

"I'm bothered by a lot of things that have to do with Jessica," he admitted.

Aiden gave him a knowing look. "So it's like that. You have a thing for her."

"I'm trying not to."

"Probably a good idea. The family has pretty much adopted Jessica. If you mess around with Jessica and break her heart, there will be hell to pay."

"I know."

"But she is very attractive," Aiden said.

"Yeah," Sean said with a nod as he met his brother's gaze.

"Still, you're a musician. You can get any hot girl you want. Leave this one alone. Your life will be a lot easier."

"I completely agree," he said, but knowing it would be best to leave Jessica alone and doing it were not exactly the same thing.

Seven

"Can I have another piece of cake?" Kyle asked Jessica.

She shook her head. "You already had one big piece."

"But I'm still hungry," Kyle whined.

"You can have a snack when we go home. Go say goodbye to Brandon. It's time to leave."

"Can't I just stay here tonight?"

"No. We're going to stay in the new house tonight." She could see thunderclouds gathering in her sugared-up six-year-old, and quickly added, "Tell Brandon we'll pick him up for school tomorrow."

Kyle gave her a sulky look but did as he was told. As he left the room, she walked over to Nicole, who was cleaning up the kitchen. Most of the family had left, and the few remaining guests were chatting in the living room.

"Shouldn't someone else be doing that?" Jessica asked. "You're the birthday girl."

"Everyone has already done way too much. Are you leaving now?"

"Yes. I want to get Kyle to bed since it's a school night."

"Thanks for coming. I know it's been a busy weekend for you. By the way, Emma told me Sean got all worked up about the house. I guess I should have been more sensitive. I'm sorry about that. I hope the house is going to work out."

"I'm sure it will. I'll see you tomorrow."

After leaving the kitchen, she went down the hall and gave Aiden and Chloe a smile as they passed by. Then she went into the guest room to grab her purse. She ran straight into Sean. "Sorry, I didn't see you," she said, trying to ignore the sudden tingle of her nerves. "I thought you left a while ago."

"I was talking to Aiden. I'm on my way out now."

"Me, too. I'm just grabbing my bag." She walked past him to retrieve her purse from the desk. As she turned to leave, she found Sean blocking the doorway, an odd expression on his face. "What?"

He stared back at her for a long moment, some internal battle playing out in his eyes. Then he said, "Nothing, never mind. You can go."

"Thanks for the permission," she said dryly.

"I didn't mean it like that."

"Do you even know what you mean?" she challenged. "You are the king of mixed signals, Sean. You like me one minute and hate me the next. You kiss me like there's no tomorrow, and then you can't bear to stand next to me in a crowded room. What is your problem?"

"You. You're my problem. And while everything else you said is true, I don't hate you. I wish I did."

She let out a breath. "It's fine, forget it. I'm just tired, and a little on edge, and I'm taking it out on you."

"You're nervous about going back to the house, aren't you?"

"Well, I shouldn't be, because it's stupid."

"I'm the one who spooked you. I'm sorry."

"It's fine."

"Is it?"

"Well, it will be."

"Why don't I follow you home? I can come inside, take a

look around, and make sure everything is okay."

She stared at him in astonishment. Those were the last words she'd expected to hear come out of his mouth. "You want to go into Stacy's house after dark?"

He stiffened. "I'm trying to think of it as your house, Jess. And it's the least I can do for making you nervous. There's nothing wrong with that house, and I shouldn't be putting the monsters of my eight-year-old nightmares onto you. In fact, going there at night would probably be a good step towards vanquishing those monsters."

She wasn't so sure about that. But all she said was, "All right. I'm going to get Kyle. I'll meet you out front—unless you change your mind again."

"I'm not going to change my mind," he promised.

—➤➤◄◄◄—

He really wanted to change his mind!

Sean pulled up in front of the Emery house as Jessica parked in the driveway. The house was completely dark and the nearby streetlight threw eerie shadows down the street. As a kid he'd been in the house dozens of times, often at night, and he'd never been scared. But he couldn't remember those times now. They were all behind a wall of flames and his last haunting images of Stacy.

She'd laugh at him if she were here. She'd loved to tell ghost stories. One of their favorite activities was to set up a tent in her room and turn off all the lights? Stacey would hold up a flashlight and whisper a story that always started with the same words, *It was a night just like this…*

He'd loved her stories and had helped her make up even creepier, bloodier tales. But none of those stories had been real. The lights had always come back on, and everything had been normal.

"Sean?" Jessica called.

Her voice penetrated through the fog in his brain. She was standing on the porch. She'd opened the front door and turned on the light in the entry. He could also see a light on upstairs now. Kyle had obviously gone up to his room.

Well, if a six-year-old could do it...

He got out of the van and walked up to the house. "Sorry, I was just checking my phone," he lied.

"Everything looks fine. You can go home."

Now that he'd made it to the steps, he wanted to go inside. "Actually, I'd like to see Stacy's photo album." He'd been thinking about that album ever since Jessica had mentioned it.

She gave him a doubtful look but waved him inside. "It's still up in the attic. I'll get it for you. Let me just make sure Kyle is getting ready for bed. Tomorrow is a school day.

He followed her up the stairs and into Kyle's room, which had once belonged to Stacy's brother, Blake. Jessica had turned her son's room into a kid's paradise. Bunk beds with bright red and orange-checkered comforters and matching fluffy pillows took up one corner of the room. On the opposite wall was a bookcase filled with books and games, a desk with crayons, paints and paper, and along the other wall was a toy chest overflowing with trucks, blocks, action figures and stuffed animals. Kyle knelt on the floor in the middle of the room, playing with a model airplane.

Kyle looked up and gave Sean a happy smile. "Hi Uncle Sean. Look what Ryan gave me."

"That's cool."

"Ryan said he's going to teach me how to fly planes when I'm bigger."

"That will be fun."

"Kyle," Jessica interrupted. "You're supposed to be getting ready for bed."

"Five more minutes," Kyle pleaded.

"You had five minutes. Put the plane away and go brush your teeth."

Kyle grumbled but got up and headed for the bathroom.

"Sorry about the uncle part," Jessica said. "Nicole thought it would be easier to give Kyle the same relationship to everyone in your family as Brandon has."

"Kyle can call me whatever he wants. I have no problem with uncle." He paused. "You did a great job on this room, Jess. It feels light and happy."

She smiled with pleasure. "I hope so. I always wanted a room like this. Maybe not so much boy stuff, but I get to relive at least some of my childhood fantasies through Kyle." She cocked her head to one side, giving him a speculative look. "Being in this room doesn't bother you?"

He shook his head. "I didn't spend much time in here. Stacy's room might be another story."

"I haven't done anything with her room yet. Right now there are just boxes and extra furniture in there, most of which came out of the master bedroom. I keep the door closed so Kyle doesn't get into things. Do you want to see it?"

"Not tonight." He wasn't quite ready to face that old memory. "I would like to see her photo album though."

She nodded and they made their way into the attic. Jessica turned on the lone light, pulled a pink album out of a box and handed it to him.

"Here you go," she said. "I'm going to get Kyle in his pajamas."

After Jessica left, he opened the album. The first few pictures didn't mean that much to him. Stacy as a baby didn't resonate with him, but when he got to the photos of them together, his heart started to pound. Seeing her blue eyes stare back at him now made him realize that he hadn't actually looked at her face in a picture since the night she died. She'd always been in his head, her features obscured by the flames and the smoke. But this was the girl he remembered. This was his friend.

She'd been a happy kid, a lot like Kyle, he thought, always curious, willing to try new things, make new friends. She'd loved playing at his house and getting involved with all his siblings, while he was usually happier to be on his own.

As he flipped through the pages, he found his tension easing. And, occasionally, a smile crossed his lips. Stacy had had a short life, but it had been good.

He closed the album and put it back in the box. Then grabbed another album to look through. This was the family album. There were date nights between Stacy's parents, birthday parties for the kids and a New Year's Eve celebration with all the neighbors that included Sally Watson and her husband, Kent, Brett Murphy and his first wife, Natasha, and even his own parents, Jack and Lynda. There were also a few shots of Sara's parents. They'd certainly all done a lot together; they'd been a tight group.

He was about to turn the page when his gaze caught on one photo in particular. There were about ten adults sitting around a bonfire at the beach, but in the shadows, the camera had caught Sally and Robert in a rather intimate pose. They were huddled together. Robert had his arm around Sally's waist as she leaned in to say something to him.

Had there been something going on between Robert and his next-door neighbor? Sally was an attractive woman. Sean searched the photo for her husband, but Kent didn't seem to be there. He turned to the next page and found a couple of more photos where Robert and Sally seemed to be together while their spouses were nowhere to be seen.

"Sean."

He jumped at the sound of Jessica's voice.

"Sorry, I didn't mean to startle you," she said. "What are you looking at?"

"Pictures from the old days." As she came to his side, he pointed to a photo taken at New Year's Eve. It was a crowded party, everyone in cocktail dresses and dark suits and there in the corner were Sally and Robert again. They weren't doing anything wrong, but there was something about the way they were always so close together that disturbed him. "I found a lot of shots of Sally and Robert looking a little too cozy. What do you think?"

"They just look like they're at a party."

"There are other shots." He flipped back to the beach bonfire. "What about this?"

"They do appear to be very friendly," she said slowly, lifting her gaze to his. "Do you think something was going on between them?"

"I don't know. But if they did have an affair, that would give Sally a reason to be concerned about what's in these boxes."

"Would she really be worried about a twenty-year-old affair coming to light?"

"She's still married, isn't she?"

"Yes. But even if we found a picture of the two of them in bed together, we wouldn't take it to her husband."

"She might not know that."

He had barely finished speaking when they heard a sudden loud crash that came from somewhere below.

"What was that?" Jessica asked, dashing for the door.

"It sounded like it came from the outside," he said, following her down the steps to the second floor landing.

Jessica stopped to take a quick look in Kyle's room. Then she pulled the door shut. "He's fast asleep."

"Let's check the downstairs," he said, jogging down to the first floor. There was nothing out of place in any of the rooms, so they went through the kitchen and out the side door to the driveway. The trashcans had been upended, a plastic bag spilling out of one of them. "I think we found the problem." He pulled the can upright and stuffed the garbage back inside. "It was probably raccoons, Jess. We get a lot of them around here."

She wrapped her arms around her waist as she gave a tight, worried nod. "Sure. Let's go back inside."

After they went into the house, Jessica turned the dead bolt and gave him a wide-eyed nervous look. "That driveway seems to make me nervous every night."

"I really think it was just a raccoon, Jess. I can't tell you how many times they knock the cans over at my parents' house."

"You're right."

"You don't look convinced."

"I'm tired. And I just need to get used to this house."

"Do you want me to hang out for a while?"

Indecision played through her eyes, but in the end she shook her head. He didn't know whether to feel disappointed or relieved.

"No, I'm good," she said. "You don't need to babysit me. I've been taking care of myself for a long time. I'm a tough girl."

"You are tough, but you're also really soft in all the right places."

Her quick intake of breath matched the new spark in her eyes.

"Sean," she warned. "You're about to mix the signals again."

He stared back at her in bemusement. "You can read my mind, can't you?"

"It's not hard when you look at me the way you're looking at me. And don't think I don't want to kiss you again, because I do, but we can't keep crossing the line. You can't have me, and I can't have you. So you should go home. It's the right thing to do."

"I'm really bad at doing the right thing." He cupped her face with his hands and gave her a long kiss. She resisted for a second, and then her mouth opened under his. She tasted like chocolate and wine, like everything that was good and bad for you at the same time. He thought he could kiss her for a couple of days and it wouldn't be long enough. Every kiss made him want another and another. He finally broke away, sliding his mouth along her jawline, swirling his tongue around her ear lobe and then he whispered in her ear. "Goodnight, Jessica."

"Goodnight, Sean," she murmured, her sweet, sexy gaze sending out an invitation that didn't match her words.

It took all his strength to walk out of the room. He hadn't wanted to come into this house and now he didn't want to leave, but he had to leave. In a few hours, the sun would rise again, and with it would come all the reasons why he and Jessica did not belong together. He just wished he could remember some of those reasons now.

Eight

➤➤➤⤜⤛⤜⤛

Sean woke up early, put on some running shoes and ran across town, ending up at the coast. The fog was still thick on the beach, sending a cool misty spray against his face as he ran. He didn't mind the cold morning. It felt refreshing and invigorating. He needed to clear his head and refocus his priorities.

On his way back, he stopped by the local market to pick up coffee and a bagel. Then he headed home. He ran into his youngest sister, Shayla, in the driveway. Shayla had dark blonde hair and eyes that mixed between light blue and gray depending on what she was wearing. Today she had on black slacks and a purple sweater over a white top.

"Hi stranger," he said, giving her a hug. Despite living a few yards from the main house, he hadn't seen Shayla since he'd moved in. "Where have you been hiding?"

"At the hospital. I seem to spend my life there."

He saw the tired shadows under her eyes. "It's been a grind, hasn't it?"

"Yes, but I love it, too."

"You're going to make a hell of a doctor," he said, knowing it was the truth. Shayla had an IQ that was close to genius. She'd skipped a grade to graduate from high school at sixteen and was now finishing up her first year of residency at the age of twenty-five. In addition to her brains, she also had a big, caring heart. That combination was going to be great for her patients.

"I hope I'll be good. I've applied to do a global health rotation in Africa," she said. "If it goes through, I'll have a chance to experience health care in a third world country."

"That sounds adventurous and challenging."

"I've been in the classroom or the hospital for so many years, I think it will be good for me to get out into the world. It's only for two months. Dad isn't too thrilled about my idea. He thinks it might be dangerous."

"Will it be dangerous?"

She shrugged. "I don't know exactly where I'll be sent yet. But I hope I'll be able to do some good."

He nodded, very proud and impressed by his little sister. "You're amazing, Shay."

"It's about time you realized that," she said dryly. "But I haven't gotten chosen yet. We'll see what happens. Hey, I'm sorry I missed your show the other night."

"No problem. There's always another show."

"Is there? Emma said you didn't have anything planned for the next few weeks. Are you guys recording?"

"We're going to do some of that," he said vaguely, not wanting to get into his other plans until he knew how they were going to work out.

"I better go."

"See you later." As he left Shayla, he couldn't help thinking that she was probably going to outshine them all with her ambition and drive.

After downing his bagel and coffee, he picked up his guitar and started to strum. A melody began to take shape. Then he tried out some of the words going through his mind, *soft lips, hard shell, fragile, strong, should but couldn't,* and he knew he was writing about Jessica, about the push-pull he felt whenever she was around her, wanting what wasn't good for him and what wasn't good for her.

His phone rang, and he set down the guitar, thinking it was a good time for an interruption. "Hello?"

"Hi Sean. I have some information for you," Emma said. "I located the Emery case file."

There was an odd note in her voice. "And?" he asked, his pulse quickening. "Do you know how the fire started?"

"No, the investigation was inconclusive."

His heart sank. "So that's that."

"I'm not sure."

"What do you mean?"

"I'm concerned as to why the investigative report is so short. And some attachments appear to be missing. There's usually a case file an inch thick when two people perish in a fire. This report is barely three pages."

"Why would that be?"

"I don't know. It strikes me as very odd, because Dad worked that fire, and the Emerys were his friends. He would have made sure the investigation was thorough."

"Maybe he didn't have that much power twenty years ago."

"Maybe," she said, clearly unconvinced. "I'm going to do a little digging. I'm on my way to a meeting right now, but can we meet this afternoon? Maybe around one?"

"Sure. Where? Your office?"

"Why don't we meet at the Emery house? I'd like to walk around the property. I know it's been redone, but I think it would still be helpful for me to see the layout. I already checked with Jessica, and she said she'd be home then."

"What did you tell Jessica?"

"Nothing. I just asked her if she'd be home, and she said she would be. You have until one o'clock to decide what you want to tell her."

After spending the morning volunteering in Kyle's classroom, Jessica got back to her house just before one. She was very curious as to why Emma and Sean were coming over. It had to be about the fire. Sean must have asked Emma to look into it.

She pulled into the driveway, and as she got out of the car she saw Sally watering some plants in her yard. She would have been happy to just wave and go inside, but Sally had other ideas. She immediately set down the hose and came through the trees that separated their properties.

"How's the cleanup going?" Sally asked.

"Great," she said, feeling a little awkward. The phone call she'd overheard the other night still lingered in her mind as well as the photos she'd seen of Sally and Robert Emery. Were those photos the reason Sally was worried about Jessica being in Helen's house? There hadn't been anything that scandalous, although they might not have found everything yet.

"Have you discovered anything interesting?" Sally asked.

"Like what?" she countered, curious to hear what Sally would say.

Sally hesitated, then gave a light wave of her hand. "Oh, I don't know. Helen had a penchant for antiques. Maybe you'll find an ugly old vase that turns out to be incredibly valuable."

"So far I haven't seen anything like that. But if I did, the profits would go to Helen."

"Oh, of course. Not that Helen needs the money. Her husband left her quite well off." Sally paused. "I saw you talking to Brett Murphy yesterday. What did you think of him?"

"He seemed very nice," she said, trying to stay carefully neutral.

"He was probably courting your vote. He's running for

County Supervisor this year."

"He didn't mention that." She wondered about the note of dislike in Sally's voice. "Are you two friends?"

"Not for a long while. Brett can't be trusted. He's very charming, but he always has an agenda. Don't ever forget that."

She thought Sally probably had an agenda, too. Unfortunately, she didn't know what either of them was up to. She turned her head at the sound of a car. Sean parked his minivan at the curb and got out.

As he walked toward them, Sally said. "Goodness, is that Sean Callaway?"

"Yes," Jessica said.

"I'll be." Sally waited for Sean to join them and then said. "I can't believe it's you, Sean. I haven't seen you in years, not since you were a teenager."

"Hello Mrs. Watson."

"Please. You're grown up now. Call me Sally."

"How are your daughters?"

"They're good. Tanya is married. Blair is engaged. Christie is still single," she said with a sparkle in her eyes. "You and Christie should get together, catch up. Unless..." She looked from Sean to Jessica. "Are you two together?"

"No," they both said at the same time.

"Jessica is a friend of the family," Sean added.

"I see. How are your parents?" Sally asked. "I haven't seen them in ages."

"They're doing great."

"I heard your grandmother has Alzheimer's."

"Unfortunately, yes," he said. "She has good days and bad days, but she's hanging in there."

"Good for her."

"There's Emma," Jessica said as Emma pulled up behind Sean's van.

"Well, it's quite the family affair," Sally said, giving

Jessica a thoughtful look. "I didn't realize you were connected to the Callaways."

She didn't know what to say to that. She certainly didn't feel like explaining her relationship to a woman who had already shown her love to gossip. In the end, she said. "The Callaways have been wonderful to me."

"It was nice to see you again, Sally," Sean said.

"You, too, Sean," she replied. "Jessica, I'm sure I'll see you soon."

She had a feeling that would be sooner than she wanted, but she simply smiled and walked across the lawn to greet Emma. Out of the corner of her eye, she could see Sally watching them.

"Sorry I'm late," Emma said. "My meeting ran long."

"It's fine. I just got here," Sean told her.

"Let's go inside," Jessica suggested. The last thing she wanted to do was get into a discussion in front of Sally Watson. She led them into the kitchen and gave them both an expectant look. "So, what's going on?"

"I asked Emma to look up the case file on the fire," Sean explained. "I got to thinking that I didn't know how it started, and I was curious."

"I figured this was about the fire. So how did it start?"

"I don't know for sure," Emma replied. "What I do know is that the fire began in the garage. Because there are usually accelerants in a garage—paint thinner, gasoline, lighter fluid and cleaning chemicals—a fire in that area is highly combustible. Common household items can become explosive, and that's apparently what happened. The fire spread to this room and the room across the hall, which I believe was Robert's office, and there was also damage to the living room and dining room. Basically, the entire first floor was involved."

"And no one could tell how it started?" Sean asked. "How does the garage suddenly catch fire?"

"In an interview with Lana Emery, she stated that they'd been having problems with the car starting. One theory was that Robert Emery was working on the car, and a spark ignited something flammable nearby." Emma paused, her expression serious. "Mr. Emery's body was found in the garage. An autopsy wasn't possible, because of the condition of the body."

Sean's jaw tightened. His face was pale, and his eyes dark. "What about Stacy? What do you know about her?"

"The television was on in her bedroom," Emma said. "The fire didn't reach that part of the house, but there was certainly heavy smoke."

"But she—she was badly burned," Sean ground out.

Emma nodded. "It's possible that she smelled smoke or heard her father call out to her and went down to investigate and got caught in the fire. She was able to get out of the house, but she died at the hospital a few hours later. She was not able to make any kind of statement. She was unconscious upon arrival at the E.R."

Sean blew out an audible breath. "What else?"

"Unfortunately, there's not much more I can tell you. Mrs. Emery's initial interview was cut short because she was hysterical. And the subsequent interview revealed no new information." Emma paused. "Dad also filed a report as a first responder. His account corroborated what I just told you. He also reported seeing black smoke when he arrived, which supports a chemically-based fire."

"So that's it?" Sean asked.

"For now. I'm going to see if I can track down the investigator. He's retired but he might remember something."

"From twenty years ago?" Jessica asked doubtfully.

"When a child dies in a fire, you usually don't forget," Emma said.

"But what other questions do you have?" Jessica asked, feeling like she was missing something. "It sounds like everyone was on the same page. They believed the fire to be accidental."

Emma nodded. "That was the consensus then, but I don't understand why the investigation was so short. There were only two witness statements, one from a Harriett Conover who lives in the house at the corner and the other from a Jason Danvers who apparently lives two streets over. I find it difficult to believe that no one else in this neighborhood came out to see what was apparently a raging fire."

Jessica glanced at Sean. He'd gone rigid at the discussion of eyewitnesses. He sent her a warning look, but it was unnecessary. She had no intention of telling Emma he was there that night. This was his trauma. He needed to deal with it in his own way.

"There was also no investigation into the Emerys," Emma continued. "I wonder if Robert or Lana had any reason to want to burn down their house."

"What reason could that be?" Sean ground out.

"Insurance money."

"They wouldn't set fire to the house when they were in it," Sean said.

"Sometimes people get caught up in fire, especially if it's explosive. There was also a note in the file that Robert had recently left his job. His wife said he'd been working at home, looking for employment and doing some freelance work. But no one spoke to his employer or any of his clients. Frankly, I think this was a shoddy investigation. I know we have forensic technology now that's a lot better than it was twenty years ago, but that still doesn't explain why basic investigative procedures weren't followed."

"What are you getting at Emma?" Jessica asked.

"I don't know yet. But I'd like to do some investigating myself. I'll probably come to the same conclusion, but I must admit my curiosity is piqued. So walk me around the house.

How do you get into the garage?"

"It's through the hallway," Jessica said, leading Emma across the hall and into the garage. She didn't know where Sean went, but he didn't come with them. He probably needed a few minutes to catch his breath. It wasn't that Emma had declared the fire was anything but an accident, but she had raised some doubt. It would have been better if the findings had been cut and dried. Then maybe Sean could have let it go.

"I pulled up the blueprints of the original house," Emma said as she walked around. "It looks like this garage was rebuilt to the same dimensions. Where did all this furniture come from?"

"Mrs. Emery's bedroom. I had to move her pieces out so I could move mine in."

Emma glanced over her shoulder, then said. "What's going on with Sean, Jessica? What don't I know?"

She was taken aback by the direct question. "You should ask Sean that."

"I don't think he'll tell me."

"You should try," she said, not willing to share anything Sean had told her in confidence.

Emma gave her a speculative look. "Sean keeps saying there's nothing between you. But I don't believe him."

"We're just—friends." Or at least they were trying to be.

"Well, as a friend, I hope you'll look out for him. Sean doesn't get emotional or upset about anything. I haven't seen him this worked up…" Her voice trailed away. "Well, the last time was probably when Stacy died. I'm worried about him. I know that Sean blames himself for letting Stacy leave our house, but I feel like there's something I don't know."

Jessica shrugged. "You should ask him," she repeated.

"All right. I can see that I will get nowhere with you. I'll do some digging and see what I come up with."

"I can't imagine what you could find that would make any

of this better."

"I don't know either. But Sean asked for my help, and he rarely asks for anyone's help, so I know it's important to him. If there's information to be found, I'm going to find it. Tell Sean I'll be in touch."

"What if you can't find out anything?"

"Then we'll be no worse off than we were before."

Jessica wasn't so sure of that. She couldn't help feeling that Sean should have left it all alone, because digging in the embers might bring that fire back to life, and who knew who would be destroyed this time? She very much hoped it wouldn't be Sean.

Nine

After Emma left, Jessica went upstairs and found Sean standing in the doorway of Stacy's room.

"Sean? Are you okay?"

"It's not the same. I know you told me it wouldn't be, but I had to see for myself." He turned to face her. "Did Emma leave?"

"Yes. She said she'd be in touch."

"What do you think about what she told us?"

"I don't know. Emma seems like a smart investigator, so I trust her to do what she needs to do."

He gazed into her eyes. "You think it's a bad idea."

"Let's just say I'm not sure it's a good idea. Sometimes the past is better left alone."

"You're probably right," he conceded. "Although it's more likely Emma will find nothing. The first investigator might have been lazy, but that doesn't mean he was wrong."

"No, it doesn't. By the way, Emma knows you're hiding something from her. Why don't you at least tell her where you were that night?"

"Maybe I will at some point—if it's important. In the meantime, I need to get out of here. Are you free? Do you want to take a ride with me?"

"I thought we were trying to stay away from each other."

"Let's start later. I could use the company."

And how could she resist that plea? She seemed to have absolutely no willpower when it came to Sean. "All right. Nicole is picking up the boys from school and keeping them until dinner, but I do have to meet Helen at four o'clock."

"No problem."

"Where do you want to go?"

"Let's find out."

Ten minutes later, Jessica buckled her seatbelt as Sean pulled away from the curb. She was happy to get out of the house. Moving there was starting to feel like the worst idea she'd ever had. She was also foolishly excited to spend a little more time with Sean. She didn't know where they were going, but she was happy to let him take the lead. She'd been on her own, in charge of every decision for almost two years now, and it was nice to just be driven somewhere.

She glanced out the window, watching the streets of San Francisco pass by, thinking how much she was starting to like her new home city. San Francisco was a lovely mix of neighborhoods, many with their own culture. It was also a picturesque city with its steep hills, famous cable cars, and wide, sweeping bay views. She even appreciated the fog that came in every night and eventually disappeared somewhere around midday, only to come back in again as the sun went down.

San Francisco had charm and history. It was a lot different than Las Vegas, where she'd spent many years of her life. It was also more urban and exciting than Angel's Bay, her most recent home. She'd liked that beautiful seaside town with its warm people and legends of shipwrecks and gold, but Angel's

Bay had been Travis's town. San Francisco felt more like her.

As Sean made a couple of decisive turns, she asked, "So where are we going?"

"You'll see."

"You're being mysterious."

"It's easier to show than to tell."

"Okay, now I'm intrigued."

He flashed her a smile, and she was happy to see his earlier tension had disappeared.

"Just the way I want you," he said.

"What is this part of town called?"

"The Haight. You've probably heard of Haight Ashbury. It was made famous in the sixties when the flower children and hippies descended on San Francisco."

"I have heard of the Haight. My mom spent a summer here."

"Maybe the Summer of Love," he said lightly. "The neighborhood has changed in the last forty years, but it hasn't strayed too far from its roots of rebellion."

She could see that, noting the eclectic mix of tattoo parlors, vintage clothing stores, and even a used record store. "I can't believe someone still sells records. Who could play them anymore?"

"I still have a record player. It belonged to my biological mom. I remember her putting on records when she ironed. It's one of my very few memories of her."

"Wow, I don't ever remember my mother ironing. She just threw things into the dryer and let them spin."

He grinned. "That usually works for me."

"Look at that—Madame Elisabeth's Dance Studio," she said, pointing out the window at a very old building. "That place was famous. My mom took tap lessons there."

"It looks like it's been closed for a while."

"Madame Elisabeth died about seven years ago. I

remember reading about it. She was a real character in the dance community. She danced into her seventies if you can believe that. I met her when I was a kid. She came to one of my mom's dance classes in Vegas. I remember that she had bright red hair and really red lipstick. She was not a person to be ignored." Jessica paused. "Sad that the studio is closed. I've actually been thinking about taking a dance class. It's been three years since I danced. I'm starting to miss it."

"I'm sure there are other studios in the city."

"True. I'll have to look into it once I get Kyle settled into a routine. Sharing parenting duties with Nicole has actually given me a little more time than I had before. And until I figure out what I want to do for money, I might as well dance."

"It's nice that you don't have to decide something right now."

"I'm lucky that Travis left me a nest egg, but eventually I will need a job. All I've ever done is dance. I guess it's time to learn something new."

"Is it? Why not dance?"

"I'm getting too old, it's a lot of night work, and there are just a lot of reasons why not," she finished, waving her hand in the air.

He shot her a thoughtful look. "You seem to have a love-hate relationship with dancing, Jess. Why is that?"

"Well, on one hand, dancing was the only thing my mom and I shared, and it was the only thing that she ever watched me do. She even admitted I was good. When she taught at the dance school, we were together a lot, but when she was dancing in shows or in music videos, she was gone. So, dancing took her away from me, too. She loved being on stage much more than she loved being a mom. I was an accident. She didn't really want a child, but she couldn't bring herself to get rid of me."

"Because she loved you," Sean said.

"She did—in her own way. Sometimes that way was difficult to understand."

"I get that."

She knew he did, because while her mom was quite different than Jack Callaway, both she and Sean had had trouble relating to their parents. But Sean had been lucky to have a second parent in Lynda. She'd only had her mother.

"I don't think you're too old to dance," Sean continued. "Not if Madame Elisabeth danced into her seventies."

"She was special."

"What about teaching?"

"I have considered that, but I'm not sure I could follow someone else's style or program."

"You could start your own dance school."

"That sounds like a really big job."

"You know how they're run. You told me you practically grew up in a school."

"I also know they're a lot of work. And I don't know much about running a business."

"You can learn."

"I also want to give Kyle a good childhood. I don't want him to grow up the way I did, with a mother who was always at work."

"That will never happen, Jess. You are not your mother. And sometimes kids need to see their parents going after their dreams. It can be inspiring."

"Watching my mother go after her dream just pissed me off."

"Well, she didn't do it the right way."

"That's true," she murmured.

Sean turned down an alley and parked next to a building. "We're here."

"Which is where exactly?" she asked, looking around. All she could see were the back doors of a bunch of warehouse-type buildings.

"Come on, I'll show you."

They got out of the car, and he led her toward a door with a sign that read Ashbury Studios.

"Is this a music studio?" she asked. "Is this where you record?"

"It's where I'm going to record—when it's done." He opened the door and waved her inside. "Watch your step. We're still in the construction phase." He flicked on the light switch and she could see a long hallway covered with drywall. He led her down the hall, pointing out some smaller rooms along the way. "These are the rehearsal rooms that we'll be renting out. Then we have two studios, one for groups and another for solo artists." He opened a door at the end of the hall and waved her inside. "This is the main studio or the live room as we call it."

She glanced around the large space. It was modern in design but the exposed beams gave the room a warmer tone. At the far end of the room was a panel of glass that led to a smaller room.

"That's the control room where the engineers will work," Sean explained. "We should have the console installed next week."

Her brows drew together as she tried to keep up. "You keep saying we. Who's we?"

"My partner, Hunter Thomas."

"Your partner? Wait a second." She gave him a questioning look. "This is your studio? You're the owner?"

He gave her a proud smile. "Surprised?"

"Yes," she admitted. "When did all this happen? Why doesn't anyone in your family know about it?"

"Because it's still a work in progress. Hunter and I have known each other since we were in high school. We played in a band together at one point. Then Hunter decided to become a sound engineer and producer and made his way to L.A. We always kept in touch. We had this dream that one day we'd open our own studio. Well, last year Hunter and his brother inherited this building from their grandfather. Hunter's brother lives in New York and didn't want anything to do with the property so he sold me his half."

"That must have been expensive."

"It was. But I've been saving money for a long time. I've lived pretty cheaply, knowing that I wanted to be ready in case an opportunity presented itself. Luckily, Hunter's brother was able to give me a deal."

She stared at him in astonishment. "I didn't think you were the plan-ahead type."

"Only when it comes to music," he conceded. "I made some good money last year, not just with the band, but with some songs that I sold to some big artists."

"This is amazing."

"Not yet, but I hope it's going to be amazing. We envision it as a multi-purpose studio, because so many people can record on their computers now. But they still need rehearsal space, lessons, and advanced engineering facilities. We're going to provide all that. And we're going to rent the upstairs space out as well and use that to bolster the bottom line."

She could hardly believe the man she'd thought of as a free spirit was talking about profit margins and bottom lines. There were a lot more layers to Sean than she had imagined. "I'm impressed. The space is great, the location is good, and you know the music business inside and out. It's the recipe for success."

"We'll see. Let me show you the lounge."

He led her through a door at the far side of the studio. The lounge was a large room with comfortable brown leather couches, a warm, brightly colored throw rug, and a small kitchen. Along one wall was a display of guitars signed by famous musicians. She picked one up and read the inscription.

"John Mayer?" she asked in wonder.

Sean nodded. "We opened for him a few years back. When he heard about the studio, he sent over the guitar."

"That's incredible. You have some good connections."

"Some."

"How have you kept this a secret?"

He shrugged. "It hasn't been that difficult. I haven't been around the family much the last year. I would like to keep this a secret awhile longer, so if you don't mind keeping it to yourself, I'd appreciate it."

"Why don't you want anyone to know?"

"Because my family has a lot of opinions, and they don't hesitate to share them. Hunter and I have a plan, and I don't need anyone else's input. We're going to host a grand opening next month and I'll announce it then."

"You're going to blow everyone away."

"It's just a music studio, Jess, I'm not curing cancer or anything."

"Don't do that. Don't put it down," she said with a forceful shake of her head. "Music is part of our culture and should be protected and nurtured. Every generation defines itself by the songs of their youth. It's the background beat to their lives. It's not unimportant. With every lyric, every melody, you create a legacy. Don't pretend that's not important."

Sean stared at her, his eyes dark with emotion. "Well, I don't know what to say."

"You can say I'm right."

"You are right. You're also pretty wonderful. So wonderful I could kiss you right now."

Her stomach flipped over. "Who's stopping you?"

"Not you?" he questioned.

"Not me," she said, as he moved towards her. Her impassioned speech had set her pulse pounding, and at this moment she couldn't think of one good reason why she shouldn't kiss him.

He put his hands on her hips, his blue eyes compelling her to look at him. "Are you more interested in me now because you think I might have a bank account and a savings plan and a nine-to-five job in my future?"

She shook her head, knowing there was an edge of seriousness behind the light question. "No, I'm interested, because you're really, really sexy. And I get butterflies in my stomach when you look at me the way you're looking at me. I know we're not supposed to do this anymore, but maybe just one more—"

He cut off her sentence with his mouth. Desire shot down her spine at the searing heat of his lips. She wrapped her arms around his neck and closed her eyes, drinking in the pleasure of his taste, his touch. Sean overwhelmed her senses and lit up her desire. He made her aware of every nerve ending, every sensual needy point of desire. When she was with him, she felt very feminine, eager to take his hard edges into her soft curves.

She wanted to really know him, to get past the teasing and the playful to the deep and the passionate. Sean had a soulful side that came out when he sang and also when he kissed. He was much more complex than she'd realized at first. There were layers and layers, and she wanted to reveal every single one.

But if she could strip Sean's layers away, then he could also strip hers. And where would that leave her? With the guard walls down, he could hurt her. She didn't want any more pain.

But what if there wasn't pain? What if the passion never ended?

Sean's mouth slid from her lips and he kissed his way down the side of her neck. When his fingers crept up under her top, teasing her abdomen, she wanted his hands all over her. This was moving way beyond a simple kiss. She had to stop it.

And she would—in a second—or two. Maybe three. But it was Sean who finally broke away.

"You're making me crazy, Jess." His blue eyes glittered like diamonds in a dark sky.

"Likewise," she said. "I feel like you've cast a spell over me."

"I think you're the witch."

"We're being reckless, walking the high wire without a net."

He smiled. "I won't let you fall."

"You might," she whispered.

The humor in his eyes faded.

She took a step back, putting some air between them. Things had gotten way too serious, and that was her fault.

A door banged, and a voice rang through the quiet, "Sean? Where are you?"

"In here," Sean yelled back.

As a man came into the lounge, Jessica smoothed down her clothes, feeling like a guilty schoolgirl caught making out in the classroom.

The man looked like a surfer, tall and skinny with blonde hair, brown eyes, and a deep bronze tan. He wore faded jeans and a blue t-shirt with palm trees on it.

"Well, well," he said, giving them an interested smile. "What do we have here?"

"This is Jessica Schilling," Sean said. "Hunter Thomas."

"You're Sean's business partner," she said.

"Among other things. Nice to meet you, Jessica."

"You, too. Sean was just showing me around."

"Was that all he was showing you?" Hunter teased.

Jessica felt her cheeks turn red. "Uh…"

"Leave her alone," Sean said. "It's not like that."

She didn't know what Sean meant by that comment, but something passed between Sean and Hunter. Then Hunter nodded. "Got it. So, I'm glad you're here, Sean. I just talked to the sound guys, and the board will be delivered next Monday. We're actually ahead of schedule now, if you can believe it."

"That's great."

"If you can be here during the installation, that would be helpful."

"I'll make it happen."

"Good." Hunter paused and then said, "I'm going to do— something else."

Alone again, Jessica wanted desperately to clear the air. "Hunter seems like a good guy."

"He is." Sean gave her a thoughtful, concerned look. "What you said before, about falling—"

"I was just rambling. It didn't mean anything."

"I think it did mean something. I don't want to hurt you, Jess. I don't want to take advantage of you in any way."

"I won't let you hurt me, and you didn't take advantage. I wanted to kiss you. You wanted to kiss me. And for a while, we let the crazy run, but sanity has returned."

"Damn that sanity," he said lightly.

She smiled. She was relieved to see humor back in his eyes.

"Do you want me to take you home?" he asked.

Yes would definitely be the right answer, but she hesitated. "I don't know. I'm kind of hungry. Is there a good ice cream place around here?"

"As a matter of fact there is. It's not a cold shower, but it might cool us down."

She hoped he was right.

Ten

<small>⟶⟫⟪⟵</small>

After saying goodbye to Hunter, they walked out of the studio. The morning fog had lifted, and there was nothing but blue skies overhead. As they walked down the street, Jessica got an even better feel for the neighborhood. There were a couple of cafés on the street including a burger place, a French bistro, and a noodle house. A clothing boutique, a small organic foods market, a juice bar, and a new age shop showing crystals in the window rounded out the block.

"This is a fun neighborhood, Sean. I like the vibe," she said. "I think you're going to be happy and successful here."

"And I like the way you think. Just for that, I'm going to buy you a double scoop ice cream cone."

"Now you're talking."

He opened the door to an ice cream and candy store called Carolina's. The shop was a kaleidoscope of colors with candy dominating one side and ice cream the other. After perusing the menu, she ordered pecan praline ice cream in a cup while Sean selected mint chip on a sugar cone. They took their ice cream over to one of the small tables by the window and sat down.

One bite, and she was in heaven. "This is delicious." She dipped her spoon for another bite.

"I know," he said, as he licked his cone. "They make the

ice cream on site. It's all organic, whatever that means."

Watching his tongue curl around the ice cream made her blood run hot again, and she decided to concentrate on her own dish. When she finished the last bite, she set the bowl down and wiped her mouth with a napkin. "It's a good thing this place is not close to my house, or I might be here every day."

"You'll have to come visit me at the studio."

"I'm sure you'll be busy."

"Never too busy for you." He finished his cone and then said, "So, Jess."

"Yes," she said warily.

"We've been talking a lot about me. Let's talk about you. Aside from my raining on your parade about the Emery house, how is everything else going for you here in the city?"

"Better than I expected."

"You don't miss Angel's Bay?"

"I miss my friends, Charlotte and Kara, but I don't miss my mother-in-law or any of the other Schillings for that matter. And I don't miss being surrounded by Travis's things. It's not that I want to forget him, because I don't. He was a wonderful man and he treated me better than anyone had ever treated me in my life. But I can't live in sadness, and everything in that house reminded me of him. It was his home long before it was mine. He picked out every piece of furniture, every painting, and every piece of tile. When I married him, I walked into a life that was already in place. I had a husband, a child and a house. It was a package deal."

"Didn't you want to change anything, put your own stamp on the house?"

"There were some things I didn't care for, but Travis and Kyle were happy, and being with them made me happy, so I told myself who cares if there's an ugly painting on the wall of my bedroom. That isn't important."

He gave her a grin. "You hated that painting, did you?"

"It was so hideous," she admitted. "It was one of those swirly dark paintings that are supposed to be important and mean something but kind of look like vomit."

He laughed. "I know exactly what you mean."

"But Travis's first wife had picked it out on their trip to Europe, and there was a whole long story that went with it. I'm sure Travis would have been fine if I took it down; I just didn't want to make waves. He loved his wife, and she died too young, and it was sad."

Sean nodded, but there was an odd look in his eyes that she couldn't quite read.

"What are you thinking?" she asked.

"That you molded yourself into Travis's life."

She heard the criticism in his words. "His life was great. Why wouldn't I do that? It's not like I had something better."

"But you have a personality and a point of view. You're not a pushover. At least, you don't seem that way to me."

"I don't think I was a pushover with Travis either," she said slowly. "Well, maybe I was a little. He was older than me. My mom thought I was looking for a father figure, but I never saw him that way. What I saw was a confident man who knew what he wanted, and he wanted me. He stated his intentions. He wasn't afraid to go all in. He was very different from most of the men who came through Vegas."

She paused, then continued. "When Travis asked me to marry him, I thought I'd won the lottery. All I ever wanted was a home and a family to love. Being married to Travis was a dream come true. Maybe I would have come more into my own as time went on. But we weren't even married two years when Travis died. And it was so abrupt, so shocking. I talked to him an hour before his accident, and everything was great. Then he was dead."

"That must have been awful." He shook his head, compassion in his eyes. "I can't even imagine."

"I was in shock for probably a year. What kept me going was Kyle. I had to make a life for him. I didn't want to let Travis down, so I tried to keep everything the same. I thought that maybe Kyle wouldn't feel the loss of his father so much if I did that. I even left that stupid painting on the wall. It was a foolish thought, but I didn't have any other ideas. I was floundering. When Kyle was kidnapped, it shocked me back to reality. The way Travis's mother treated me during that time, the lies she told, made me realize that we were never going to have a relationship. I was just punishing myself by continuing to try to make friends with her and continuing to be shot down. I knew that I couldn't keep living Travis's life, because Travis was gone, and he wasn't coming back. I needed to give Kyle a mother who was aware and present. That's what I'm trying to do now." She took a breath and let it out. "I am talking way too much."

"Not at all. I asked."

"And the shorter answer is that I am doing wonderfully well here in the city. It's been a great change. Your family has been terrific. I've found my feet again, which is a good feeling. I'm still figuring out a lot of stuff. Sometimes I look at Nicole and think I am nowhere near as good a mother as she is, but she inspires me to do better."

"She's been at motherhood longer than you, and she still stumbles. She's the first to admit that."

"Yeah, but Brandon is a lot more difficult to deal with than Kyle. She is so patient with him, so positive and determined and just amazingly strong."

"I can't argue with that. She impresses the hell out of me. In fact, I could say that about every one of my siblings. I ran into my youngest sister, Shayla, earlier today and she told me that she's going to Africa to treat patients in remote villages so she can better understand the global medical challenges." He shook his head in bemusement. "My whole family is made up of super overachievers. I don't know what the hell happened to me."

"Nothing happened to you. You're building a business as we speak, and it's going to be fantastic."

"I hope so, but in the scheme of things—"

She cut him off with a shake of her head. "There is no scheme of things. We all have to do what we're meant to do. And I don't think every single sibling is an overachiever. Nicole told me that Colton got his third speeding ticket of the year last week."

He smiled. "Ah, my little brother, Colton. Once he hit middle school, I could usually count on him to take some of the heat off of me. And before that there was Aiden, but then Aiden had to get responsible, become a husband and a father."

She smiled back at him. "Well, you still have Colton. From what I understand he's kind of a hell raiser."

"Yeah, but he's a firefighter, so in my father's eyes, he can do no wrong."

"I don't think your dad was too happy about the speeding tickets."

"Colton has always liked to go fast, whether it's in a car, on a snowboard, in a boat...you name it, he'll race it. Hopefully, they don't let him drive the fire truck."

Jessica glanced down at her watch, suddenly realizing how long they'd been chatting. "We should go. I need to get back to my house so I can grab my car and meet with Helen."

"Right. I forgot about her. Why don't I go with you?"

His suggestion was more than a little surprising. "Uh, I don't know, Sean."

"Why the hesitation?"

"She's never mentioned the fire to me, which means it must be too painful for her to think about. She's an elderly woman now. I don't want to upset her."

"I'm not going to upset her. I just want to say hello."

"That's a little hard to believe."

"I knew her as a kid."

"I thought she lived in San Diego then."

"She visited at Christmas and in the summer."

"And you're not going with the intention of asking her questions about the fire?"

"What would I ask her? She wasn't there."

"Then why do you want to see her?"

He sighed. "I don't know. Maybe I just want to spend more time with you."

"Yeah, right." She didn't believe that for a second.

"It will be fine, Jess. I don't have a hidden agenda."

"All right. You can come, but tread carefully. I don't want to get evicted. It was a big job to get unpacked. The last thing I want to do is move again."

———◆◆◆———

Helen Emery resided in an assisted living facility near the UC San Francisco hospital. The wing that Helen resided in showed no sign of the medical services being provided on the opposite side of the building. Thankfully, Helen didn't need more than general assistance and meals yet.

Helen's apartment was on the third floor. Jessica knocked on the door, and a moment later it was opened by a tiny, gray-haired woman with hazel eyes.

"Jessica. Hello. It's so nice to see you. Who's your handsome friend?" Her brows knit together. "Wait, I know you, don't I? You're one of the Callaways. You have those handsome black Irish looks, dark hair and blue eyes, a dangerous combination for a woman," she added, giving Jessica a pointed look.

"Tell me about it," she muttered.

"I am a Callaway. I'm Sean."

"Oh, Sean." Her eyes softened. "Stacy's little friend. Not so little anymore."

"No," he said tightly. "It's been a long time."

"Yes, it has. And yet it sometimes seems like yesterday that my sweet granddaughter was asking me to braid her hair and watch her throw a softball. She took after me, you know. I was an excellent softball player in a time when women were not supposed to be good at sports." She paused. "Where are my manners? Please come in."

As they walked into the apartment, Helen waved them toward the couch. "Please sit down. I'm eager to hear how you like the house."

"I like it very much," Jessica answered. "I've got our bedrooms set up and the kitchen as well. I've only taken a quick look at the attic. I thought before I got started, I should go over what you want to do with the more personal items."

Helen's shoulders sagged, and she seemed to lose a little of the brightness she'd had only a moment earlier. "I hate to even think about what's up there. I know I should have cleaned it all out years ago, but I just couldn't bear it." She glanced at Sean. "That's where I put all of their things after the fire." She looked back at Jessica. "I never told you about the fire, did I?"

"No, but Sean filled me in."

"It was unbelievably sad. My son and my granddaughter perished in that fire. I wasn't sure at first if I could move back there, but someone had to take care of things. Lana had taken Blake and gone to her sister's home. She wanted nothing to do with the house. I put everything she left behind up in the attic. I kept thinking one day she might want something, but she never came back."

"I did find some photo albums," Jessica said. "One belonged to Stacy. Do you think her mother would want it now?"

"I don't know. As I said, I haven't spoken to Lana in

years."

"What about Blake?" Sean interjected. "Have you talked to him? I always wondered what happened to him."

"I tried to keep in touch with them that first year, but then Lana moved out of her sister's house, and her sister told me that Lana needed time and space to recover. She'd get in touch with me when she was ready. I guess she was never ready, because I never heard from her again."

Jessica frowned. "I'm surprised she wouldn't want her son to know his grandmother."

"It was hurtful to me. I'll admit that I didn't have the best relationship with Lana, but my son loved her, and I respected her as his wife. I certainly loved my grandchildren."

"Why didn't you and Lana get along?" Sean asked, leaning forward, his forearms resting on his thighs.

"I always felt like she demanded a lot from Robert. She wanted to live a certain lifestyle, and if Robert had to work every weekend in order to provide that lifestyle, she was okay with it. I thought she was a little hard on him when he decided to quit his job. The stress was making him ill, but she couldn't stand the idea of him not bringing home the big money. He was an investment banker. It was a very stressful job."

"I understand that he quit his job a few weeks before the fire," Sean said.

"Yes. It was rather abrupt. He told me he finally realized he couldn't do it anymore. He'd missed spending time with his family." She blinked back a tear. "I wish he'd quit it sooner. At least he could have enjoyed more than two weeks of freedom before he died." She pulled a tissue out of her pocket and dabbed at her eyes. "I'm sorry. I can't talk about the fire. It's too sad."

"We understand," Jessica said. "Getting back to the photo albums. Should I try to find Lana or Blake? I don't know that I'd be successful, but I could try."

Helen hesitated. "Maybe you should try. I'd like to see Blake again. He's all grown up now. He might be married with children. I might be a great-grandmother and not even know it. Not that he'd probably be interested in seeing me. They know where I've been the last twenty years, and they've never tried to get in touch."

Jessica wondered why Helen hadn't tried harder to reconnect with her grandson. She had a feeling Helen hadn't told them the whole story.

"I could help Jessica look for Lana and Blake," Sean offered. "And we could ask my brother-in-law for assistance. Emma's husband is a police detective."

Helen smiled. "That Emma was such a delightful girl, a real live-wire. So she married a police detective?"

"This past Christmas," Sean said.

"Well, that's lovely."

"Do you still have Lana's sister's address or phone number?" Jessica asked. "We could start with her."

"I think so. As you know, I never throw anything away. Just a moment." Helen got up and walked over to a small desk. She pulled out a thick, weathered address book and flipped through the pages. "Here it is, Connie Bristol. She lives in Carmel, or at least she used to. I'll write it down for you. Unfortunately, the phone number was changed a long time ago. I crossed it out and wrote disconnected."

As Helen jotted down the address, Sean looked at Jessica. "That's not that far away—a two-hour drive."

"It's a long way to go without knowing if she lives there anymore. If her phone was disconnected, she might have moved."

"Only one way to find out."

Helen handed Jessica the address. "I hope you can find Lana. I don't want to throw those albums in the trash, but there's no one else I can give them to."

"I'll let you know what we come up with," Jessica said, getting to her feet.

"If you do talk to Lana, tell her..." Helen's voice trailed away. "Goodness, I don't even know what you could tell her. I suppose you could say that I'm sorry we let so much time go by." She paused. "Maybe that's not the right thing to say. Oh, I don't know. It's never been easy with Lana."

"I'll tell her that you hope she's well and that you'd love to see your grandson again," Jessica suggested.

Helen gave her a watery smile. "That's perfect. You're a good girl. I'm glad I rented the house to you."

Jessica smiled back at her. "I'll talk to you soon."

"It was nice to see you again, Sean."

"You, too," he said.

They'd barely left the apartment when Sean said, "I think we should drive down to Carmel tomorrow."

"What makes you think Lana's sister will give us Lana's address even if we do find her?"

"Because we have something that Lana might want," he said pointedly.

"Stacy's photo album," she said, meeting his gaze.

"Exactly. Lana should have it, or her brother, if he wants it. But at the very least, they should know it still exists. What do you say?"

"Let me check with Nicole. Usually, I take the boys after school on Tuesday, but if she can do it, then I'll feel more comfortable going that far away. We can probably get down there and back by two, but I don't want to cut it that close."

"Sounds like a plan. Shall we check with Nicole now? Didn't you say you had to pick up Kyle before dinner?"

"And you don't mind playing chauffeur?" she asked, as they walked down the hall.

"You're helping me out. It's a two-way street."

"Am I helping you?" she asked with a frown as he pushed

the button for the elevator. "What do you want to get out of all this, Sean?"

"I'm not sure, but at the very least, I think I owe it to Stacy to get her photo album back to her mom."

The elevator dinged, and when the doors opened, Jessica was surprised to see a familiar face.

Eleven

--->=>>≪≪<≈--

"Brett," she said in surprise. "What are you doing here?"

"Visiting Helen, of course." He glanced at Sean, his gaze narrowing. "I'm sorry. Have we met?"

"A long time ago, Mr. Murphy. I'm Sean Callaway."

"One of the Callaway kids, I should have guessed that," Brett said with a nod. "I used to throw batting practice to you and your brothers. One of the kids, I think it was Burke, had a killer swing." His gaze moved to Jessica. "I didn't realize you and Sean were friends."

"We are," Jessica said, not wanting to get into a more complicated explanation. "Sean's sister, Nicole, is the one who told me about Helen's house."

"How is Helen doing?"

"She looks well."

"I don't know how she's going to handle you giving away all her things. I'm still surprised she agreed to let you do that."

The way he said the words made Jessica feel like she was somehow taking advantage of an old lady.

"I'm going through the things at her request," she reminded him.

"Have you found anything interesting yet?"

It was the same question Sally had asked her. "Not really,

no. I haven't seen any of the signed baseball cards you gave Blake," she added, remembering his earlier question. "But I've just gotten started."

"Let me know if you do."

"Speaking of Blake," Sean interrupted. "Have you kept in touch with Lana and her son?"

A spark of something that looked like anger flashed through Brett's eyes. "Lana? No. I haven't talked to her since she left San Francisco. She was destroyed after the fire. She wanted nothing to do with the old neighborhood."

"So you don't know where she is now?" Sean asked.

"I just said I haven't spoken to her," Brett said with annoyance. "Why do you ask?"

"We're trying to find Blake and Lana. We have some pictures they might want," Sean replied.

"What kind of pictures? Were they at Helen's house?"

"Family stuff," Sean said with a vague wave of his hand.

"I wish I could help you," Brett said. "Are you sure Helen wants you to contact Lana and Blake?"

"She gave us Lana's sister's address," Jessica said.

"That surprises me. She's never had anything good to say about Lana."

The elevator doors opened again, and Jessica took the opportunity to say, "We should get going. We'll see you later."

"Sure."

Once the doors closed, she turned to face Sean. "Did Brett get a little nervous when you mentioned the pictures?"

"I don't know about nervous, but he was definitely interested."

"Yes, too interested. I don't know what it is about Brett and Sally. They're both perfectly nice to me, but I get an odd vibe from them. And they've each taken time to warn me about the other. But maybe I'm just imagining that they have some hidden motive for talking to me. If there had never been a fire, would I even think twice about offers to help from two friendly neighbors?"

"But there was a fire. You can't take that out of the equation. Hopefully, if we can find Lana, she'll be able to tell us everything we need to know."

"I hope so," she said, but she had a feeling that was a long shot.

Sean's mind was spinning as he drove Jessica to Nicole's house. Somehow he'd gone from wanting to know the origin of the fire to wondering if Stacy's death had not been an accident at all. Not that he thought anyone wanted to kill an eight-year-old girl, but what about her father? Or what if Robert's father had killed himself and Lana had covered it up to get the insurance money? He really needed to talk to Lana. Tomorrow couldn't come soon enough.

"Looks like baseball has started," Jessica murmured, as he turned down Nicole's street.

Kyle, Brandon and Ryan were in the front yard. Kyle was playing catch with Ryan while Brandon dug through a pile of rocks at the edge of the garden.

"I didn't know Kyle was a baseball player," he said.

"This will be his first year on a team. Ryan signed up to coach. They're both over the moon about it."

Sean grinned. "As I recall, Ryan was a good baseball player. Kyle is in great hands."

"I'm very happy that Kyle has someone to teach him how to throw a ball, because I definitely throw like a girl." She glanced over at him as he stopped the van. "What about you?"

"I definitely do *not* throw like a girl."

She smiled. "Were you a star athlete?"

"I played sports when I was young. But once I got into music, that took all of my time."

As they got out of the car, Kyle shouted, "Hey, Mom. Watch this."

Ryan gently tossed a tennis ball to Kyle. The ball hit the mitt, and Kyle somehow managed to awkwardly hang on to it. He held the ball up with a gleam of triumph in his eyes.

"I did it. I caught the ball," he said.

"I saw that," Jessica said, clapping her hands. "Good job."

"Kyle is a natural," Ryan said, walking over to join them. "He might be my first baseman when the league starts."

"Aren't you getting a little ahead of yourself?" Jessica asked.

"I know talent when I see it."

"Can you throw me more balls, Ryan?" Kyle pleaded.

"Actually, we need to go home and make dinner," Jessica said.

Kyle's face fell. "Just a few more, please?"

"Why don't you go inside and say hello to Nicole, Jessica?" Ryan suggested. "I think she had something she wants to ask you."

"All right, I'll be back in a few minutes."

As Jessica headed into the house, Ryan tossed the ball to Sean. "Why don't you throw to Kyle? He needs to get used to different people throwing to him."

"Okay." He strode toward the driveway so there was a good ten feet between him and Kyle. "Ready, Kyle?"

Kyle nodded, holding up his mitt. Sean tossed the ball, but it was a little too low, and the ball went right past Kyle, landing at Ryan's feet.

"Sorry, buddy. Give me another chance," Sean said.

Ryan grabbed the errant ball and tossed it back to him. "Aim for the mitt," Ryan advised.

Sean followed his suggestion and did everything he could to put the ball right in the sweet spot of Kyle's mitt. Kyle caught the ball and did a little spin of excitement.

Sean laughed. "Did you teach him that spin, Ryan?"

Ryan grinned back at him. "That's all him. Kyle does everything with enthusiasm."

Kyle threw the ball back to Sean, and for a few minutes, Sean concentrated on nothing but getting that ball into Kyle's mitt over and over again. He wanted to build the kid's confidence. Then Kyle would be ready for bigger challenges.

Several minutes later, Nicole and Jessica stepped out on the porch. "I've talked Jessica into staying for dinner," Nicole said. "But she tells me you're her driver, Sean, so you have to say yes, too."

"What are you having?" he asked.

She rolled her eyes. "I'm sure it's better than whatever fast food place you were planning to hit up on the way home."

"That's not an answer."

"Grilled chicken, rice, vegetables and chocolate pudding for dessert. Kyle and Brandon made it."

"Sold," he said.

"I'm thrilled," Nicole said dryly. "It will be ready in about twenty minutes."

"I'll help you," Jessica said, following Nicole back into the house.

"Why don't you and Brandon go wash up?" Ryan suggested to Kyle. "It's getting dark."

"Not that dark," Kyle protested.

Ryan tousled Kyle's hair. "Don't worry, kid. There will be lots of baseball to come." He paused, turning towards his son. "Brandon, time to wash your hands for dinner."

"I'll get him." Kyle ran over to Brandon and knelt down next to him. He put his hand on Brandon's arm, and then a minute later both boys ran into the house.

"That's amazing," Sean said, struck by the twins' silent communication. "Kyle didn't even say anything to Brandon."

"I know. Nicole and I both wish we could connect to

Brandon like that. But at least our son has a link to the world through his brother. Brandon also gets less agitated now that he has Kyle with him. There are fewer tantrums, moments of frustration. It's like everything is right with his world as long as his brother is nearby. Sometimes, we wish we could have Kyle every second of the day, but we're trying not to completely take over. We want to respect Jessica's relationship with Kyle, too, give them their space. It's not easy, especially for Nicole. You know how impatient she can be."

Sean nodded, very aware of his sister's tendency to want results really fast. "I'm glad it's working out so well. I know Jessica is happy with the situation, too."

"She's been great, very easygoing and flexible." Ryan paused, a reflective glint in his eyes. "It's strange how that kidnapping changed everything for the better."

"Have you ever heard from the biological parents or grandparents again?" Sean asked. The biological grandmother had been the mastermind behind the kidnapping, wanting to reunite her daughter with her children.

"The grandmother is in jail, and the mother is still in rehab. One day we might possibly consider talking to her, but that's a long time from now. Why don't we go inside? Dinner should be about ready."

When they entered the kitchen, Kyle and Brandon were sitting at the kitchen table looking at a book together. Nicole was cutting up garlic bread, and Jessica was tossing shredded carrots into the salad. It smelled like garlic and tomatoes, like home, and Sean felt an odd pang of longing for more moments like this. Not that he wanted to spend his dinners with Nicole and Ryan, but with Jessica and Kyle…maybe.

That thought was a little terrifying. He'd never considered himself to be a family man. And while he liked a home-cooked meal every now and then, his life was about music and travel, a different city, a different hotel, a different woman…

But the woman he was interested in looked very comfortable in this kitchen. She was exactly where she wanted to be. She'd spent her life wanting more family, and he'd spent his life wanting less.

"What do you want to drink?" Ryan asked, interrupting his thoughts. "We have beer and wine left over from the party. Also plenty of soda."

"I'll take a soda since I'm driving."

"Jessica?" Ryan asked.

"Well, since he's driving, I'll have a glass of wine." She set the salad bowl on the table, and took the seat across from Kyle.

Sean sat down next to her.

Kyle took a sip of milk, then gave him a bright smile and said, "Did you know that sharks don't have any bones in their bodies, Uncle Sean?"

"I did not know that."

"Did you know that a whale shark has more than 4,000 teeth?" Kyle pressed.

He grinned. "I didn't know that, either."

"Kyle," Jessica interrupted. "Sean doesn't want to know about sharks."

"Actually, I'm learning a lot," he said.

"Do you know what the biggest shark in the world is?" Kyle asked.

"Is it the one with all the teeth?"

Kyle nodded. "Yep. It's the whale shark." He looked over at his brother. "Brandon drew a really good picture of a shark at school today. Let's show it to Uncle Sean."

Brandon didn't say anything, but when Kyle slid off his chair, Brandon followed.

"Brandon is a fantastic artist," Jessica said. "Have you seen his work?"

"I remember seeing a sketch from when he was kidnapped. He drew the restaurant where the kidnappers stopped."

"That's right," she said. "I forgot about that."

"It's a savant skill," Nicole said, as she brought the platter of chicken to the table. "Brandon has a photographic memory and the ability to recreate what he sees. It's how he relates to the world."

Brandon and Kyle returned to the room, and Kyle handed the picture across the table to Sean.

"Wow," he murmured, impressed. "This is great. Good job, Brandon."

Brandon stared down at the table in front of him.

"We saw a movie about sharks in school, and then Brandon drew that picture," Kyle said.

"I didn't realize Brandon and Kyle were in the same class," Sean said.

"Brandon is in a special education program, but since Kyle came to town, he's been sitting in the regular classroom for a few hours," Nicole explained. "So is everyone ready to eat?"

"I am," Kyle proclaimed loudly.

Jessica laughed and looked over at Sean. "My son is enthusiastic about everything. It's hard to be cynical around Kyle."

"Yeah," he said with a nod, wondering how old he'd been when he'd lost that joyful and hopeful spirit.

And then the answer came to him. He'd been eight. And he'd just lost his best friend.

"Do you want some salad?" Jessica asked, passing him the bowl.

"Absolutely." he said, pushing the past back where it belonged.

Jessica felt a little too happy, she thought, as Sean drove her and Kyle home from Nicole's house around seven-thirty. Dinner had been fun, and she'd enjoyed listening to Sean and

Nicole's stories about growing up in the Callaway family. She'd liked their teasing interaction, and she'd been fascinated by their wonderful family adventures. She'd also enjoyed watching Kyle interact with Sean. The two seemed to have an instant rapport. Not that that was surprising. Both Kyle and Sean got along well with people.

That reminder drove the smile off of her face. Sean was a popular guy. She knew that first hand. She'd seen the women drooling over him at the club the other night. And *that* was his life. Not family dinners that started at six and involved children rambling on about sharks. Sean had been nice, kind, but this was not his life; it was hers. And she couldn't let herself start thinking that their two worlds could merge into one.

It just wasn't fair that this man had to be the one who touched her on both a physical and emotional level. She could handle the attraction if that's all it was. But she liked him, too. He was smart, funny and creative. And they connected through music. He was about the song, the melody, the lyrics, and she was about putting moves to the music, but in the end it was all about artistic expression. Travis had never known that side of her. She'd been a dancer when they'd met, but she'd given it up the second they got married.

As Sean had suggested, she had lost a little of herself in the marriage, but that had been her choice. It wasn't a choice she'd make again though. She knew herself better now. She was older, stronger, and more independent, less willing to let a man's life define her.

Of course she still had to define herself. Once she got Helen's house cleared out, she needed to focus on her next move, whatever that was going to be.

Sean pulled up in front of the house. "Do you want me to come in so you don't have to go in alone?"

She hesitated, knowing she would like nothing better than to keep the evening going. But at some point she was going to have to learn how to say no.

Before she could answer, Sean's phone buzzed.

He took it out of his pocket to read the text.

"Is that from Emma?" Jessica asked.

"No, it's from Tim; he's in my band. He wants me to meet him at a club in North Beach. There's a drummer he thinks I should hear."

Another reminder of Sean's real life. She'd be reading stories to her kid and in bed at ten, and he'd be drinking with friends at a club. They could not be more different. "You should go."

"I might."

"Why wouldn't you go? Isn't that what you do?"

He frowned at her tone. "Am I missing something?"

"No." She knew she was deliberately baiting him, just because she was annoyed and frustrated, and mostly angry with herself for wanting a man who was completely wrong for her in a lot of ways. It was just too damn bad he was good for her in so many other ways. "It's been a long day."

"Are you sure that's it?" He glanced toward the back seat. "Kyle is conked out back there if you're worried about him overhearing."

"There's nothing to overhear. You should meet your friend. I'll see you tomorrow."

"You know, Jess, I'd be the first to admit that I rarely know what women are thinking, but I can generally tell when they're pissed off at me."

She shook her head. "I'm not mad at you."

"Then who?"

"Myself."

"Why? What did you do?" he asked lightly.

"I started to like you."

"Then my friend texted, and you remembered I was a musician," he said.

"We lead really different lives, and we both need to remember that."

"I haven't forgotten."

"Well, then you're doing better than me. I need to get Kyle inside and up to bed."

"You're still coming with me tomorrow, right?"

"I know I shouldn't, but yes, I'm still coming."

Relief flashed in his eyes. "Thank you. I'll try not to cross any lines, Jess."

She was going to try, too. She just didn't know if she'd be successful.

Twelve

⟶⟫⟨⟵

Tuesday morning Jessica got Kyle off to school and then gave herself a long talk about keeping things friendly with Sean but not getting any more personally involved with him. Today was about finding Lana, hopefully delivering Stacy's photo album, and maybe putting the old fire to rest. If they did all three, it would certainly be a good day. And if she refrained from kissing Sean, it would be even better. Not as much fun, but definitely better.

Sean arrived just before nine. She walked out to his van with two photo albums in her hands, the family album, and the one belonging to Stacy.

Sean met her on the sidewalk, his jaw stiffening as he looked at the pink album. "Maybe put that in the back," he suggested, pulling open the side door of the van.

As she put the albums on the seat, she noticed two sleeping bags tossed in the back. She hadn't remembered seeing them yesterday. "Are you going camping?"

"What?"

"The sleeping bags."

"Oh, no. Tim returned them to me last night. I usually keep them in the van in case I have to sleep in the car. He borrowed them a couple of weeks ago."

"And you need two bags?"

"It's warmer that way."

"Especially if someone, maybe a female, is in the other one," she suggested.

He gave her a long look. "You're right. It *is* warmer that way."

She frowned and then closed the door so she wouldn't have to think about Sean and some hot girl hooking up in a sleeping bag. She got into the passenger seat and buckled her seatbelt while Sean slid behind the wheel.

"Everything all right?" he asked.

"Sure, let's go."

They drove for at least ten minutes in total silence. It was not a comfortable quiet, at least not on her part. She was on edge. She'd been on edge since Sean had dropped her off the night before. Actually, she'd been on edge since Friday night when she'd kissed him for the first time.

"So," she began. "About the woman in the sleeping bag."

He shot her a wary look. "What are you talking about?"

"Your love life. I'm curious."

"What do you want to know?"

"Who was the woman in the sleeping bag?"

"Her name was Mary Lynn, and it was about six years ago, I think. Yeah. It was the summer we toured through Nashville. She was a country singer, beautiful voice, beautiful body."

"Did you love her?"

"No, but she was fun."

"Have you loved anyone? Have you had a serious girlfriend?"

"That's personal, isn't it?"

"Well, we've gotten rather personal, don't you think? Besides that, we're friends. Friends share. I've told you about Travis. Let's hear your story."

He didn't answer right away, his attention on the road as he changed lanes, then he said, "I was in love when I was nineteen. Her name was Shelby. She was an artist. We went out for about a year and a half. Then she had an opportunity to get into an art program in Paris. She wanted me to go with her, but I didn't have any money, and my band was here. We were just getting going and good things were happening."

"So she went to Paris."

He nodded. "And she fell in love with a French guy and never came back."

"Did she break your heart?"

"She definitely put a dent in it. But we were young. Who knows what would have happened if she'd stayed?"

"That was a long time ago, Sean. No one since then?"

"Not really. When I'm focused on my music, I'm not a good boyfriend, at least that's what I've been told," he said dryly. "And I can't say anyone is wrong. I do get tunnel vision when I'm writing a song or working on a melody. Everything else seems to fade away." He glanced her way again. "I just confirmed what you already think of musicians, right?"

"Yes, but I also understand your commitment to the song. When I was dancing a difficult piece, I'd get lost in the movement. I'd think I'd only been in the studio for fifteen minutes, and it was really two hours." She reflected on what else he'd said. "Maybe you just never met anyone who made you want to focus on them instead of the music."

"That's very possible. Or maybe no one like that exists."

"You don't really believe that, do you?"

"I might."

"How can you speak so cynically about love when your songs are filled with emotion? Your lyrics about love are powerful and deep and sometimes really raw."

"I write and sing about the fantasy, what people want to hear."

She shook her head in disbelief. "No way. Your songs are

too personal. When you sing, it's like you're telling me a story that's important for me to hear and that I'll be changed forever after I hear it."

"That's really what you think when you listen to my music?" he asked, shooting her a thoughtful look.

"Yes, it is. I downloaded a couple of your songs, and I've listened to them a lot. My favorite is *Moonlight Girl. She walked out of the light and into my heart*," she quoted. "Those words don't come from a cynic. You want to know what I think?"

"Does it matter if I don't?"

"I think you put up a front, a wall of indifference. And that wall keeps everyone out. I don't know if you're afraid of getting hurt or what, but in your real life you're extremely guarded. In your songs, you're wide open." She saw his jaw tighten and thought she'd hit a nerve. "Maybe you need to find a way to merge those two."

"Or maybe I don't. I'm pretty happy with my life."

"How could you be when you don't let anyone in? You're building this incredible studio, and no one in your family knows about it. You let them think you're a loser when we both know that's not true."

"In my father's eyes, it is true."

"Your father has no idea who you really are. But that's not his fault, because you don't let him in."

"I don't know what you want me to say," he muttered.

"I just want you to be who you are. Be honest. Be upfront. Say what's on your mind and not what you think other people want to hear."

He gave her a sharp, challenging look. "Are you sure that's what you want me to do?"

A shiver ran down her spine. "I think so," she said, suddenly not so sure, because judging by the look in his eyes, he was about to tell her something she did not want to hear.

"Okay. Let's start with this. I want you, Jessica. I think you're smart, sexy and gorgeous, and I'd really like to take you to bed and spend a few weeks there. But I'm not good at relationships, and I've never made a long-term commitment to anyone or anything besides my music. That's not the guy you want, is it?"

She should definitely say no, that wasn't the guy she wanted, but she was a little hung up on the image of them in bed together. "No," she finally said. "That's not the guy I want."

"Okay then. We've both been honest. Are you happy now?"

She sighed. "No."

"Well, I don't know what more you want."

"I want to apologize," she said slowly. "I think I got a little carried away analyzing your life."

"You absolutely did," he agreed.

"I'm sorry."

A few moments passed, and then he said, "You weren't completely wrong though."

She wanted to ask which part she'd been right about, but she decided to leave well enough alone. "Do you mind if I turn on some music to get rid of the awkwardness that's now between us?"

He smiled. "More honesty. I like it. And I'd love some music."

－➤➤◀◀◀－

An hour later they arrived in Carmel, a seaside town that catered to an upscale class of residents and tourists. The downtown area was filled with expensive antique shops, art galleries, clothing boutiques and restaurants. At the far edge of town was the famous Pebble Beach golf course where celebrities and pros gathered each year for a tournament.

Jessica would have liked to look around, but they weren't here to sightsee. They were on a mission to get Lana's phone number and address from her sister, Connie Bristol.

Jessica had a feeling their mission was going to be a difficult one. The fact that Helen had not spoken to or seen her daughter-in-law or grandson in twenty years was very odd. There was more to that story than they knew.

Sean turned into a residential area and drove slowly as they looked for the address. Connie lived in an older part of town, the homes a mix of small single story structures and new or remodeled two-story homes. Connie's house was one of the bigger ones on the block.

Sean parked and looked at Jessica. "Ready?"

"I guess. This is your past, so I'm going to let you lead."

"All right. Let's go."

"Should I bring the albums?"

"Not yet. I don't want to hand them over to Connie. I want to give them to Lana or Blake."

"Okay." They got out of the van, and walked up a nicely landscaped path to Connie's front door. Sean pressed the bell, and they waited.

"I hope she's home," Jessica said. "It would be a shame to have come all this way for nothing."

"There's a car in the driveway and a light on inside."

He'd barely finished speaking when the door opened. A woman with dark brown hair and brown eyes gave them a suspicious look. She appeared to be in her early fifties, so she was the right age to be Lana's sister.

"Can I help you?" she asked.

"Are you Connie Bristol?" Sean asked.

She gave them a wary look. "Yes, who are you?"

"I'm Sean Callaway and this is Jessica Schilling. A long time ago, I was friends with Stacy Emery. In fact, I lived right around the corner."

The woman's face paled. She drew in a sharp breath. "Why are you here now?"

"We're looking for Stacy's mother, Lana. I understand you're her sister."

"How did you get my address?"

"From Helen Emery. Jessica recently moved into Helen's house. We found a photo album belonging to Stacy. We thought Lana might want it."

"You can give it to me. I'll see that she gets it."

"I'm afraid that we're going to need to give it directly to Lana," Sean said, his tone firm and determined.

Connie hesitated. "Lana doesn't want any contact with Helen."

"She doesn't have to have contact with Helen, just with us," he said.

Jessica could see the indecision in Connie's eyes. "Can I ask why Lana is still so angry with Helen?" she interjected. "Helen told us that she hasn't seen Lana in years. Or her grandson, Blake."

"Helen never liked Lana. She treated her terribly. I don't know all the details, but I know she was awful to my sister."

"This isn't about Helen; this is about Stacy," Sean said. "I owe it to my friend to see that her mother gets her photo album."

"I'm not sure Lana would want it," Connie said. "It would just be a painful reminder of the terrible loss she suffered."

"That should be her decision, don't you think?" Sean asked.

Connie stared back at them. "Wait here." She shut the door.

Sean let out a breath and dug his hands into his pockets as he turned to face her. "What do you think?"

"I think she's calling her sister. Or maybe her sister is inside."

"I don't understand what happened between Lana and Helen. It was obviously big enough to last beyond Robert and Stacy's deaths and then another twenty years."

"I can kind of understand it. If I didn't see my former mother-in-law ever again, I'd be okay with it."

"But you will see her because of Kyle."

She sighed. "You're right. I will, because I can't deprive Kyle of his grandmother, no matter how awful she is. But I'm going to keep the visits as minimal as I can."

"Lana obviously didn't feel a need to keep Blake close to Helen at all."

"Maybe it was the house, the fact that Helen moved in after the fire. Maybe Lana didn't like that."

"She was gone; she didn't want it. Why would she care who lived there?"

"I guess we won't know until we talk to her. Hopefully, that will happen."

Ten minutes passed. Jessica was beginning to think Connie had deserted them when the door finally opened again.

Connie handed Sean a piece of paper. "I spoke to my sister. She said she'll see you. This is her address. She lives in Seascape, it's about thirty minutes north of here."

"I know where it is," Sean said. "Thank you."

Connie didn't bother to answer, just gave a nod, and closed her door.

"We got her address," Sean said, a pleased smile in his eyes.

She wondered if he was going to look quite so happy when they actually met Lana, because seeing Stacy's mother again was bound to raise some painful memories.

***

It took them close to thirty minutes to get to Lana's home,

which was a two-story townhouse in a development near the Seascape Country Club. Sean found a parking spot near the front of her building.

"I wonder if Lana married again," Jessica mused. "We should have asked Connie."

"I doubt she was going to tell us anything about her sister."

"True." As Sean put his hand on the door handle, Jessica said, "Wait."

He gave her an expectant look. "What's the problem?"

"What do you want to get out of this, Sean?"

"I want to give Lana her daughter's photo album."

"And..."

"I don't know beyond that," he admitted.

"Are you going to ask her about the fire?"

"I'd like to hear what she knows about it, but I'm going to play it by ear." He tilted his head. "What are you worried about, Jess?"

"I'm worried about you. I don't have a good vibe when it comes to Lana Emery. And I don't want her to hurt you."

"How could she hurt me?"

"I don't know," she admitted.

"She was always nice to me when I was a kid."

"I'm probably worried about nothing."

"Let's find out."

Thirteen

Sean thought he was ready to see Lana again, but when she opened the door and he found himself looking into Lana's eyes—eyes that reminded him so much of Stacy, his confidence faltered. Jessica's question echoed through his mind. *What did he want out of this meeting?*

Was he looking for answers or absolution from the guilt that had plagued him for so long?

Or was he hoping that Lana would rip into him, that they would finally have the confrontation he'd always been afraid was coming? Because he couldn't imagine why in the world Lana wouldn't blame him for Stacy's death.

Swallowing hard, he drew in a deep breath, realizing that Lana was staring just as hard at him as he was at her. She was twenty years older than when he'd last seen her, but she'd aged well. Her shoulder-length hair was golden blond, not a trace of gray. Her skin was flawless, her figure thin and toned in a pair of tight black pants and a silky white top with a thick heavy necklace.

He cleared his throat. "Mrs. Emery," he said, finally finding his voice.

"Sean Callaway. Even if my sister hadn't told me you were coming, I would have recognized your blue eyes anywhere.

You were such a cute kid, but here you are—all grown up." She shook her head in bemusement. "I don't know why I'm surprised. Blake is an adult now, too. But in my mind you're still eight years old—frozen in time."

She'd been frozen in time for him, too. But looking closer, he could see lines of age around her eyes and mouth. He searched for a way to begin the conversation. He'd told Jessica he'd take the lead, but now he didn't know where to start.

Lana's gaze moved from him to Jessica. "And you are?"

"Jessica Schilling. I'm renting your old house."

"Where's Helen?"

"She moved into an assisted living facility last month," Jessica answered. "She hired me to go through her house and determine where everything should go, what should be given away, and what should be thrown out."

"Is Helen dying?" Lana asked, her tone somewhat cold.

"Uh, I don't think so," Jessica said. "She told me that she couldn't drive anymore and needed to be in a place where it was easier to get transportation and help with meals. But I don't think she's sick."

"It's hard to picture Helen as a frail old lady," Lana said, a tart edge in her voice.

"She said the two of you haven't seen each other since Stacy and Robert died."

"I doubt Helen has missed me. She hated my guts. She never thought I was good enough for her son."

"I know what that feels like," Jessica said with a nod. "I had a similar experience with my mother-in-law."

Lana's tension seemed to ease at Jessica's words, and Sean was extremely grateful that Jessica had taken control of the conversation. They needed to build a rapport with Lana, and thanks to Jessica, that's exactly what was happening.

"Helen was extremely judgmental," Lana continued. "Robert refused to stand up to her. He would never take my side. As far as he was concerned, his mother could do no wrong." Her lips tightened. "Helen blamed me for the fire. She told me I should have been at home, I should have taken care of the car. I should have made sure there were fire extinguishers in the garage. She had a million criticisms for me, never mind the fact that I was mourning my husband and my child." She shook her head in disgust. "Everyone else saw Helen as this sweet lady, but I saw the other side of her, the nasty side. When I left San Francisco, I vowed never to see her again."

"You probably don't want to hear this, but Helen asked me to tell you that she was sorry," Jessica said.

"You're right. I don't want to hear it." Lana straightened. "More importantly, I don't believe it. If she said that, she had a reason."

"She did say that she missed her grandson."

Lana gave an unrepentant shrug. "She can say whatever she wants, but she never tried that hard to see Blake. She's always known where my sister was. She gave you Connie's address, didn't she?"

"Yes."

"You found me in one day. Helen could have done the same, if she really wanted to. She didn't. And Blake has another grandmother, so he hasn't missed out on having a grandparent. Anyway…my sister told me that you have something that belonged to Stacy."

"Yes, her photo album, and there's a second album as well," Jessica answered. "I'll get them from the car."

"Can we come in and speak to you for a few minutes?" Sean asked, as Jessica went back to the van to retrieve the albums. He didn't want to just hand over the books and leave. "I'd like to hear what Blake is doing. I've thought about him often over the years."

Lana hesitated and then tipped her head. "All right. Come

in." She left the door open for Jessica, then ushered him into the living room.

The décor was a mix of white and chrome, modern sofas and chairs with expensive art on the walls. The far wall of the living room was all glass and looked out over a beautiful patio and the golf course beyond.

Jessica entered the room and set the albums down on the coffee table. Sean took a seat on the couch next to her while Lana settled in the armchair across from them.

"So tell me about Blake," Sean said.

"He owns a website design company," Lana replied. "He's doing really well, and he's getting married this summer to a beautiful girl. Theresa is a pediatric nurse."

"That's great. Blake always liked to draw."

"From when he was a very young boy," Lana agreed. "Stacy never cared much for coloring."

Sean smiled. "No, she didn't. Too much sitting involved. She liked action. She always wanted to throw a ball, climb a tree or ride bikes."

Lana's face paled, and she swallowed hard. "I don't think I can do this. I don't talk about Stacy. Not ever."

"I'm sorry," he said quickly. "I didn't mean to say anything painful."

"Just hearing her name is painful. I think about her every day. I think about how much she's missed, how she's never going to fall in love, get married, or have children. She's never going to laugh or sing or make funny faces. I'll never hear her tell me that she loves me." Her voice broke, her lips trembling as she struggled for control. "I'm sorry. This is why I don't talk about her. It's too hard."

"It's okay," he said gently, feeling a knot growing in his throat. He'd locked Stacy away, just as her mother had done. Thinking or talking about her had brought pain, so he'd stopped doing both. And he'd only been her friend. It had to have been a thousand times worse for her mother. "I miss her, too."

"You were so close to each other." Lana gave him an emotional smile. "I remember one time when your mother and I were watching you two play at the park. I don't remember which one of us said it, but it was something along the lines of, wouldn't it be fun if you and Stacy grew up and fell in love and had one of those love stories that started when you were in kindergarten and never ended."

Her words made him uncomfortable. He'd loved Stacy as an eight-year-old loves a friend, nothing more. Whether they would have even stayed friends forever was a question that couldn't be answered.

"I'm sure Stacy would have grown up to be a beauty. She would have had her pick of men." He cleared his throat. "Do you mind if I ask you a few questions about the fire? Since Jessica moved into the house, I've been thinking more and more about that night. I was too young to understand what happened then, but I'd like to understand now."

"What do you want to know?"

"How did the fire start?"

"They said it started in the garage, that a spark, possibly from the car, ignited the paint thinner and some of the other cleaning solutions that we stored out there."

That backed up what Emma had told him. "Was there something wrong with the car?"

"We'd been having trouble getting it started that week. One of the firefighters suggested that Robert might have been working on the car, but that didn't really make sense to me. My husband was not the kind of man who worked on automobiles. The only thing he knew how to do was change the oil. He might have put up the hood and taken a look, but beyond that…" She shrugged. "I didn't see how that could start a fire." She paused, frowning. "However, it's possible he went into the garage to smoke. I wouldn't let him smoke in the house, and he was trying to quit, but when he got tense, he liked to light up a cigarette."

"Did the firefighters find any cigarettes or a lighter?" Jessica put in.

"I don't really know. They sent me a report a few weeks after the fire, but I didn't look at it."

Sean was beginning to see a pattern. Lana didn't look at anything that bothered her.

"Was your husband tense because he'd quit his job?" Jessica asked.

"He was stressed out, yes, but it was his decision to quit. I don't really know what happened between him and his partner. Robert came home one day and said he was done. Helen, of course, blamed me. She said I put too much pressure on Robert to make money, but he was plenty ambitious on his own. In fact, he was a workaholic. He lived for his job. The kids and I always came second. You must remember how many times we had dinner without him, Sean."

"I do remember he wasn't around a lot," Sean said. "But getting back to the night of the fire..." He drew in a breath for strength and then said the words he should have said a long time ago. "I don't think I ever had a chance to tell you I was sorry for letting Stacy go home without telling anyone."

Lana stared back at him. "I was angry when I realized what had happened. I didn't know Stacy was at our house until I saw the ambulance and your father told me that Stacy was on her way to the hospital."

"I am so sorry," he repeated.

She blinked back a tear. "I wanted to scream at you. I think your father knew that. He wouldn't let me near you."

Sean was surprised to hear that. It wasn't like his father hadn't been angry with him, too.

"Your mother reminded me that you were only eight years old, and how could I blame such a young child for an innocent mistake."

"I blamed myself. I still do."

"We all have guilt to carry, but you didn't start that fire, and nothing will change what happened."

Silence followed her words. Lana finally looked at the albums on the table. She pushed the family album aside, then laid her hand on the cover of the pink album. She traced Stacy's name written in red ink on the front. A tear dripped down her cheek. "Oh, my God," she whispered. "My baby girl. I can't open it. I can't see her. Please take it away."

Jessica hastily picked up the album.

"The other one, too," Lana said. "I don't want those memories. I'm married to someone else now."

"What about Blake?" Sean asked. "Would he want the albums to show to his kids one day?"

"Blake doesn't talk about Stacy either."

He wondered if that was because Blake didn't want to upset his mother. "Would you mind if I asked Blake?"

"I'll ask him, but later. He's happy now. He's caught up in his wedding plans. I don't want to take him back to that unhappy time in our lives. Could you hang on to the albums for a while?"

"Sure," Jessica said. "It's going to take me a while to go through Helen's things, so I can tuck these away for a few months." She paused. "There may be other things in the house that belong to you. Helen didn't throw anything away after she moved in. The neighbors told me they offered to help her clear things out, but she always turned them down and said she wasn't ready."

Lana straightened in her chair. "What neighbors?"

"Sally Watson and Brett Murphy." Jessica answered.

"They both still live there?"

Jessica nodded. "Yes."

Lana didn't look happy about that fact. Sean wondered

why. "I'm surprised you didn't keep in touch with them," he said. "I thought you were all good friends."

"I thought so, too. Don't get involved with either of them," Lana said. "Trust me, you'll be better off." She got to her feet. "I don't want anything in the house. Throw it away. I don't care."

"But you do want me to hang on to the albums until you speak to Blake?" Jessica asked.

Lana hesitated.

"Stacy put that album together," Sean interjected. "She picked the pictures that meant something to her. It's her life. It was too short, but it's still important. I know it hurts to remember, but don't we owe it to her not to forget?"

Her lip trembled. "You must think I'm a terrible person."

"I think you're in pain."

"Because it's my fault that she's dead."

"What do you mean?" he asked.

She drew in a breath. "Never mind. Keep the albums for me, and give me your phone number. I'll talk to Blake, and I'll let you know."

"All right." Sean gave Lana his phone number and then he and Jessica walked out to the van. He got inside but made no attempt to start the engine.

Jessica turned sideways in her seat. "Are you okay?" she asked, worry in her eyes.

"That was rough."

"Did it feel good to apologize?"

"That part did feel good. I never had a chance to face her until now. I'm sure I saw her at the funeral, but we didn't speak."

"Your father kept her away."

"Yeah, go figure."

"Did you get any of the answers you wanted regarding the fire?"

"Some, but now I have more questions. Like why did she say it was her fault?"

"She probably felt guilty because she wasn't at home. When Kyle was kidnapped, I blamed myself for sending him to the birthday party alone even though he was going to be well supervised by other people, or at least that's what I believed. Obviously, he wasn't that well supervised. Anyway, Lana has probably gone over that night in her head a million times. She was on a field trip with her other child, right? Maybe she thinks if she hadn't gone on the field trip, hadn't sent Stacy to your house, hadn't gotten home later than she anticipated, everything would be different."

"You're probably right. I don't know why I keep trying to make an accident into something else."

"You're looking for a reason for Stacy to be dead, but there may not be one." Jessica paused. "I will say though that Lana's comments about Helen have made me wonder if I've completely misjudged the woman. I thought she was a sweet lady, but Lana makes her out to be a bitch."

"And what about Lana's warning not to get involved with the neighbors?" he said.

"That was weird," Jessica said with a sigh. "I wish she would have explained. It's those kinds of statements that keep making us think there's more to the fire than what we know."

"Right?" he asked, seeing the agreement in her eyes.

"Yes. I feel like everyone we speak to has a secret."

"And we don't know if it's the same secret."

"No, we don't. However, I don't believe we're going to get anything else from Lana," Jessica said, glancing back at the townhouse. "I'm not sure you'll ever hear from her again."

"Maybe not. Or perhaps she'll talk to Blake and he'll want the albums."

"It would be interesting to talk to Blake."

"I doubt he would have any information. He was six years

old at the time of the fire. He probably only knows what his mother told him, and I don't think she told him anything."

"So what now? Shall we head back to San Francisco?"

He hesitated, not quite ready to focus on the long drive. "It's early. How about some lunch?"

"I could eat. Do you want me to look up restaurants on my phone?"

"I have a better idea. How do you feel about a picnic on the beach? It's a little cold, but I could use some fresh air.

"That sounds perfect. Let's do it."

Fourteen

They stopped at a deli a few miles away and picked up sandwiches, chips, drinks and cookies for dessert. Fifteen minutes later, Sean unzipped one of the sleeping bags from the van and spread it out on a wide sandy beach.

"The sleeping bag does come in handy," Jessica said with a smile.

"More times than you know, and most occasions don't involve sex," he said with a grin. "I know I let you think that earlier, but I'm usually in the bag alone."

"What about Mary Lynn from Nashville?"

"She was one exception, but that was a few sleeping bags ago."

"So why did you lie? You didn't want to ruin your rock star image?"

He gave an unrepentant shrug. "I knew what you wanted to hear."

"I didn't want to hear that," she protested.

"Sure you did. You wanted another reminder that I'm not someone you should be interested in. But then you couldn't stop thinking about having sex with me in the sleeping bag," he teased.

She wished she could say he was wrong. "You think you

know everything."

"I think I'm getting to know you."

"Let's just eat," she said, thinking that the beautiful deserted beach and the cozy blanket were setting the scene for something a little more exciting than lunch. But she could exercise some self-control, couldn't she?

She knelt down on the blanket and started unpacking their lunch.

"We certainly got a lot of food," she said, handing him his turkey and cranberry sandwich. She pulled out the chips, salads and cookies and put them on the blanket between them, then settled in to unwrap her baguette with turkey and veggies.

"It's good," Sean said a moment later.

It was good. Not only the food, but also the entire scene. There was not another soul on the beach, which probably wasn't unusual for a Tuesday morning in February. But it was a beautiful day, the sun rising high overhead, white puffy clouds dotting the bright blue sky, a light breeze bringing in the salty smell of the nearby sea. The waves were gentle and rolling, adding to the restful atmosphere. She felt more relaxed than she had in a very long time.

"That hit the spot," Sean said, crumpling up his empty wrapper.

"That was fast."

"I grew up in a family with eight kids. If you didn't eat fast, you went hungry."

"I can't see Lynda allowing that to happen," she said dryly.

"Okay, the truth is I skipped breakfast."

"The most important meal of the day?"

"Yeah, yeah, I know, but I'm not usually awake for breakfast."

"I used to be like that," she said as she finished her own sandwich. "Late nights dancing led to late mornings. It seems like a million years ago that I was living in a one-bedroom apartment with two other girls, Marley and Fran. Marley and I shared the bedroom, and Fran slept on the pullout couch in the living room. We shared one very small bathroom and if you were the last one into the shower, you could expect only cold water." She smiled to herself, thinking that despite having no money, those days had been fun, too. "Marley was a dancer. We were in a lot of the same shows together. Fran was a blackjack dealer. We all worked late nights, so breakfast was usually around noon."

"Do you keep in touch with them?"

"Texts and emails, the occasional phone call. I have to admit I pulled away first. I married Travis and pretty much ditched everything in my life. I don't know why I thought I had to make such a clean break. I guess I was a little defensive about my Las Vegas background when I got to Angel's Bay. When Travis's mother heard I was a dancer, she immediately thought stripper. There's nothing wrong with stripping, but I didn't do that. I think I tried too hard to erase that part of my life just so I would fit in better." She sighed, feeling a little sad. "I really liked those girls. I'm sure I probably hurt their feelings. I feel badly about it all."

"Maybe you can reconnect."

"I've been thinking about it," she admitted.

"Don't just think about it, do it."

"I'm not sure how receptive they'll be."

"Only one way to find out." He paused. "Getting back to Angel's Bay, you should never feel you have to apologize for who you are or try to be someone else. You accused me of that last night, saying I always try to play the bad guy, the black sheep of the family. Well, maybe you've tried too hard to be the good girl."

He wasn't wrong. "So, you're giving me a taste of my own medicine," she said lightly.

He grinned. "How's it going down?"

"A little bitter," she admitted.

He stretched out on his side, propping his head up with his hand as he gazed at her. "Tell me more about Vegas. Where did you dance?"

"Everywhere. There are shows at all the venues now. I'm good at acrobatics, which is a big part of many of the productions. And I don't mind spinning on a wire a few hundred feet in the air, so I never had much trouble getting work."

Surprise filled his eyes. "I had no idea you were so fearless."

"When I'm in a show, flying in a harness, I'm playing a character, and I want to bring that character to life, so I can be brave. I know they're not going to let me fall. Real life tends to be far more scary."

"I get that. When I'm on stage, it feels like another world."

"A world you command. You're a natural performer, Sean. You come to life under the lights."

"Apparently, so do you. I'd like to see that sometime."

"I doubt that will happen. My acrobatic days are over, and that's okay. I developed those skills because they were marketable, but my first love for dance is ballet, then comes lyrical and contemporary routines." She paused. "Actually, I love it all."

"That's why you need to be involved with dance again, either as a dancer or as a teacher."

"I need to make sure that I'm a good mom first. It's the one role I don't want to screw up. I owe that to Travis."

"You're a great mom. Kyle is happy. You need to make yourself happy, too. That's what you owe to Travis."

She stared at him, searching for the right words. "Sometimes I'm afraid to dream again."

"Why?"

"Because I dreamed of love, marriage, family, and I got all

that, and then it got ripped away. It was hard to go through that pain. I don't know if I could do it again. Loving someone is a huge risk, even bigger now because Kyle is part of the picture. I have to protect not only myself but also him. I have to be careful. I can't get things wrong."

"You're tying yourself up in knots, Jess. Do you want to spend your life being too afraid to make a move because it might be the wrong move?"

"I know that sounds boring, but it's smart. It's safe. It's what I need to do."

He shook his head with a frown. "It's not you. You're creative and passionate. And you want to fly. I know you do. You just told me how fearless you were."

"On stage, not in real life," she said, feeling a little desperate to convince him, because his words were making her restless, making her want to believe that maybe he was right.

"In real life, too. You're the girl who met a man, got married and changed her whole life for love."

"And look how that turned out?"

"Not because you were wrong, because there was an accident. You can't let fear stop you from living. I know it's easy to say and harder to do. But you have to try. You're too young to stop dreaming. You deserve to have everything you want."

"It's not just about me. It's about Kyle. You don't understand because you don't have a kid. But I can't be selfish. He has to come first."

"I understand that. But Kyle deserves a mother who's happy, too."

"Maybe not," she said shaking her head. "My mom was happy, but I sure as hell wasn't. Maybe if she'd been a little less happy, my circumstances would have improved."

"You know that's not true. And again, you're not your mother."

"Stop talking," she said, putting up her hand.

He opened his mouth, but she leaned forward and put her fingers against his lips.

"I mean it," she added. "I know you're trying to be encouraging or supportive or something, but you're making my head spin."

"Because you know I'm right," he mumbled against her hand.

She got to her feet, knowing that he wasn't going to stop talking until she was too far away to hear him. She walked briskly toward the sea, ignoring Sean's plea to come back, his apology for pushing too hard. She didn't want to talk to him right now. He was too passionate, too persuasive. He almost had her convinced that he was right.

Was he right? Would playing it too safe only hurt Kyle in the long run?

Why was it so difficult to know the right thing to do?

With her pulse racing, she walked along the water's edge, letting the repetitive motion of the tide slow down her heartbeat. She tried to clear her mind, to stay in the moment, concentrate on the seagulls, the horizon, the rocky cliffs ahead.

Eventually, she ran out of beach. She stopped and turned and saw Sean about ten feet behind her. "You followed me."

"You were upset," he said. "You weren't looking where you were going. I didn't want you to get knocked down by a rogue wave."

She was more likely to be knocked down by him.

He moved closer. "Are you okay, Jessica?"

"I'm fine."

"You don't look fine. I shouldn't have pushed my opinion. I don't like when other people do that to me, so I'm sorry. But I still don't think I'm wrong."

She sighed. "Maybe you're not completely wrong."

"Yeah? What part was I right about?"

"I do want to be happy. I just don't want to let Travis down."

"Why do you keep saying that?"

"Because when Travis picked me to marry, everyone around him had doubts about me. When Kyle got kidnapped, those same people looked at me like I was the worst mother in the world. And I know it wasn't my fault, and everything is good now, but there's still a part of me that is afraid I'm not up to the challenge, that maybe Travis should have picked someone else to be Kyle's mother."

"He picked you for a reason. He saw in you everything he wanted. When you doubt yourself, you doubt him."

"I never thought of it that way," she said slowly.

"You'll figure it all out, and it doesn't have to be today." He brushed the hair out of her eyes and gave her a tender smile. "For the record, I think you're amazing at pretty much whatever you do. I have every confidence that you will be a fantastic mother, dancer, business woman, whatever you want to do. You're the only one setting limits. No one else is."

Her eyes watered. She tried to blame the wind, but it was him, all him.

His gaze darkened as he ran his knuckles down the side of her cheek. Then his hand was under her chin and she was lifting her face to his, because kissing him on this wild, deserted beach seemed the absolute right thing to do. It was over way too fast, cut short by the ringing of Sean's cell phone.

She stepped back as he pulled his phone out of his pocket, telling herself that the interruption was good, because the beach was a little too empty, and the sleeping bag was a little too close.

She wrapped her arms around her waist, feeling a chill without Sean's arms around her, without his lips on hers. She was getting addicted to kissing him. Each kiss seemed better than the last. And while she told herself every time was the last time, there always seemed to be another tempting moment.

"Emma," Sean said. "What's up?" He listened and then said, "I can't hear you very well. Let me call you back in a few minutes, okay?" He hung up the phone, his jaw tightening, his eyes glittering with anticipation. "Emma has some news. Let's pack up and get in the car. Then we'll call her back."

→→►◄←←

Ten minutes later they were in the front seat of Sean's van with Emma on speaker.

"So I tracked down the fire investigator," Emma said. "His name was Jackson Randall. Unfortunately, he passed away two years ago. So that's a dead end. However, I also did some research into Robert Emery's financial records. At the time of his death, he had over four hundred thousand dollars worth of debt. Twenty years ago, that was even more money than it is today. He'd recently quit his job, which didn't make sense, since he owed so much money."

"Where are you going with this?" Sean asked.

Jessica had a feeling she knew exactly where Emma was going, and she didn't think Sean was going to like it. She put a hand on his thigh. She could feel the tension in his muscles.

"I'm wondering if Mr. Emery decided he was worth more dead than alive," Emma replied. "He had two life insurance policies totaling about six hundred thousand dollars. The insurance paid off because the fire was ruled an accident."

"Why wouldn't the investigator have considered that theory?" Jessica enquired.

"That's a good question. He didn't interview anyone related to Mr. Emery's former employer, and his interview with Mrs. Emery didn't include any questions regarding Mr. Emery's state of mind."

"I don't think Mr. Emery would have killed himself with

Stacy in the house," Sean put in.

"Unless he didn't know she was in the house," Jessica interjected. "The TV was on upstairs. Robert was in the garage. Maybe Stacy didn't announce her arrival. Maybe she just went straight up to her bedroom."

"Jessica has a point," Emma agreed. "And the fact that Mr. Emery's body was found away from the entrance into the house from the garage suggests that he was overcome by fire too quickly to even attempt to get out. Which could also back up the theory that he deliberately planned it that way."

"There's one other theory," Sean said. "Lana told us that she wouldn't let her husband smoke in the house. He was trying to quit, but with all the stress, he'd been sneaking cigarettes out in the garage."

"No cigarette butts or a lighter were found," Emma said. "But that's interesting. How did you come to talk to Lana?"

"Helen gave us Lana's sister's address," Sean replied. "We got the sister to tell us where Lana was. The conversation was painful. Lana could barely speak of the fire."

"Aside from the cigarettes, did she tell you anything else? Did she tell you why Robert quit his job?"

"She said Robert didn't share his work with her, mostly because she was annoyed that he was always working so much. She didn't know why he quit or what his plans were."

"So that still needs to be figured out. I think you and Jessica should talk to Mr. Emery's business partner, Clark Hamilton. As far as I can tell, Robert and Clark started the company, which was called Clark and Emery Investments, when they were in their mid-twenties. They'd been working together for almost ten years when Robert quit. It would be interesting to know why he suddenly left a firm that he'd founded."

"Wait a second," Jessica interrupted. "Did you just say Sean and I should talk to Clark Hamilton?"

"Unfortunately, yes. I'm on my way to the scene of a three-alarm fire in the Garment District. There's one known victim and possibly other fatalities. The fire has jumped to the building next door, and there's an evacuation underway. I'm going to be tied up for a while on this, at least the next three or four days. I'm certainly happy to follow up next week, but if you want to move faster, I'll give you Mr. Hamilton's address."

"I'll take it," Sean said, jotting down the address on his phone. "Thanks, Emma."

"Let me know if you find out anything. I'll get back on this as soon as I can."

"Are we seriously going to go talk to Mr. Emery's business partner?" Jessica asked, not liking the idea at all.

"It's a good lead."

"For an investigator, but neither one of us is that."

"We're just going to ask him a few questions."

"Why would he even talk to us?"

Sean thought for a moment. "We'll use the same excuse we did today. You're cleaning out Robert's house, and you found something that might belong to him."

"And what would that be?"

"I don't know. We'll look in the attic when we get back. There has to be something we can tie to him." He gave her a pleading look and an irresistible smile. "You're not going to make me go by myself, are you?"

She should really do just that, but she couldn't seem to say no to him. "All right. I'll go with you, but you're going to have to help me find something in that attic that we can pass off as belonging to Mr. Hamilton."

"Done."

She let out a sigh. "At what point are you really going to be done, Sean?"

"I don't know, but I'm not there yet."

Fifteen

When they got back to Jessica's house, Jessica let Sean inside so he could get started on the search for something to take to Clark Hamilton, then she hopped in her car to get Kyle.

Alone in the house, Sean wandered down the hall, noticing fresh flowers on a side table and a large green plant in the corner of the dining room. Jessica had taken down the heavy and very formal dining room draperies and replaced them with simple cream-colored shades. The room was brighter and lighter now. She was starting to add personal touches to the décor, which made him happy, not only because she finally had a house that she could make hers, but also because it was starting to feel less like the Emery house and more like Jessica's home.

He walked into the kitchen and pulled a soda out of the refrigerator. As he unscrewed the top, he perused the artwork Jessica had displayed on the fridge. Some of the pictures were very childish, basically stick figure drawings, which had to have been done by Kyle. Others were brilliant detailed sketches that had Brandon's artistic flourish. The pictures were another reminder that there was a new family in the house.

He finished his soda and tossed it in the recycle bin and then forced himself to go upstairs. Jessica had agreed to go with him to see Clark Hamilton; he needed to hold up his end of the bargain. He made his way into the attic and started digging through boxes, looking for something masculine, something that might have related to work or to the two men. He couldn't imagine what that would be.

He pulled another box off a deep shelf and set it on the floor, coughing as a flurry of dust kicked up. When the dust cleared, he saw a very old desktop computer that had been hidden behind the box. On the side of the monitor were a bunch of colorful stickers.

His heart skipped a beat. He knew this computer. It used to sit in Robert's office, and occasionally he and Stacy had been allowed to play a game on it when Robert was at work. One day Stacy had gotten bored and put stickers all over the screen.

The computer was over twenty years old. It probably didn't work anymore.

But if it did…

What would be on it?

He hesitated for another second and then grabbed the tower that housed the hard drive. He didn't see a plug anywhere nearby so he took it downstairs to the kitchen, then dashed back up to the attic to grab the screen, keyboard and the mouse. A plastic bag of cords was nearby so he took that as well, hoping one of those power cords would work.

It took him a few moments to set up the computer and hook everything together. Then it was time for the moment of truth. He pushed a button and was thrilled when the hard drive began to whir. The screen flickered, and a beach scene appeared on the screen. One by one the programs began to populate.

It worked! He could hardly believe it.

The sound of a car door closing told him that Jessica was back. A moment later she came in through the side door with Kyle. Kyle dropped his backpack on the floor and came running over, excitement in his blue eyes.

"What's that, Uncle Sean?"

"It's a very old computer," he said, meeting Jessica's surprised gaze. "I found it in the attic. It's Robert's computer."

"It looks like Stacy's with all those stickers."

"She put them on there, but this computer belonged to her father. I wasn't sure it would work, but it seems to be trying to load."

"Do you think Robert kept financial records on there?"

"We'll see."

"Can I help?" Kyle asked.

"Not right now," he told the little boy, feeling bad when he saw the disappointment in Kyle's eyes.

"Sean has to see if it will work first," Jessica told her son. "And you're going to help me make dinner, right? Go put your backpack in your room and then we'll start cooking."

"Okay," Kyle said, taking his backpack and heading out of the kitchen.

Jessica sat down at the table, her eyes sparkling. "This could be a big clue."

"I hope so. The first step is to see if we can get into the files. By the way, I didn't find anything to take to Clark Hamilton yet. I saw the computer and got distracted."

"Understandably so. I can look later. Do you want to stay for dinner, Sean? I'm going to make tacos."

"Sounds great."

As Jessica stood up, a knock came at the kitchen door. She shot Sean a quick look, then opened the door. "Sally, hello."

"I saw you and your son come home," Sally said. "I wanted to drop off these homemade cookies."

"That's nice of you."

As Jessica took the plate of cookies, Sally peered around her. "Is that Sean?"

At Sally's question, Jessica reluctantly took a step back so

Sally could enter the kitchen.

"Mrs. Watson," Sean said, getting to his feet.

"If I'd known you were here, I would have brought you some cookies, too." She'd barely finished speaking when her gaze moved to the computer on the table. Her face paled, and her lips tightened. "That's—that's Robert's computer," she murmured, confusion and surprise in her voice. "Where did you get that?"

"It was in the attic," Sean said, wondering about her reaction. "Is something wrong?"

Sally put a hand to her chest. "No. It just took me back in time, that's all. I can't believe that computer survived the fire. I thought Robert's office was completely destroyed."

Her words raised a question in Sean's mind. If the computer had been in the office next to the garage, why hadn't it been destroyed? And why wouldn't it have been in that office? He couldn't remember Robert working in any other room.

"Does it still work?" Sally asked, as she inched closer to the table.

He had the sudden urge to cover the screen, but there was nothing for her to see, just basic computer icons.

"I just started it up," he said.

Sally's gaze moved to him, and he could see worry in her eyes. "Perhaps you should turn it off."

"Why?"

"Because the information on there is private. If anyone should have that computer, it's Helen or Lana, or possibly Blake. It doesn't seem right for you and Jessica to look through Robert's personal files."

"Robert died twenty years ago," Sean said. "And Helen hired Jessica to go through everything in the house. That includes this computer."

"If there's anything of a personal nature, I'll let Helen

know, and she'll decide what should be done," Jessica added.

Sally's gaze moved from Sean to Jessica and then back to the computer.

"Is there something on the computer that's personal, Mrs. Watson?" Sean asked, deciding to confront her.

She gave him a startled look. "How would I know that?"

"You seem upset," he said bluntly. "And very concerned about what we might find."

"It's not concern exactly," she said slowly. "Seeing that computer brought back painful memories, that's all. Of course, you're right. You have to go through everything, and obviously Helen trusts you both." She blew out a breath. "It still makes me sad to think about Robert and the terrible way he died."

"It sounds like you and Robert were close," Jessica said.

"We were neighbors," Sally replied quickly, a mask coming down. "Everyone in the neighborhood was close back then."

"Were you close enough to know why Robert quit his job?" Sean asked.

She shook her head. "No, that was odd. He loved his job. But he was also very ambitious, and I'm sure he had plans to move on to something bigger and better. He was always talking about making more money, moving into a bigger house, and sending the kids to private school. I'm sure he would have accomplished all that if he hadn't died. He was very good at picking the right investments and ruthless enough to know when to cut his losses."

As Sally finished speaking, Kyle ran into the room. "I'm ready," he announced. He stopped and gave Sally a curious look. "Hi."

"This is my son, Kyle," Jessica said. "Kyle, this is Mrs. Watson. She lives next door."

"Do you have any kids I can play with?" Kyle asked.

Sally smiled. "No, my kids are all grown up. Sorry."

"That's okay. Mommy, can I have some juice?"

"Sure. Thanks again for the cookies, Sally."

"I hope you enjoy them," Sally said. "Nice to see you again, Sean."

As the door closed behind her, Jessica said, "Sally looked at that computer like it was a snake about to bite her."

"Yeah," he said, sitting back down in front of the screen. "Let's see if we can find that snake."

----➤➤◄◄◄----

Jessica wanted to huddle next to Sean and look through the computer files, but she had a hungry six-year-old on her hands and mom duties came first. She set Kyle up with a block of cheese and a grater and showed him how to grate the cheese. While he was doing that, she sautéed ground beef and then cut up onions, tomatoes, lettuce, peppers and some avocado.

While she was cooking, Kyle talked non-stop, jumping from subject to subject, so fast she could barely keep up. But all she really cared about was how happy he was. He liked his school, his friends, his brother, and was excited about learning how to play baseball. He also loved Nicole, every other sentence starting with Nicole did this or Nicole told me that. In the beginning, she'd felt a twinge of jealousy and had worried that Kyle might like Nicole better than her. But she'd gotten past that, telling herself that it wasn't a competition; the more people who loved Kyle the better.

When dinner was just about ready, Kyle got down from the chair to run up to the bathroom, and she came around the counter to see what Sean was up to. He'd been quiet for at least twenty minutes.

"Well?" she asked.

"I was able to get into some of his document files. But there are a lot of business files, and so far nothing has jumped out at me as being incredibly important. I'd like to get into his email, but I don't know what his password is. I've tried a bunch of combinations."

"Maybe play off his kids names," she suggested.

"I already tried everyone in the family as well as sports teams. Nothing is coming through."

"What about hobbies? Did he play golf, tennis, baseball? Was he a fisherman? Did he hunt?"

"As far as I know he was a businessman and as Sally said, he liked making money."

"How about a family pet?"

"They had an old cat named Harvey," he said slowly. "I forgot about that cat."

She frowned. "Please tell me he didn't die in the fire."

"No, he was an outdoor cat. I don't know what happened to him. I assume Lana took him with her." He typed in *Harvey* and the mailbox opened. "You are brilliant, Jessica."

"I have my moments," she said, peering over his shoulder. "The inbox is full of messages, almost twelve-hundred."

"Let's start with the mail he got the week before he died."

Sean scrolled through the messages and then paused. "Gingerbabe1. That's an interesting address." He opened the mail and whistled under his breath. "It's from Sally. *Meet me tonight. Make sure Lana doesn't know. You won't regret it, Sally.*"

"No wonder Sally looked nervous when she saw the computer. This certainly implies the two of them had something going on, although it's not gushing love."

"We need to keep looking."

"Later," she said as Kyle returned to the kitchen. "Dinner is ready, and I don't want to talk about things in front of Kyle. He has a tendency to repeat things he hears to other people."

"Are you talking about me, Mommy?" Kyle asked, as he climbed into the chair across from them.

She ignored his question and said, "Did you wash your hands? Let me see."

Kyle held out his hands and she gave them a quick inspection.

"Good boy. I'll get your taco."

"Can I help?" Sean asked.

"No, everything is ready. Just let me know what you want on your taco."

"I'll take whatever you've got."

"That's easy."

A few minutes later, Jessica sat down at the table to eat. It felt a little surreal to be having a family dinner with Sean, the second in a row. Last night she'd had Nicole, Ryan and Brandon as a buffer. Now she only had Kyle. And despite the fact that her six-year-old was entertaining Sean with stories about school, she still felt like the dinner was somewhat—intimate.

Worse, it felt comfortable and right, as if the three of them were a family, and she could not let herself think like that. This was not Sean's scene at all. He was just hungry and in the middle of something. That's the only reason he'd stayed.

"I'm done. Can I have dessert?" Kyle asked.

"You can have one cookie. Take your plate to the sink."

Kyle did as he was told, spilling a little on his way to the counter, but he did manage to set the plate down and grab a cookie before heading up to his room.

"That kid can talk," Sean said with a smile.

"Tell me about it. I really try not to stop listening, but sometimes it's hard." She got up to clear the table. "Do you want to get back to those emails?"

"I can help you clean up."

"It's fine. I can handle it, and I'd really like to know if Sally sent Robert any other messages."

She took the plates to the kitchen while Sean opened the

computer again. While she rinsed off the dishes and loaded the dishwasher, Sean went through the mail.

"There are two more messages, both from the day before the fire," he said. "Here's the first one. *I feel guilty, Robert. But sometimes you have to pay for what you want. You know that better than anyone.*"

"That sounds ominous and cryptic," Jessica said returning to the table. "What does the other one say?"

"*Brett knows. Did you tell him? I have to deal with him now and that's going to cost more.*" Sean looked up from the computer. "Sounds like an affair with maybe some blackmail mixed in."

"No wonder Sally looked like she was going to pass out when she saw the computer."

"Yes, but while Sally and Robert having an affair is interesting, I'm not sure whether their relationship had anything to do with the fire."

She frowned. "That's true. I feel like it's one step forward and two steps back."

"I wouldn't go that far. A secret affair would at least explain why Sally was worried about you being in the house. She still wants to protect her secret."

"Maybe I should tell her that I don't care what she and Robert did, and I have no interest in revealing anything to anyone."

"Why don't you wait on that? Let's see what other secrets this computer has to tell. We may have only hit the tip of the iceberg."

"You're right, but it will take days to go through everything. And while I'm excited to learn more, maybe we should continue this tomorrow. I need to spend some time with Kyle before he goes to bed."

"And you'd prefer me to get out of your hair."

Actually, that wasn't what she wanted at all. She'd love for

Sean to stick around, to play games and read stories with Kyle and do all the things parents with young kids did. But Sean wasn't Kyle's father, and they weren't a couple.

As Sean gazed back at her with his deep blue eyes, a shiver ran down her spine, and she was suddenly very aware that her chaperone was all the way upstairs.

She cleared her throat. "You should go home, Sean. I have to be a mom for a while."

"You already said that. Do you think I'm going to forget that? Do you think that being a mom makes you less sexy, less kissable?"

She caught her breath at his provocative words. "I don't think I should answer that question. You need to go."

"You go first."

It was a dare, and one she really should accept, but she couldn't seem to move.

Sean's eyes drew her in, and her gaze fell to his mouth. She wanted to kiss him again. She needed to kiss him again. They both moved at the same time, their mouths colliding somewhat awkwardly. He lifted his head and smiled. "Let's try that again."

He covered her mouth with his and the warm, branding kiss sent tingles down every nerve. He tasted spicy, like jalapenos and hot sauce, and she couldn't get enough. His arms came around her back, holding her close, as if he were afraid that she would move, end the kiss, but that was the last thought in her head.

"Mommy!"

The loud call made her jump back. She gave Sean a dazed look and then got to her feet as Kyle came into the kitchen.

Kyle's face was red, and there were tears streaming from his eyes. "What's wrong?" she asked, dropping to her knees in front of him, checking for cuts and blood, but she didn't see anything. "Did you hurt yourself?"

"I broke Ryan's plane," he sobbed, holding up two pieces of a model airplane. "I was trying to fly it, and it hit the dresser, and it broke. He's going to be mad. He's never going to teach me how to fly."

"Oh, honey, it's okay."

"It's not okay," Kyle wailed.

"Let me see that," Sean said.

Kyle handed over the pieces of the plane. "Can you fix it?" he asked, taking a moment out of crying to give Sean a hopeful look.

"Do you have some glue?" Sean asked Jessica.

"There's probably some in the laundry room. I'll get it."

She ran into the adjoining room and got the glue. When she came back, Kyle was sitting on Sean's knee and looking at him with adoration as Sean explained how he was going to try to fix the plane. His patience and tenderness touched her heart. Sean might not think of himself as a family man, but she thought it was a role for which he was quite well suited.

Sean had definitely won her son over.

He'd won her over, too.

She handed him the glue. "Here you go."

"Okay, give me a little room."

Jessica pulled Kyle into her arms, and they both watched Sean put the plane back together. A few minutes later, it was whole again.

"You're going to need to let it dry," Sean said. "Don't play with it until tomorrow and then be a little more careful. Maybe this plane just stays in the airport for a while."

"Okay," Kyle said happily.

"Can you say thank you?" Jessica urged.

"Thank you, Uncle Sean." Kyle left her arms and gave Sean a big hug. Then he ran back upstairs.

"You're his hero now," she said as Sean got to his feet.

"Some problems are easy to solve." His expression turned

somber. "For the record, Jessica, I've never been a hero. Those are the other guys in my family. I'll see you tomorrow."

He left before she could tell him that while he might not think he was a hero, she knew one six-year-old boy and one twenty-seven-year-old woman who thought differently.

Sixteen

—➤ ➤ ◄ ◄—

Sean drove home, feeling restless and frustrated and generally pissed off. Jessica was to blame, beautiful, sexy Jessica, with her big brown eyes, and soft full lips. She kissed like a dream. She made him lose all sense of time and place. He wanted her, and he couldn't have her. And he wasn't just falling back on some trumped up reason not to get involved in a relationship, like he'd done before. These reasons were real and undeniable and they were never going to go away.

Jessica was always going to be tied to his nephew, his sister, his family.

So what? He asked himself. What if things didn't go wrong? What if they went right?

But when the hell had they ever gone right?

Frowning, he got out of the car. As he walked up the driveway, his thoughts moved from Jessica to Kyle. Her little kid, with his blond hair and blue eyes, had looked at him like he was a hero. But it was nothing to fix a model airplane. He could do the easy stuff. The hard stuff was another matter.

And he'd seen the look in Jessica's eyes when she'd watched him with Kyle. Danger bells had gone off in his head. She was a single mom, looking for a dad for her kid. He wasn't father material. He wasn't husband material. He liked his freedom. His life was one of movement and change.

A sexy single mom and her cute kid weren't going to change all that. Were they?

He had to admit he enjoyed having dinner with them. He liked being part of a family again. He'd almost forgotten what that felt like. But Kyle and Jessica weren't his family. If anything, they belonged to the Callaways.

With a sigh, he unlocked his door. He was just about to step inside when he heard his name called.

He looked down the stairs and saw his father standing by the side door.

"Can you come down for a minute?" Jack asked.

He really wished he had a good reason to say no, but he didn't. So he nodded and walked back down the stairs.

Jack had disappeared into the house by the time he got there. Sean entered through the laundry room, walking into the big country kitchen that had been remodeled about ten years ago, but the large oak table where he'd done his homework still sat in its nook by the window.

His father was sitting at that table now. He had his computer open, and a mug of coffee sat next to it.

"Just made some coffee if you want some," Jack said.

"I'm good." Sean took a seat at the table. "What are you working on?"

"I'm catching up on some emails. There doesn't seem to be enough time in the day."

Sean nodded, already out of casual conversation. When it came to his dad, he never knew what to say.

"I spoke to Emma earlier." Jack lifted his gaze from the computer and fixed his sharp blue gaze on Sean's face. "She's looking into the Emery house fire. Was that at your request?"

He hesitated and then decided there was no point in prevaricating. "Yes. When Jessica moved into the house, I started thinking about the fire and realized I never knew how it started."

"You didn't think to ask me?"

"Emma is an arson investigator," he answered carefully.

"And I was there that night. I ran into that fire. You don't think I might have some answers?"

He saw the disappointment in his father's eyes and tried not to feel guilty about bypassing his dad, because this was the very conversation he'd hoped to avoid. "Emma said that you didn't have any information that wasn't in the report. Is that incorrect?"

Jack's lips tightened. "No."

His father might have faults, but he was always honest. "That's what I thought."

"Your mother told me I was too hard on you after the fire. And later I realized she was right. I took out my anger and frustration about the tragic deaths of two people on you, and you were just a child."

Sean was stunned at the apology. He didn't know what to say.

"I tried to talk to you about it," Jack continued. "But you shut me out after that. I thought eventually you'd get over it, and things would go back to normal, but I realize now that that was the beginning of the end for us."

"Until this past week," Sean said slowly, "I didn't realize that fire was a turning point for us, but you're right, it was. You were hard on me, but I deserved it. Stacy might be alive if I'd told someone she left. I have to live with that for the rest of my life."

Jack gave a regretful shake of his head. "I don't want you to live with that guilt. The fire was an accident. No one was to blame, least of all you. I'm sorry I put that on you." He paused. "How can I help you now?"

"I don't know," Sean said, taken aback by the offer. "Emma said the investigation appeared to be incomplete, that certain protocols weren't followed. I wonder why, especially since you were on that fire, and you knew the Emerys personally."

Jack nodded, his jaw tightening. "She mentioned that. I don't know what happened. I spent quite a bit of time detailing my findings at the scene with the investigator. But only one page of my report is apparently in the file. I don't know why the rest is missing, but I can tell you that there was no evidence that the fire was anything but an accident."

"Robert was in a lot of debt. His widow collected more than half a million in insurance money."

"I did not know about the debt, but the fire didn't look like suicide. I knew Robert. I can't believe he would have killed himself. He wouldn't have done that to his wife and children even if he was having money problems."

"Did you know that Sally and Robert were having an affair?"

Jack's jaw dropped. "I did not. Are you sure about that?"

"Not one hundred percent sure, but it looks like there was something going on between them."

"Well," Jack said, lapsing into quiet as he thought about what Sean had said. "I find that surprising. Robert wasn't a man to cheat on his wife."

"Maybe you didn't know him as well as you thought," Sean suggested.

"Maybe I didn't."

"Emma said there were other problems with the report," Sean added. "The investigator said there were only two witnesses at the scene, but there were more than two people watching that house burn."

Jack's gaze bored into his. "How do you know that?"

Sean quickly realized his mistake. He'd just backed himself into a corner and judging by the look on his father's face, he wasn't going to be able to get out of that corner without coming clean. It was time to tell the truth. He just didn't know if he could do it.

"Sean," his father pressed. "What aren't you telling me?"

He took a deep breath and then said, "I was there that night."

"You were where?"

"Outside of Stacy's house."

"That's impossible."

"No, it's not. I saw the smoke from my bedroom window." He paused as the memory flashed through his head. "I didn't know the fire was at Stacy's house, but I knew it was close by. I left my room, and I went downstairs. Mom was cooking dinner in the kitchen and helping Drew and Emma with some homework. She didn't even see me walk through the room. I knew I wasn't supposed to go outside, but I was drawn to the fire."

He took a breath and then continued. "When I got around the block, I realized it was Stacy's house. I was shocked and scared. I didn't know what to do. I just stood there. And then the front door opened and Stacy came running out." He swallowed a lump in his throat. "She was on fire. The flames were lighting up her hair, and she was screaming. She looked across the street. I think she saw me, but I don't know. Then the fire engines arrived. I saw you run to her. You wrapped her in something and threw her on the ground."

"Damn," his father murmured, shaking his head in disbelief. "I had no idea. I never saw you."

"You were a little busy. You know what I did next? I ran home. I went upstairs, got into my bed and I pulled the covers over my head. When you and Mom came to see me later that night, I already knew what you were going to say." He paused. "Stacy was dead, and it was my fault."

"Why didn't you tell me?" Jack demanded.

"I was already in trouble for letting Stacy go home."

"You shouldn't have been out there. You were eight years old. You knew you weren't supposed to leave the house by yourself."

Sean thought it only fitting that his father should focus only on what he'd done wrong and no other part of the story. "Well, I was there, and I saw Stacy, and I couldn't get that image out of my head for years. When Jessica moved into that house, it all came back to me. That's why I asked Emma to look into the fire. I want to put it to rest, but I can't do that until I know why it happened."

"It was an accident, Sean. I really believe that."

"If that's what it comes down to in the end, then I'll believe it, too."

"You're so stubborn."

"Apparently, we have one thing in common."

Lynda walked into the kitchen and gave them both a pointed look. "You were both doing so well," she said with a sigh. "I had a feeling it wouldn't last. I was listening," she added. "And I'm not going to apologize."

"So you heard everything?" Sean asked.

She met his gaze, sympathy and compassion in her eyes. "I can't believe you never told us you were at the fire, Sean. It was such a big secret for you to carry. No wonder you couldn't sleep for months after that fire. I feel like I should have known. I obviously missed something that night."

"There's enough of us taking blame for what happened that night, don't you start, too," he said. "You didn't miss anything. I kept the secret from you. I didn't want you to know, and as the years passed, I tried to put it behind me. The only reason I told Dad now was because he asked me how I knew there were other witnesses. I saw at least six to seven people from the neighborhood huddled on the street together, so it didn't make sense to me that none of them were questioned."

Jack frowned. "It doesn't make sense to me either. I know

some of my guys talked to the neighbors. I'm going to talk to Emma about the investigation, and I'll see if I can help."

"I appreciate that."

"This explains so much, Sean," Lynda said. "Your sudden aversion to all things having to do with fire. You wouldn't go down to see your father at the firehouse after that night. You avoided the firefighter picnics. You stiffened when you heard a siren. I had a feeling it had to do with Stacy, but now that I know you saw her come running out of her house, I can see why you had to stay away. I just wish you'd told us."

"There was nothing you could do."

"That's *not* why you didn't tell us. Do you know what I think?" she asked.

He was afraid to ask. "What?"

"You wanted to be punished, and not the simple punishment we would have handed out for leaving the house. No, keeping the secret kept you in pain for a long time, and it was pain you thought you deserved. But you didn't, Sean, and you need to let it go."

His mother's words hit him like a punch to the gut. He didn't know if he was punishing himself, but he did know that he needed to find a way to move on. "I'll be able to let the past go when I know everything there is to know about that night," he said.

"Sometimes the truth doesn't set you free," Lynda said.

"Sometimes it just makes you hurt all over again," Jack added.

His parents were smart people. He hoped they were both wrong.

Jessica got into Sean's van on Wednesday morning with a brown paper bag in her hand. "What's that?" he asked curiously.

"Our excuse to see Mr. Hamilton." She reached into the bag and pulled out a carved statue of an elephant. "What do you think?"

"I'm not sure," he said. "Do you have a story to go with that?"

"As a matter of fact, I do," she said with a sparkle in her brown eyes. "I found a box labeled India. Inside was this elephant as well as photos of Mr. Hamilton and Mr. Emery on a business trip to Kashmir. There were pictures of them in front of the Taj Mahal and with various business associates. It's easy to assume that this elephant belonged to Clark and might even be valuable."

"Very smart," he said approvingly.

"I thought so," she said with a smile. "I'm starting to feel like a detective."

"I'm starting to feel like an idiot for getting into all this," he murmured.

She frowned. "Okay, what happened between last night and this morning, because you were still feeling pretty gung ho when you left my house last night?"

He sighed. "I ran into my parents when I got home. I had a chat with dear old dad."

"Really. What did you tell him?"

"Everything." He glanced over at her. "All of it, Jess."

"I'm surprised. How do you feel?"

"A little lighter for getting the big secret off of my chest, but at the same time I wonder what the hell we're doing now. My dad was on the scene. As an experienced firefighter, he knew what he was looking at, and he saw no sign that the fire wasn't an accident."

"Did you tell him what else we've discovered?"

"Some of it—the debt, the possible affair—but it still doesn't quite add up to suicide or anything else."

"Anything else being…"

"Deliberate."

She met his gaze, her brows drawing together as she gave him a thoughtful look. "You're not talking about Robert setting the fire himself anymore, are you?"

"It occurs to me that if he was having an affair, maybe someone was angry."

"That someone being Lana. You think she would have killed her own husband and daughter?"

He heard the doubt in Jessica's voice, but he had an explanation. "Lana didn't know Stacy was in the house," he reminded her.

"You're right." Jessica settled back in her seat. "Well, that's another theory."

"It could explain why Lana said the fire was her fault."

"I thought that was just mother's guilt."

"Maybe it was. Like I said, I don't know what we're doing."

"We're following clues. Emma thought it was a good idea for us to talk to Mr. Hamilton. We have this elephant to show him. I say we go and talk to him and then decide if we want to do anything else. Even though you're frustrated, I don't think you're ready to quit yet, Sean."

"You're right. Let's talk to Clark."

Fifteen minutes later they parked in an underground garage, then made their way up to the twenty-second floor of a building in the Financial District. The glass door was engraved in gold with the name Hamilton and Associates. They stepped into a plush lobby, decorated with thick carpet, large black leather sofas, Impressionistic paintings and an ornate antique desk in the corner.

A young woman in her twenties sat at the reception desk. She gave them a friendly smile.

"Can I help you?" she asked.

"We're here to see Mr. Hamilton," Sean said.

"Do you have an appointment?"

"No, but we have something for him."

"I can give it to him. He doesn't see anyone without an appointment."

"I'm afraid we're going to have to deliver it personally. Can you tell him that we have something for him from Robert Emery, his former business associate?"

The woman gave the bag in Jessica's hand a curious look and then reached for the phone. "What's your name?"

"Sean Callaway."

She punched in a number, then relayed Sean's message. Then she said, "Mr. Hamilton said he can spare you five minutes." She got up from her desk and led them through another pair of glass doors, down a long hallway, to the office at the end. After a quick knock, she opened the door and waved them inside.

Sean had seen evidence of wealth in the outer office, but Clark Hamilton's private office was a designer's dream. And it wasn't just the furniture that was impressive, it was also the floor-to-ceiling view of the San Francisco bay just behind his desk.

Clark stood up as they approached. He was extremely tall, at least six-foot-five. He had brown hair that was streaked with gray and a dark moustache. He wore an expensive suit with a white shirt and red and black striped tie. He gave them an enquiring and somewhat wary look.

"How can I help you?" he asked.

"I'm Sean Callaway and this is Jessica Schilling."

"I met a Jack Callaway once."

"My father," Sean said.

"That makes sense. My receptionist said you have something for me that has to do with Robert Emery?"

"Yes," Jessica said, stepping forward. "I moved into Mr. Emery's former house last week. His mother, Helen, asked me to go through all the things her son left behind after he died and make sure that anything of a personal nature goes to the person who might want it." She cleared her throat and sent Sean a quick look.

He knew exactly what she was worried about. She didn't want to hand over the elephant without finding out more about Clark and Robert's relationship.

"It's our understanding," Sean said, drawing Clark's attention to him, "that you and Robert worked together."

"For ten years," Clark said, bitterness in his eyes. "Robert was at the top of his game, a brilliant investor, but he got greedy. He wanted a bigger cut. He wanted to make the kind of money his clients were making. So he crossed a line. He betrayed me. That's when I fired him."

Sean was surprised by his answer. "I thought he quit."

"I let him tell people that because of our long friendship. It wasn't true. He should have gone to jail for what he did."

"How did he betray you?" Jessica asked.

"He stole money from me, the firm, and some of our clients."

"He didn't die with any extra money in the bank," Sean pointed out.

Clark gave him a sharp look. "How would you know that?"

"The investigation into the fire revealed that Robert was in quite a bit of debt at the time of his death."

"He lost the money he stole in the stock market," Clark said. "He wasn't so brilliant after all. So what do you have for me?"

Jessica pulled out the elephant. "I thought this might be valuable. Robert left it in a box with your name on it. It was with some pictures taken in India."

"Robert bought that elephant for his son," Clark said, making no move to take it out of Jessica's hand. "You should give it to Blake."

"Oh, I didn't realize," Jessica said. "It had your name on it."

Clark uttered a harsh, bitter laugh. "Probably his idea of a joke. Was there anything else with my name on it?"

"Not that I've discovered so far," she replied. "But there are quite a few boxes to go through."

"I thought everything was lost in the fire."

"Apparently not," she said. "I guess the upstairs didn't suffer that much damage, at least that's what people tell me."

"Why isn't Lana cleaning out the house?" Clark asked.

"She's not interested. It's too painful for her."

"So you've spoken to Lana?" Clark asked.

"She's remarried and lives in Seascape," Sean answered, drawing Clark's attention back to him. "She told us that Robert quit his job and wouldn't say why."

"That's simple. He didn't want her to know what he'd done."

"Why didn't you blow the whistle on him, call the cops, put him in jail?" Sean asked. Clark didn't seem like the kind of man who would let someone steal from him and do nothing about it.

"I thought about it. I even threatened to do just that. But Robert and I had been close friends for years. We were like brothers. We had started the firm together. In the end, I just wanted him to leave, so I could rebuild my business."

"It sounds like Robert was in a bad place," Sean said. "Not only was he caught stealing, he lost the money he stole and also his job. You weren't going to give him a reference, so what was he going to do for work?"

Clark shrugged. "I have no idea."

"When did you speak to him last?"

"About a week before he died."

"What was his frame of mind?" Sean asked.

"He was angry, desperate to get his job back. I told him we were done."

"Do you think Robert was capable of killing himself?"

It was a shocking question to ask, but Clark didn't react with surprise. Instead, he said, "I wondered about that myself, but it's my understanding that the fire was believed to be accidental."

A knock came at the office door.

"Come in," Clark said.

The receptionist stepped into the room. "Your next meeting is here."

"Tell them I'll be right with them." Clark gave them a brief smile. "I'm sorry, but as you heard, I have another appointment. Miss Conway will show you out."

"Thanks for your time," Sean said.

"If you do find any papers relating to the business Robert and I had together, I would be interested in seeing those. I still have a few questions about what he did with the money," Clark said.

"I'll let you know," Jessica said.

The receptionist led them out to the lobby.

They didn't speak until they got back into the car.

"I don't understand why Clark would let Robert just walk away from the job," Sean said, as they fastened their seatbelts. "It doesn't seem like the action of a sharp, ambitious man who'd spent years building a business that depended on trust.

"They were friends," Jessica said. "Clark felt some loyalty to Robert, which stopped him from calling the police. He wanted Robert gone but not destroyed."

"I suppose that makes sense," he said, but he wasn't entirely convinced. Then again, he didn't know what he would do if Hunter stole from him. Maybe friendship and loyalty would trump criminal punishment. Maybe he would do the same thing as Clark.

"So what do you want to do now?" Jessica asked.

"I guess I'll fill Emma in on the conversation and see if she has any other ideas."

"I really think it's looking more and more like Robert killed himself. Think about it. Robert was at the top of his game. He was a superstar. Then he crossed a line. He stole money, lost his job, and apparently lost the money he stole. He has an affair with Sally. He's not getting along with his wife. Then he dies, and Lana ends up with half a million dollars. No one knows about the terrible mistakes he made. His reputation is intact. His wife is out of debt. It makes sense."

"You make a good case," he said as he started the engine. "I just wish we had some proof."

"Well, unless we find a suicide note, I don't think we're going to come up with any."

As he drove out of the parking garage, he glanced at the dashboard clock. It was almost eleven. "Are you in a hurry to get home, Jess? I need to run by the studio and drop off a check for Hunter. It won't take long."

"That's fine. I guess we can spend a little more time together."

He gave her a smile. "We're friends, right?"

She smiled back at him. "You're the most complicated and challenging friend I've ever had."

"Right back at you."

Seventeen

--➤➤◄◄◄--

While Sean spoke to Hunter in the control room, Jessica decided to explore. She found a staircase and went up to the second floor where she found what she presumed to be Sean's office. She was impressed with the state-of-the-art computer set-up and the artistically designed décor. A glass table served as a desk, and along one wall was an extensive display of photographs and music awards.

She moved closer. The first few photos were of bands. Then there was a close-up of Sean on the guitar on some outdoor stage, a line of majestic mountains as the backdrop. Her heart skipped a beat at the sight of him in action, his wavy brown hair blowing in the breeze, his fingers on the guitar, and an intense expression on his face as he sang into the microphone.

She could almost hear the music and the female screams of excitement. She'd seen Sean in a small, intimate club, but here he looked like a rock star. She moved to the next shot which zoomed out, showing the thousands of fans surrounding the stage. As she'd imagined, there were dozens of girls in the pit looking up at Sean with pure adoration.

How could one woman ever compete with that? How could one woman ever be enough for a man who got this much attention on a daily basis?

Maybe that's why there'd never been just one woman for Sean.

"Are you impressed?" a female voice asked.

Jessica whirled around in surprise. A stunning blond, looking very much like a supermodel, gave her a smile. Dressed in a super short skirt with a camisole top, a leather jacket, and three-inch heels, the woman was close to six-feet tall. She had long, silky straight hair that reached her waist, and her eyes were like a cat, a mix of gold and green. Those eyes were now filled with amusement.

"Speechless, huh? That usually only happens when the guys are actually in the room," the blonde said. "So who has you hot and bothered? Hunter or Sean?"

Jessica hadn't even seen Hunter. Her gaze had only been on Sean. "I'm sorry," she said, stumbling a little. "Who are you?"

"Pamela Becker. And you?"

"Jessica Schilling. I'm with Sean. I mean, I'm a friend of Sean's," she hastily corrected.

"So it was Sean who put that dreamy look on your face. That's good, because Hunter is my boyfriend."

Jessica wasn't surprised to hear that. This was exactly the kind of woman a musician would be with.

"So, you and Sean are friends. How did you meet?"

"That's a long story."

"Sounds like it might also be an interesting one."

"Not really. Did you say you and Hunter were together?"

"For almost a year. We met at that concert." She tipped her head toward the photo Jessica had been looking at. "Actually, it was at the after party. Hunter went to Coachella to see Sean play. I was there doing a photo shoot for one of the sponsors." She grinned. "It was lust at first sight. Then it turned to love."

Pamela's words reminded Jessica of her other life, the life

she'd led before Travis and Kyle, where concerts and musicians and booze-filled nights created instant couples. Usually, those nights were filled with regrets, but apparently Pamela and Hunter had gotten lucky.

"Are you sure you and Sean aren't more than friends?" Pamela asked.

"Yes," she said quickly.

"Too bad. He's a good guy, a really good guy, just in case you're wondering."

"I already know that," she said. But a part of her felt like she didn't know the guy in the photograph at all. And while that guy attracted her, he also scared her to death. She couldn't let herself forget that Sean had more than one side, and at heart he was probably more like that rocker on the stage than the man who had listened to her son talk about sharks for an entire dinner.

"Know what?" Sean asked, startling her with his sudden appearance in the doorway.

"Uh, nothing," she said.

His gaze narrowed. "What did Pamela tell you?"

"I told her you were a good catch," Pamela said.

"And I told her I wasn't interested in catching you," Jessica put in. "That we're just friends."

"Right. Just friends."

His gaze clung to hers for a long moment, and despite what she'd said, she felt a shiver run down her spine.

Pamela cleared her throat. "Sure. I totally believe both of you. Where's Hunter?"

"Downstairs," Sean said.

"Then I'll leave you two alone to do your *friend* thing," Pamela said as she left the office.

Jessica had been alone with Sean a lot the last few days, but now felt different. Maybe it was because they weren't focused on solving an old mystery at the moment. "I like the photos," she said, searching for something to say. She tipped her head toward the wall. "You really have played all over, haven't you?"

"It's been quite a ride."

"I didn't realize you played such big venues."

"On occasion." He gave her a speculative look. "Something bothering you, Jess?"

"No. Are you ready to go?"

"Almost. I want to show you something first."

"What's that?"

"Come with me."

"You're being mysterious again," Jessica complained as they walked out into the hallway.

He shrugged. "I don't have words. You just have to see it."

Sean opened a door and led her into a large open space. Sunbeams danced off the hardwood floors.

"This is the space we're planning to rent out," Sean said.

She walked into the middle of the room. "It's great. I love the floors."

"The light is really good up here, too."

"I'm sure you won't have any trouble renting it out."

"But we want to make sure we have the right tenant, someone who fits in with the creative nature of our business. I was thinking a dance studio might be perfect."

A nervous flutter ran through her stomach as she shot him a questioning look. "When did you start thinking that?"

"A few days ago, when you told me that you've been thinking about opening a studio."

"Thinking about it is a long way from doing it," she said, but she couldn't deny the spark of excitement his suggestion had elicited. "That's just a dream."

"That's how the music studio started. Sometimes dreams become reality."

"You prepared for your dream. You saved money. You

found a partner. You had a plan. I just have an idea."

"You don't have to decide right this second, Jessica. Think about it." He paused and waved his hand around the room. "Wouldn't this be a great place to dance?"

She thought so. In her mind, she could hear the music, see a room full of dancers, kids, professionals, couples, older people looking to recapture the moves of their youth.

"You're practically swaying," Sean teased. "You can see it, can't you?"

"I can," she admitted. "But there's no way I could afford to rent this space. And even if I could come up with the money to invest, I have no business experience whatsoever."

"But you know the world of dance."

"I left that world, Sean. I'm a mom now. I have other priorities."

"You always make it sound like being a mom makes it impossible for you to be anything else. The only person putting limits on your life is you."

She wondered if that were true. She glanced around the room again. "It is a beautiful space."

"Show me what you've got, Jess."

"Excuse me?"

"One or two moves, a spin. That's all I'm asking."

"I don't think so," she said, fighting the urge to give in to the persuasive look in his eyes. "There's no music."

"I'm betting you don't need any. You hear it in your head." Sean folded his arms in front of his chest. "I played for you. It's your turn to dance for me."

"I don't have the right shoes or clothes," she said, making one last protest.

His steady stare told her he wasn't going anywhere until he got what he wanted.

She turned her back on him and walked to the center of the room, to a triangle of sunlight. She could feel the warm beams of light on her head. And like any good dancer or performer, she knew how to use that light to her advantage.

Not looking at him, she closed her eyes and let the music inside her head play. It was what she'd always done. From the first time she'd gone to dance class and had been asked to perform in front of others. She always took a moment to center herself, to let her mind float away from reality to the dance ahead.

And then she was moving—a step, a turn, and then another turn. Her hands and arms were graceful and light. She was a bird in the sunlight, freed from its cage, ready to take flight, and that's exactly what she did.

She left everything behind—all the stress, the anger, the grief, the guilt, and the worry. The emotions that gripped her and grounded her far too often evaporated with each step. She felt free and happy.

So she spun, and she spun, and she spun, until she was dizzy and laughing.

Until Sean caught her in his arms.

Then she came back to earth.

She came back to him.

Kissing Sean seemed the absolute perfect finish to her spontaneous dance.

He seemed to feel the same way, his warm mouth answering her eager lips, his tongue sliding inside, deepening the connection between them. She wrapped her arms around his waist as the music playing through her head wrapped around both of them in a dance of desire, attraction, love.

The music in her head came to a screeching halt. She forced herself to break the kiss, to halt their movement, to stop the madness.

But while she'd come to her senses, Sean still gazed at her with amazement and wonder.

"That was better than anything I've ever seen," he said.

"You were almost flying. It was incredible. Do you know how talented you are, Jess? How special?"

His gaze clung to hers. She felt incredibly touched by his words.

"You have to dance," he continued, passion in his voice. "Or teach. Or both. You have a gift. You can't not use that gift."

"I have used it. I've danced for many, many years. But it wasn't enough. I wanted more."

He shook his head in confusion. "I don't know how Travis could have watched you dance and then let you quit."

"I couldn't dance in Angel's Bay. And that was his home, where he needed to be. Don't judge him. He didn't make me quit. I chose to quit."

"Then you can choose to come back."

"I'm too old."

"You're twenty-seven."

"That's old in dancing years."

"There's still a place for you in that world, Jess. Maybe you can choreograph or inspire your students. But you can do something. And I think you want to do something. I think you need dance in your life."

"Like you need music?"

"Yes," he said with an emphatic nod. "We're both artists."

"But I chose to walk away. I chose family." She paused. "You would never do that, would you?"

His gaze darkened and a frown crossed his lips. "I'll say it again, why does it have to be a choice?"

"Because it does. Because we both know what it takes to be at the top of our professions."

She wanted him to argue with her. She wanted him to say he'd give it all up for the right person, just as she'd done. But Sean didn't say anything, and maybe that was the real answer.

"We should go," she said finally. "I need to get home. I

need to get back to doing what I was hired to do." And most of all, she needed to remember that that was her real job and this studio was just a fantasy. A really nice fantasy, she thought with a sigh, as she gave the space one last look and then turned toward the door.

-->>><<--

As Sean drove Jessica home, he felt pissed off, irritated with her and also with himself. Jessica didn't seem too happy either, and he knew why. He hadn't come up with the answer she wanted to hear, because he'd been thinking about her question, because, for the first time in his life, the easy answer didn't seem so easy anymore. But his silence had only reinforced her opinion of musicians making lousy boyfriends or husbands.

And the problem was, he couldn't even argue with her opinion. He knew what it took to be successful in the music business, and it didn't exactly jibe with being a family man.

Up until now, that had always been fine with him. Music was enough.

At least that's what he'd told himself.

But he'd been feeling restless, even before he'd met Jessica. He'd been on the road awhile. He'd seen how difficult it was to make money even with sold-out shows. He'd realized that a great song didn't always translate into cash in the bank. Which was why he'd put away every penny he could, knowing that one day he was going to have to get, as his father would call it, a real job.

He'd wanted it to be a job he could be happy in. And he thought the studio fit the bill. Whether they could make that studio successful was still a question mark, but he was going to try damn hard to succeed. Because he was a Callaway, and while most of his father's teachings had bounced right off of him, the one that didn't was that the only sure way to failure was to quit, and Callaways don't quit.

But Jessica had quit. She'd given up dance for love. And he had judged her a little for it.

Frowning, he knew that had been wrong. But when she'd danced in that circle of light, she'd looked like an angel, a fairy, some otherworldly spirit, who had literally stolen the breath right out of his chest. And he'd known with a certainty that Jessica was meant to dance. He'd never seen her so alive as he had in that empty space where she'd found some music in her soul and given it movement.

He pulled up in front of her house and didn't bother to turn off the engine, knowing that he could not go inside. He was feeling way too many emotions to be alone with Jessica right now. He needed to put some real space between them.

Jessica put her hand on the door and then paused. "I don't want to fight with you, Sean."

"Are we fighting?"

"Aren't we?"

He sighed. "We were just having a heated conversation. Sometimes we Callaways get a little carried away with our opinions."

"That's the first time I've heard you refer to yourself as one of the Callaways," she pointed out.

"I have more of my father in me than I thought. He loves to tell people what they should do. I've been on the receiving end of his unasked-for advice, and I shouldn't have tried to tell you what to do. Sorry."

"Well, you did make me think. That's not the worst thing in the world."

"Good. We're not going to do anything with that space for a while, so keep it as an option."

"I will." She paused. "When do you want to look at Robert's computer again?"

"I'm not sure," he said. He did want to go through the rest

of the emails, but now didn't seem like a good time. "I'll call you later."

"It will have to be much later. I need to go into Mom mode right now. I have to clean the kitchen and do some laundry before I pick up the boys. Then it's on to the park and the library. Pretty exciting stuff, huh?"

"It sounds like a busy afternoon."

"Are you going back to the studio?"

"No. I'm meeting my band for a practice session. We use the back room of a furniture warehouse owned by my drummer's uncle. Pretty exciting stuff, huh?" he said, echoing her words.

Her smile eased the tension that had grown between them. "I guess your life isn't always glamorous."

"No one's life is. It just looks that way from the outside."

As he finished speaking, he saw Sally come out of Brett's house. She paused when she saw them sitting in the van. Then she gave a quick wave and hurried back to her home.

"I thought Brett and Sally didn't like each other," he muttered.

"They sure act like they don't when they speak to me. I wonder what they were talking about."

"Maybe she told him we found Robert's old computer."

"Why would he care?" she asked.

"Didn't one of Sally's emails to Robert say *'Brett knows and it's going to cost more'*?"

Jessica stared back at him. "I forgot about that. Maybe Brett was involved in Sally's blackmail scheme. Hopefully, it will become clear when we go through more of the emails."

"Why don't we touch base later tonight? We'll figure out our next move."

"Do we have a next move?" she asked, doubt in her voice.

"Definitely," he said. "We're going to solve the puzzle, Jess. We're getting closer every day."

Eighteen

They weren't getting closer to an answer; they were just creating new questions, Jessica thought, watching Sean drive away. Still, Sean had a confidence that she very much admired, and she hoped he would get the answers he needed. She wanted him to be able to move on from the trauma of his childhood. But they'd talked to just about everyone involved and while they'd gotten bits and pieces, none of those pieces were forming a clear picture. Maybe they never would. Maybe no one's life could be re-examined and put together like a puzzle.

She thought about her own life and what a crazy mosaic that would make. She certainly wasn't the same person today than she'd been two years ago or ten years ago. Actually, she wasn't even the person she'd been yesterday, because this afternoon Sean had made her remember what it felt like to fly.

She put a finger to her mouth, remembering that kiss in the studio. It had been a perfect, heady ending to her dizzying and happy impromptu dance. For a few minutes she'd felt like herself, her real self, the girl who used to dance, who loved to move, who could hear a song in a silent room and a quiet space.

Drawing a deep breath, she looked up at the sunny sky,

thinking about how that same sun had filtered through the windows of that beautiful space. She could fill that space with dancers, music, and costumes. She could teach children to dance, to find expression through their body as well as their mind. It seemed like a wonderful plan.

But where did that leave Kyle? She didn't want to shortchange him. And even though she would try not to do that, would she be able to do it all? Or was that just another foolish dream?

Shaking her head, she realized she was still standing on the sidewalk, already losing her focus thinking about dance. She needed to concentrate on her real life, on laundry and cleanup and plans for dinner.

She was about to go inside when Brett came out of his house and crossed the street. She wasn't really in the mood to talk to him, but there was no way to avoid conversation without appearing rude.

"I'm glad I ran into you," Brett said. "Helen told me that you were going to try to find Lana, and I'm curious to know if you were successful."

"Perhaps you should speak to Helen about that," she said, not sure how much to tell him, especially since she'd just seen him and Sally together.

His gaze narrowed and anger sparked in his eyes. "Is it a secret? I knew Lana quite well when she lived here. I've wondered about her often over the years." He paused. "Helen and Lana didn't get along very well. I was actually surprised when Helen told me that she'd given you Connie's address. Why *did* she give it you?"

"Why didn't you ask her that question?"

"I was going to, but we were interrupted."

Judging by the determined look in Brett's eyes, she was going to have to tell him something. "I found some things in the attic that Helen thought Lana might want. She suggested I contact Lana's sister, Connie. Connie was able to put me in touch with Lana."

"So you did see Lana?"

"I did."

"How is she?"

"She seemed well. She looked good. She said she's remarried."

He nodded, his lips tightening. "I figured. She must have been shocked to see Sean. He and Stacy were so close. She couldn't have liked that reminder."

"I think it was a little unsettling at first."

"Did she give you any information?"

"About what?" Jessica countered.

"About the things in the house. Is she planning to come back and take a look through the attic?"

"I don't know about that. We're going to talk again as I dig deeper."

"Did she ask about me, about any of the neighbors?"

Jessica hesitated and then told the truth. "She told me I shouldn't trust anyone on this block. Apparently, she doesn't have happy memories of her life here."

His eyes darkened into hard points as he said, "Lana wasn't unhappy until the very end, until she lost her daughter. Then everything changed." He shook his head, anger rolling off of him in waves. "That damn fire ruined a lot of lives."

"Did Lana ever tell you how the fire started?" she asked, wondering if she would hear a different story from Brett than she'd heard from everyone else.

"She didn't talk to me about it, but I heard that Robert was trying to fix his car or something."

"That's one theory," she muttered.

He raised an eyebrow. "Is there another theory? Are you and Sean looking into the fire? I thought you were just cleaning out the house."

"The two seem to be going hand in hand."

"What do you think you're going to find?"

"I don't know," she replied, wishing she could take back her last sentence, because she'd just raised the level of Brett's interest another notch.

"Do you think someone set the fire deliberately?" he asked. "Do you have any suspects? Do you know anyone who would want Robert dead?"

She was taken aback by the sharpness of his words, the tension in his voice, the rapid fire of his questions. She turned it around. "Do *you* know anyone who would want Robert dead?"

Brett stared back at her. "Robert was a ruthless businessman. He worked with big money. He could have had enemies. In fact, I know he had plenty of people who didn't like him. He wasn't the most likeable guy. I'm sure Lana told you that he was a workaholic. She used to complain about him all the time."

"She did say he worked a lot," Jessica conceded.

"But Lana thinks the fire was an accident, doesn't she?"

"That's what she said."

"Then I don't understand who or what is driving the interest in that old fire. What exactly is going on?"

She certainly couldn't tell him it was Sean who wanted answers. She searched for something to say that would appease him, because she could see the anger in every tight muscle of his face and body. He looked like he could explode at any second.

"I think I've misled you," she said quickly. "There's no driving force looking into the fire. I've had some questions about the past, because I'm going through things that belonged to Robert and Stacy. But I didn't mean to imply there was anything more going on."

"I hope not," he said grimly. "This neighborhood suffered

a lot with that fire. Looking through the ashes isn't going to help anyone."

She glanced down at her watch. "I'm sorry, but I have to go. I have some things to do before I pick up my son from school."

"All right," he said, his voice distracted as if his thoughts were now somewhere else.

She had a feeling that somewhere else was twenty years ago.

"By the way," he added. "I'm running for County Supervisor in a special election. How would you feel about letting me put a sign in your yard?"

"Uh, I guess that's fine," she said, feeling awkward once again. She barely knew the man and certainly didn't have any idea if he was qualified to be supervisor, but she also didn't want to offend him.

"Great. I'll put one up later today. Thanks for the support," he said, his angry gaze turning to grateful charm.

"Okay," she said, not quite sure what to make of his changing emotions.

As she walked into the house, she felt Brett's gaze follow her to the door. Once inside, she peeked through the curtain and saw Brett pull out his phone and make a call as he crossed the street. It was highly unlikely that the call had anything to with their conversation. On the other hand, he'd certainly been very interested in her meeting with Lana and why she was looking into an old fire. Did he know more about that fire than he was letting on? Or was that her imagination putting motives behind Brett's words that simply weren't there?

All she really knew was that the man rubbed her the wrong way. He seemed like someone who was always putting on an act, playing out a role—star baseball player, devoted stepfather, civic-minded politician. He tried to come across as friendly and outgoing, but when she'd hesitated to answer his questions, she'd seen the anger in his eyes. The man had a temper, and she was going to keep her guard up around him, at least until she knew him better.

For the next few hours, Jessica concentrated on getting her own life into order. After starting a load of laundry, she straightened up Kyle's room, and then headed out on errands. After picking up the boys from school, she took them to the park for an hour so they could run off some of their pent-up energy, then it was on to the library to return books and pick out new ones, with a final stop back at Nicole's house just before five.

With Ryan on a flight to Hong Kong, Nicole asked her to stay for dinner, and since Nicole was a far better cook than she was, Jessica decided to say yes.

"Can I help you do anything?" Jessica asked, watching Nicole move efficiently around the kitchen. "Although, you always seem to have everything under control."

"It's an easy dinner tonight, spaghetti, salad and garlic bread. So don't give me too much credit. And I made the sauce on the weekend when I had more time."

"Now I have to give you credit, because my sauce comes out of a can."

Nicole smiled. "It's probably just as good." She tossed some freshly ground garlic on a loaf of bread and slid it into the oven. "How was the park? Did Brandon give you any trouble?"

"Brandon never gives me any trouble. I'm not sure what he thinks of me actually. All our communication is through Kyle. Brandon only gets a little antsy when Kyle gets upset about something. Otherwise, he pretty much goes with the flow."

"I never thought anyone would describe Brandon as going

with the flow," Nicole said, disbelief in her eyes. "At least not since he got sick. Before that, he was a happy, easygoing child, a lot like Kyle. I sometimes wonder if the boys hadn't been separated if Brandon would have gotten autism. I'll never know, and it's pointless to think about it, but it has crossed my mind. Anyway…" She wiped her hands on a dishtowel and said, "I wanted to talk to you about Sean."

Jessica stiffened. "What about Sean?"

"You seem to be spending a lot of time together."

"Because of the house. Sean is dealing with old memories about the fire."

Nicole nodded, but she didn't look convinced that the fire was the reason for their constant togetherness, and Jessica couldn't really blame her.

"Emma told me she's looking into the cause of the fire," Nicole continued. "I know that Sean and Stacy were friends, and he was very sad when she died, but I don't understand what the mystery is."

"It's kind of a long story. You should ask Sean, or Emma; they know more about it than I do."

"Sean never tells me anything, but he seems very open with you."

She didn't know how to respond to that. "We're friends," she said, feeling kind of lame for repeating a tired phrase that didn't begin to describe their complicated relationship.

"Are you falling for him, Jess?"

She met Nicole's gaze head on. "I'm trying not to. But I'm not doing a very good job." It was the first time she'd admitted that her feelings for Sean went beyond friendship, and saying the words out loud seemed to give them even more importance.

Nicole's gaze filled with worry. "I love Sean. He's my brother, and he's a great guy, but I know the way he is with women and relationships. I don't want him to hurt you, Jessica. He doesn't have a good record with commitment. When the wind blows, he tends to go with it."

"I know all the reasons why being with Sean is not a good idea."

"But you still like him."

"I can't seem to help myself. He's very likeable." She offered up a conciliatory smile. "If it makes you feel any better, Sean has been very up front about the fact that he doesn't do long-term relationships. He's not pretending to be someone he's not."

"Sometimes that honesty is more attractive," Nicole murmured.

She shrugged, unable to deny that she found Sean attractive in so many ways. "You don't have to worry about me, Nicole. I appreciate your concern, and I'm touched that you care enough about me to say something. But I can take care of myself."

"I know you can, it's just—"

Jessica cut her off knowing exactly what Nicole was worried about. "My relationship with Sean will never impact our relationship, the one between you, me, Ryan and the boys. We're a family. We're raising our kids together. That's not going to change no matter who comes into my life, whether it's Sean or someone else."

"I know you're going to fall in love again," Nicole said. "You're young and beautiful, and you should be happy. I want that for you even if it does change things in some way. But hopefully it won't."

"It won't," she said, feeling one hundred percent sure of that fact. "It's not about us; it's about the boys. Brandon and Kyle belong together, and we're both going to do whatever it takes to make that happen."

As she finished speaking, the boys came into the kitchen.

"We're hungry," Kyle announced.

"It's almost ready," Nicole said.

"Can I spend the night here?" Kyle asked, giving Jessica a pleading look. "Brandon and I want to play pirates later."

She sometimes marveled at the way Kyle spoke of their games, as if the two of them would be wielding swords and play-fighting with each other. But when she watched the two of them play, Brandon was usually sitting down and watching Kyle. Yet Kyle never seemed to feel that he was carrying the burden of the game.

"It's okay with me," Nicole put in. "You know I'm always happy to have Kyle. It makes bedtime easier, especially when Ryan isn't here to help me."

Jessica hesitated. They had a schedule, and she liked to keep to it, but saying no would disappoint not only Kyle but also Nicole and Brandon. And she wouldn't mind having the opportunity to take another look through Robert Emery's computer. "All right. You can stay."

Since they'd started co-parenting, they'd made sure that each boy had clothes and toys and personal items at each house so they always felt like they were at home, no matter which house they were in.

"Brandon, I get to stay over," Kyle told his brother.

A spark of light flickered in Brandon's eyes. Jessica glanced over at Nicole, wondering if she'd caught it, and of course she had.

Nicole blinked away a tear. "It's moments like that that keep me going, Jess. One day the flicker will stay lit, I'm sure of it."

Jessica hoped very much that that was true.

It was after eight when Jessica finally left Nicole's house. After dinner, she and Nicole had shared cleanup, homework and story time. It reminded Jessica of what it had been like when Travis was alive, when they'd been a family of three instead of two. Things had definitely changed in the last few years, but she no longer felt the weight of depression and sadness, and it wasn't just the move to San Francisco that had upped her mood, it was also Sean.

He'd brought new light into her life. He'd made her feel young again. With Travis, she'd always felt pressure to live up to his life, his family, and his stature in the community. She hadn't wanted people to see her as an immature girl, so she'd done everything she could to appear older, wiser, and even more conservative. Now, she had no pressure to live up to anyone else's expectations.

She felt like she was coming into her own. She was a young mother, and she didn't know everything, but she was trying, and she wasn't doing a bad job. Knowing how fast and short life could be, she wanted to really live her life, not keep putting things off for the future or waiting for the perfect situation to make something happen.

Travis had rescued her once, but she didn't need another man to do the same. She needed to rescue herself. Sean had made her see that earlier when he'd taken her upstairs to that beautiful room and asked her to imagine the dream she'd had for a long time. When the vision had come, it had been incredibly clear.

Her life was waiting for her to start. She just had to start. She had to throw off the fear and the worries about not being able to be a mother and a dancer and a businesswoman. Maybe she would stumble. Maybe she would even fail. But she wanted the challenge.

Feeling remarkably confident and strong, she turned down her street and then pulled into the driveway. She wanted to put her thoughts into a plan, maybe even do a little research into the local dance schools. She needed to see how much competition she would have and what kinds of programs were being offered at what price. Then she would review her finances, take a hard look at what she had and what she needed to save for Kyle. She would not do anything that would jeopardize his future.

She smiled to herself as she shut off the car and gathered her things together. She felt energized and ready to move, and she had Sean to thank for that. He'd woken her up, and now her eyes were wide open.

Maybe she'd call him, too. She had the night to herself.

A shiver ran through her at the thought of being alone with Sean, no six-year-old to chaperone, but it wasn't as if they hadn't been alone before. And they still had some things to talk about. Before she could really get started on her own plans, she wanted to help Sean tie up the loose ends from his past. Then they could both move forward.

She walked up the driveway, pausing at the corner of the house. Shimmers of light by the dining room window gave her pause. What was that?

She moved closer, shocked at the sight of glass on the ground. Her gaze moved to the window. The curtain was blowing in the night breeze.

What the hell had happened?

She couldn't believe what she was seeing. Every muscle in her body tensed as she strained to hear some sort of activity from inside, but it was quiet.

She forced her feet to move. When she got to the side door, she put her hand on the knob and turned. The door opened, and she felt a wave of fear. She'd locked the door.

Someone had been inside the house. Were they still there?

Her heart almost jumped out of her chest at that thought. She should investigate, but she was terrified, and she couldn't bring herself to go inside. Instead, she pulled the door shut, ran back to her car, got inside and locked the door. She stared at the house for a long minute, debating her options. Then she started the engine and drove down the street and around the corner. She parked in front of the Callaway's home, thrilled beyond belief to see a light on in the garage apartment.

Sean opened the door on her third knock. He looked like he'd recently gotten out of the shower, his hair damp, his cheeks freshly shaven. A pair of jeans hung low on his hips but his chest was bare, with beads of water glistening on his skin. She'd never been so happy to see him. She stepped forward, threw her arms around his neck and said, "Thank God you're home."

She took a deep breath, inhaling the musky scent of his aftershave. He felt so good, so solid, so safe, but as he pulled her into the cradle of his hips, safe turned to sexy, and the shivers that ran down her spine now had less to do with what she'd just seen and more to do with the half-naked man who was holding her in his arms.

Desire, fear, and a half-dozen other emotions ran through her, and her head was literally spinning.

"Jess? What's wrong?"

She didn't want to answer. She didn't want to make it real.

"Jess," he said again. He shifted slightly so he could see her. Then he put two fingers under her chin and lifted her face to meet his gaze. There was concern in his eyes. "You're shaking."

"Am I?"

"Yes." His arms tightened around her. "Are you cold?"

"I was," she said, but there was delicious warmth now seeping into her bones, the heat coming from Sean. She cleared her throat and told herself to focus, remember why she was here.

"Someone broke into my house," she said, finally getting the words out.

His eyes widened in surprise. "What are you talking about?"

"The dining room window near the driveway was smashed in. When I went to the back door and tried the knob, it opened. I know it was locked when I left."

"Did you call the police?"

She shook her head. "I came straight here. I should have gone inside and looked around, but I was too scared. I'm a coward."

"Don't be ridiculous," he said, his brows knitting together with worry. "The last thing you should have done was go inside by yourself." His hands dropped from her waist, as he stepped away from her. "Let me throw on a shirt and I'll check it out."

As he pulled a t-shirt over his head, she felt cold again, and she wrapped her arms around her waist. She was worried now that she'd done the wrong thing coming to Sean. She should have called the police. They would have sent someone out, someone who would be armed and who would know what to do if the burglar was still inside the house. But now Sean was going into what could possibly be a dangerous situation.

"Maybe we should call the police," she suggested, as he finished tying his shoes and stood up.

"Let me check it out first. See what we're dealing with. Did you hear anything or see anyone inside the house?"

"No, it was completely dark. There weren't any lights on. I just got home from Nicole's house. I was gone all afternoon."

"Then whoever broke in is probably gone."

That suggestion made her feel better. But when she saw him pull a baseball bat out of his closet, her heart sank again. "Do you really think you need a weapon?"

"Probably not. But I'd like to have something in my hands. Did you walk or drive?"

"I drove."

"Okay, we'll take your car back."

They left the apartment and got into her car. Her hands

were trembling, but she managed to drive around the corner without incident.

A moment later they pulled into her driveway.

"I'm probably getting all worked up over nothing," she said, trying to talk herself out of the panic that was still racing through her. "Maybe a kid threw a baseball through the window. It could just be that, right?"

"I doubt they would have unlocked your back door. Speaking of kids, where's Kyle?"

"He's spending the night at Nicole's house."

His hand tightened on the bat as he reached for the door handle. "Wait here."

She waited for two seconds, enough time for him to get down the driveway, then she got out of the car, catching up with him at the side door.

"Jess, I told you to wait," he said with irritation.

"I'm not letting you go in there alone. There could be trouble."

"Exactly," he said tersely. "Which is why you should be in the car."

"It's my house, my trouble. And I think it's better if we stick together."

"Fine, at least stay behind me."

"Happy to," she said.

He opened the door, waited a second and then stepped into the kitchen.

She put her hand on his back as she followed him into the room. "Should I turn on the light?" she whispered.

"Yes."

She flipped the switch, and the kitchen lit up. The room looked completely normal, exactly the way she'd left it, with one exception. Her gaze landed on the table—the now empty table.

Oh, my God," she murmured. "The computer is gone."

There was no hard drive, no keyboard, no mouse, and no monitor. "Someone stole Robert Emery's computer."

Nineteen

Jessica turned to Sean. Surprise in his eyes had been replaced by anger. His jaw was tight, his eyes fiercely determined. "What do you think?" she asked.

"Let's check the rest of the house," he said, heading toward the hall.

There was dirt on the floor, the trail leading to the dining room and the broken window, where they found more pieces of jagged glass.

"Looks like this is how they got in," Sean said, examining the window. "They must have gone out the side door when they took the computer." He looked around the room. "I don't see a rock or a brick."

"There are loose bricks that frame the planter outside. I didn't notice if one of them was out of place."

"That makes sense. They probably tossed it back out the window when they were done. Not exactly a high tech operation, but it worked."

After a quick glance into the living room, which looked untouched, they went upstairs and checked each of the rooms. Again, there was no evidence of a search or a robbery. Her laptop computer still sat on the bed, and in Kyle's bedroom there were video games in plain sight on the dresser. The door to Stacy's old room was open, but since the room was still jammed with furniture, it was doubtful anything had been taken. Next stop was the attic.

There were traces of dirt on the stairs. The thief had definitely gone into the attic. And why not? If they were interested in Robert's old computer, then they were interested in the past, and the attic was filled with family history.

The attic showed signs of at least a quick search. Some of the boxes had been moved around and upended, the contents tossed on the ground. But the room was a mess and there were many boxes still untouched. There was no way to tell if anything had been found or taken.

"I don't know if they ran out of time or gave up," Sean murmured.

"It would take days to look through everything in this room." Her mind wrestled with the question of who could have done this, and one name kept coming to mind. "Do you think it was Sally who did this?"

"She's certainly a suspect," he said grimly. "She had an extremely negative reaction when she saw the computer. And we know there are emails from her on it. She also had opportunity. It would be easy for her to see you coming and going. All she had to do was break the window, climb inside, grab the computer and go out the side door. Even if someone saw her in your driveway, they might not think anything about it. And who would see her? Her house is the only one facing the driveway."

"Brett could have seen her from across the street, and I don't think we can eliminate him as a suspect. After you dropped me off earlier, he asked me about our trip to Lana's house. Then he started grilling me about what we were doing here in the house. When it became clear we were looking into the fire, he got angry. He basically told me to stop, that stirring up the past was going to be bad for everyone."

"That sounds like a threat."

"He tried to veil it, but he didn't quite succeed. He asked me who I thought would want Robert dead. I turned it around on him, asking the same question. He told me that Robert had a lot of enemies, that he was a ruthless, ambitious businessman."

"That coincides with what Clark said about Robert."

"Yes. Neither Brett nor Clark seemed to like Robert. Even Lana talked crap about him," she added. "I'm not sure anyone was that unhappy he died. It almost sounds like they think he got what he deserved."

"But Stacy didn't deserve to die," Sean said harshly.

"No, of course not." She put a hand on his arm, feeling his tension. "Everyone expresses great remorse about Stacy."

"Remorse doesn't bring her back." He drew in a breath and blew it out. "Let's go downstairs."

"And do what?"

"Well, I should try to find something to cover the window until you can get it repaired. Do you have any wood around?"

"There might be some bookshelves in the garage," she offered.

"That will probably work," he said, heading toward the stairs.

"What about calling the police?"

"Why don't we start with Emma and Max?"

She liked that idea a lot. The police would probably blow them off since the only thing that had been taken was an old computer, but Emma and Max would know what to do next.

While Sean called Emma, Jessica went into the dining room to take another look at the window. Through the broken glass she could see the lights on at Brett's house across the street as well as the lights on at Sally's home. Was one of them watching her right now, maybe wondering if they'd left any fingerprints or other damning evidence behind?

A car drove down the street, and she felt even more

nervous. Was she wrong in thinking that the burglar was Sally or Brett? Maybe it was someone else entirely. Was the car going slow because they were looking for an address, or because they wanted to see if she'd come back?

Nervous tension tightened every nerve. She felt completely shaken by the break-in. This was her home. She was supposed to be safe here. But she didn't feel safe at all.

"Jess?"

She jumped at the sound of Sean's voice and whirled around.

"Sorry," he said, putting up a hand in apology. "I didn't mean to scare you."

"Everything is scaring me at the moment. I've never felt so uneasy. I feel like someone is watching us."

"Maybe they are."

She didn't like his answer. "Great."

"Sorry again. I spoke to Emma and told her what happened and what was taken. I also filled her in on what we've learned the past few days from Lana and also from Clark Hamilton. Unfortunately, Emma is working a fire and can't get away right now. Max is also tied up. She said we could call the police and make a report, but probably nothing would be done based on the fact that only an old computer was taken, a computer that was probably the target of the break-in. I also told her that Sally had seen the computer, and that we had found emails on that computer between Sally and Robert that suggested an affair or blackmail or maybe both. Emma is frustrated that she can't help us figure it all out right now, but she'll get back to us tomorrow. In the meantime, she suggested that you spend the night somewhere else."

Jessica was more than happy with that suggestion. "I guess I could go to Nicole's house, but I don't really want to have to explain all this."

"I have a better idea. Come home with me."

She immediately shook her head. "I can't stay in your parents' house."

"I'm talking about the studio over the garage. You can have the bed; I'll take the couch. You're not going to get any sleep if you stay here, Jess. You'll be listening for the next creak, wondering if someone has come back in."

Unfortunately, he was right about that. "I know I should probably stick it out."

"Why?"

She couldn't come up with a reason. "Okay, I accept your offer."

"Good decision."

Was it a good decision? Hadn't she just agreed to spend the night in a small room with a man who set her heart racing with every smile? This might be her worst mistake yet. She let out a heavy sigh.

"What's wrong now?" he asked. "I hope you know you can trust me, Jessica."

She stared back at his handsome face, his beautiful blue eyes and thick dark hair, and said, "It's not you I'm worried about; it's me."

He sucked in a quick breath as shadows darkened his gaze. "I really wish you hadn't said that."

"Me, too. I'm just going to grab a few things, then we'll go."

—⇒⇉⇇⇐—

Sean let out a breath as Jessica left the dining room. Her provocative words and the look in her eyes had put him more on edge than the break-in. But he was not going to take advantage of the situation. He was helping her out tonight as a friend. And friendship was all he was going to offer her.

As for what she might offer him…

He was trying not to think about that.

He went to the garage, grabbed the bookshelves, nails and a hammer. It took only a few moments to cover the window. Tomorrow Jessica could get someone out to replace the glass.

When he went back to the garage to put the tools back, he paused for a moment, reminded that this was where it had all started. This was where Robert had died.

A chill ran through his body. How weird it would be to die in your own garage. It seemed unimaginable, and yet it had happened. Had Stacy run into this room and seen her father through the flames? Had she tried to get to him? To save his life?

It would have been just like her. She'd been a fearless little girl. But she wouldn't have been strong enough to pull her father out, especially if he was unconscious.

Or she might not have come in here at all. She might have gotten caught in the flames that had already spread to the house.

His mind flashed on her image once again. When she'd come through the front door, she'd looked right at him.

Had she seen him that night?

He'd always wondered if she had; if she'd hoped he would save her.

But he hadn't moved, not one inch. He hated himself for that. He should have had the courage to go to her, to try to help.

"Sean?"

Jessica's voice spun him around.

She gave him an apologetic smile. "Sorry. I guess this time I scared you. Were you thinking about Robert?"

"And Stacy. I feel like I'm missing something. I don't know what it is, but it tugs at the back of my mind, some piece of information that I can't understand and I can't get out of my head."

"What could you have missed?"

"I don't know, and I don't think I'm going to be able to figure it out," he said with a frustrated sigh.

"I think it's just guilt that weighs on your mind, Sean. You have to find a way to make peace with yourself."

"I thought I had. I really didn't spend every day of the last twenty years thinking about Stacy. But now that I say that, I feel guilty that I didn't. What the hell is wrong with me?"

She gave him a soft smile. "Nothing is wrong with you. You have a big heart and a strong sense of justice and loyalty to friends."

"A lot of good that does me," he grumbled, covering up the fact that he appreciated her words more than he could ever say.

"You're a good man, Sean. Don't doubt that. Don't let one mistake from twenty years ago color your whole life. Stacy wouldn't want that."

"You never met her."

"I have met her—through her photos and her things and through you. She loved life. She loved you. You owe it to her to have everything she didn't have."

He stared into Jessica's warm brown eyes as her words resonated within him. She was right. And somewhere in his head he heard Stacy's quick laugh, as if she were happy that he was finally getting it.

"Shall we go?" Jessica asked.

"Yeah. Let's go," he said, as they left the garage.

"Should we drive or walk?"

"Let's walk."

"Through the dark neighborhood?" she asked a little nervously.

"I'll protect you," he said, reaching for her hand.

Her fingers tightened around his. "Don't let go."

He met her gaze. "I won't."

⟶⟫⟪⟵

They left through the side door. Jessica took a minute to lock it, and then they headed down the driveway. Sally's house was dark except for one light in an upstairs bedroom. At Brett's house, Sean could see the television on in the living room but no sign of any people. He wasn't worried about being attacked in the street, but he was happy to have Jess by his side as they walked down the block, because it seemed to be a night where memories were incredibly vivid, and he was once again reliving his steps on that fateful night.

The wind picked up and the tall trees swayed, and like Jessica had said earlier that night, he had the feeling someone was watching them. He was glad when they finally turned the corner. There was something about the big Callaway house that felt safe and secure.

"I hope we don't run into your parents," Jessica murmured. "I don't want them to get the wrong idea about us."

"Neither do I," he said, in wholehearted agreement. "But their bedroom is on the opposite side of the house, so with any luck, no one will see us go upstairs. It's the beauty of the garage apartment; it's very private." As they approached the house, he saw lights on in his parents' room but the rest of the home was dark. "Looks like we're good." He led her up the stairs and opened the door, ushering her inside. "It's a little messy. I didn't want to unpack since I'm only here for a short time, so I've been living out of suitcases and boxes."

Jessica nodded as she glanced around the studio apartment. "I didn't realize there was a kitchen up here."

"It used to be a rental when we were small. But as the family expanded, and the kids grew up, my parents started to use it as an extra bedroom. I coveted this apartment for years. But being sixth in the lineup of kids, I was stuck in the house while Burke and Aiden and later Drew had all kinds of crazy parties out here."

"That sounds like fun."

"I'd see hot girl after hot girl coming down the driveway," he joked.

"Your brothers are not bad looking, I have to say."

"Only my brothers?"

"You know what you look like," she retorted. "And if you don't, I'm sure one of the many beautiful girls who come to your concerts could tell you. So, Nicole and Emma didn't try for the apartment?"

"I don't know if they wanted to live here, but I suspect my father wanted the girls in the main house."

"Makes sense. Well, you're here now. You can live out all your teen fantasies," she teased.

"Don't tempt me."

She caught her breath at his words. And just like that he'd changed the air from comfortable to tense. "Sean," she began.

He didn't know where she was going with that sentence, but judging by the look in her eyes he wanted to go with her. She licked her lips, and the swipe of her tongue made his body hard. Who the hell was he kidding? He couldn't do this. He couldn't spend the night with her and not make love to her.

"I should stay in the main house," he said.

"No. I don't want to be alone."

"Jessica—"

"We can do this," she said cutting him off. "We can be friends. It will be fine."

He wanted to agree, but he had a feeling that her definition of *fine* was vastly different than his.

"Can I use the bathroom?" she asked.

"It's right over there."

He was grateful for the respite. He needed a few minutes to pull himself together so that things really would be *fine* between them.

Twenty

W hile Jessica was in the bathroom, Sean kicked off his shoes. Then he grabbed a blanket off the shelf in the closet and tossed it to the sofa, along with one of the pillows from his bed. He forced himself not to think about the night ahead—Jessica curled up in his sheets, her beautiful dark hair spread across the pillow, her body soft and warm, her lips so inviting.

Damn! It was going to be a long night.

He sat down on the sofa and picked up his guitar. He needed a distraction and music had always been able to take him somewhere else. He strummed a few random chords, trying to get his mind off Jessica, but he was still fighting the desire when she walked out of the bathroom and sat down on the edge of the bed. He tried not to look at her. But he could hear her—even the soft swoosh of her breath turned him on.

"Will you play something for me?" Jessica asked a moment later.

He cleared his throat, still not looking at her. "Sure. What do you want to hear?"

"*Moonlight Girl* is one of my favorites."

He looked down at his guitar and then played the opening chords. He'd written *Moonlight Girl* when he was twenty years old, and over the years it had been one of his most popular songs.

He could hear Jessica scoot backwards on the bed, settling against his pillows, but he forced himself to concentrate on the song.

"She came out of the shadows, her face kissed by the moonlight," he sang. *"She pulled him out of the dark, gave him hope and a spark for a life and a love that would last forever."*

The girl in the song had never really had a clear face to him, but as he finished the last few words, he lifted his gaze and looked across the room at the beautiful dark-haired, dark-eyed woman on his bed, and her face became clear. He hadn't known who he was writing about back then. The moonlight girl had been a fantasy of a love that had yet to come.

Had it come now?

"That was wonderful," she said. "Did you write that song for a girlfriend?"

He shook his head. "No."

"Really? It sounded like you were inspired by someone."

"Maybe tonight I felt inspired," he said quietly.

The smile on her face faded. "It's not fair, you know."

"What's not fair?"

"That you can seduce me with a song."

"It's not fair that you can seduce me with your eyes—your beautiful, expressive eyes that show every emotion."

She stared back at him. "What emotion do you see now?"

"Desire, attraction, uncertainty."

"My eyes told you all that?"

"Am I wrong?"

She slowly shook her head. "You're not wrong. Play me something else."

"What do you want to hear?"

"Do you ever play classical music?"

He was surprised by the question. "As a matter of fact, I do. What do you like?"

"I used to dance to *Bagatelle No. 2* by William Walton."

"One of my favorite pieces," he said, taken aback.

"Really?" she asked, her gaze meeting his.

"Yes. It's haunting, evocative."

"Like you're dancing in someone's dream," she finished.

"Or playing the score," he countered.

She smiled. "I see everything through movement."

"And I see the chords. I have to warn you I'm a little rusty on this kind of complicated piece." He got up and exchanged his guitar for another. "The strings on this will sound better." He settled back on the couch and started to play. He had a few missteps in the beginning, but as he went along, the music came back to him.

He'd spent a year training under a superb classical guitarist and he'd forgotten how much he loved playing compositions that took the guitar to another level, turning the instrument into a miniature orchestra.

When he finished that piece, he played another and another, letting the music surround them with its power and emotion.

Finally, his fingers came to rest and he looked across the room. Jessica had been so quiet, he'd wondered if she'd fallen asleep. But she wasn't asleep, and she was no longer sitting on the bed; she was walking toward him.

His heart leapt into his throat.

She stopped in front of him, her gaze full of purpose. She took the guitar out of his hands and placed it on the ground. Then she sat down next to him.

"Jess," he began.

"No talking." She put her fingers against his lips. "We're done with conversation."

His pulse began to race. He wanted to ask her if she was sure she wanted to do this, but as she drew her thumb across his mouth, all questions faded from his mind. He didn't want to talk any more, either. Nor did he want to think about all the reasons being with Jessica was a bad idea. It seemed like an excellent idea right now, and she seemed to feel the same way.

Her hand drifted across his cheek, sliding through his hair, and down to his neck. Then she put her other hand on the opposite side of his face and moved even closer. Her breath teased his face—a tantalizing torture. Then she finally pressed her mouth against his.

It might have been the absolute best kiss of his life.

He loved the fullness of her lips, the scent of her skin and hair that enveloped him in a perfume that was all Jess—only Jess.

He let her lead, enjoying her slide from tentative to certain as she grew more comfortable in the kiss, as she teased his lips apart, and let her tongue tangle with his.

She was such a mix of sweet and sexy, hard and soft, cynical and optimistic, a woman who had seen hard times and yet still seemed innocent. She deserved the best of life and the best of him, and tonight he was going to give her that.

He put his hands on her waist, his fingers moving under her top to find hot, bare skin. She pressed her breasts against his chest as her arms moved around his neck.

He slipped his tongue between her lips, deepening their connection as his hands slid up her abdomen. He could feel her tense, but when she shifted, it was only to give him more room to touch her, and he grabbed the opportunity, moving his hands up to her breasts. He was shocked and thrilled to find out she wasn't wearing a bra. His hand covered one breast, and she let out a small moan of pleasure. The sound made him even harder. There was no more going slow, no more patience for exploring. He wanted her clothes off. He wanted her naked body against his. He wanted inside.

Jessica broke away from the kiss, her lips pink, her eyes glittering with desire and need.

"Please don't say you want to stop," he said.

She smiled. "No way." She put her hands on the bottom of her top and then lifted it over her head and tossed it on the floor.

She had the most beautiful breasts he'd ever seen, her long dark hair falling across one nipple. She made no move to cover herself up, which made him very happy.

"Your turn," she murmured, helping him off with his shirt.

Then she took his hands and put them on her breasts. It was a bold, unexpected move, and he loved it. She smiled again, and he smiled back at her. His hands moved around her breasts in a teasing caress. Her nipples pebbled under his touch. And then he lowered his mouth to her breast and swirled his tongue around the point.

She put her hands in his hair, urging him on, holding him closer. He took his time, enjoying each new inch of discovery. He wanted to touch and taste her all over. He wanted to know her and for her to know him. He wanted to make every nerve ending come alive. He wanted to start a fire that would never go out.

He lifted his head to look at her. "Jess?"

She answered his unspoken question. "Yes."

"Do you want to take this to the bed?"

She shook her head. "No, right here."

"Okay, hang on one second." He ran into the bathroom, grabbed a condom and came back.

Jessica had pulled off her yoga pants and was sliding a pink thong down her legs. His mouth went dry. Looking at her bare body, he found his hands shaking as he unzipped his jeans and stepped out of them. He'd never felt such nervous excitement before.

Then she reached for his hands and pulled him down to her. "Love me, Sean."

She really didn't have to ask.

He pressed against her, wanting every point of contact—mouth, breast, hips, groin, legs. She was so soft. Her curves fit perfectly with his body as they moved together, he felt as if they were creating their own dance. Every kiss, every touch, every slide, every move brought them closer and closer together, until they were one, until he didn't know where he ended and she began, until the dam that had been building inside of him finally burst free.

—➤◄—

They moved from the couch to the bed a little after midnight. The second time they made love, Jessica took more time exploring Sean's body while he did the same to her. As a dancer, she'd never been shy about her body. It was the tool she used to express herself, and she'd been trained to be aware of every muscle, every ligament, every trigger point. Sean had hit all those triggers tonight, touching her, tasting her, teasing her, basically driving her out of her mind. And she'd loved every second of it.

She'd returned the favor, too, delighting in the hard planes of his beautiful male form, the fine spread of hair across his chest, the muscled abs that told her he spent at least some of his time working out, and the powerful arms that now held her close to his body. Her head was on his chest, his heartbeat resonating in her ear, and she didn't think there was a better sound in the world.

She felt warm, happy, loved and deliciously exhausted. Being with Sean had been different than being with anyone else. There'd been no awkward moments, uncomfortable collisions of lips or hands, no trying to figure out what pleased the other. It just flowed in a perfect, organic way. It was as if they'd known each other forever. They were in tune on an emotional as well as physical level.

The thought made her feel a little guilty. Was it wrong to be this happy, to have so much joy and passion with another man?

But Travis would want her to be happy, she told herself. He'd been a wonderfully generous man, and she would never ever regret their time together, but that time was over.

Tonight was all about Sean, sexy, creative, soulful, amazing Sean. The man touched her heart in ways she'd never imagined and the connections between them were powerful. They shared a love of music, of creating something out of nothing, whether it was a song or a dance. They'd both grown up a little lonely for different reasons. She'd been an only child of a single mother who was never around. Sean had been one of many kids, but his childhood trauma had separated him from his family, especially his father. Holding on to his secret had also isolated him from his parents and siblings.

Sean put on a front for others, but with her he hadn't been able to hide. She'd seen his pain, his struggle with guilt, his determination to find truth and justice for his friend. She'd also seen the lighter side of him, the easy, teasing grin that had brought her out of her own shell, the quick wit, the self-deprecating smile that told her he didn't take himself too seriously.

And then there was the passion, the soul-shattering kisses that had made any question of resistance on her part a joke. She'd wanted him since the first moment she'd met him. This night had been inevitable. They'd fought the attraction. They'd tried to find reasons to stay apart. But deep down she'd always known they would end up in each other's arms. It had been good—better than good. It had been perfect.

But what happened when the night was over, when the sun came up, and reality returned? How could she ever *just* be his friend? Was she about to get her heart broken all over again? Would one night of passion be worth all the pain that followed? She shuddered at the thought of hurting again. She wanted to be happy.

Sean stroked her back. "Jess? Are you okay? You seem suddenly tense and not in a good way."

She sat up abruptly, reaching for the sheet to cover herself, which seemed ridiculous since Sean had just kissed every inch of her body about ten minutes ago, but that had been ten minutes ago. "Maybe I should go home. Or sleep on the couch."

"Whoa! What did I miss?" He sat up and gave her a concerned look. "Did I fall asleep for a few minutes? Because I thought we were getting along very nicely."

"I don't feel like going to sleep, and I don't want to keep you awake," she lied.

"Jess, come on. You know you can't lie to me."

He was right. He could see right through her. "I don't know what to say, Sean. I don't know what to do now. Things have changed."

"You don't have to say or do anything. Just be in the moment. We had fun, right?"

She nodded.

"Let's hang on to that feeling for a while. We can decide if this was all a mistake tomorrow."

"Neither one of us wanted this to happen," she reminded him.

"That's not true. I wanted it to happen from the first second I met you."

"I was a mess then."

"A beautiful mess. But it was the wrong time."

"A couple of days ago you said it was also the wrong time. Maybe there's never going to be a right time, because we don't want the same things, Sean."

"We wanted the same things tonight."

"In bed we're great, I'll give you that."

"Not great, spectacular," he corrected.

"Fine, spectacular, but—"

He put his fingers against her mouth and smiled. "Let's leave it at that."

His smile made it hard to hold on to her worry, so she tried to get it back, thinking that she had to find a way to put a wall back up between them. "I can't leave it at that," she said, pushing his hand away. "Out of bed, we lead different lives. I have a child. I can't live the single, dating life with you. I can't get into random hookups and sexy text messages and late night calls. I can't do that."

"I didn't ask you to do any of that." His tone held annoyance now. "You're jumping way ahead, Jess. And I'd prefer if you stop trying to make me into someone I'm not."

"I'm sorry if that's what you think I'm doing."

"You are doing that. You're putting words into my mouth."

"Okay, but that's because I have to worry about the future. I'm usually surrounded by people who don't worry at all. It has always fallen to me to be smart. Otherwise, I pay the consequences."

"But you don't have to be smart right this second, do you?" he challenged.

"I don't know." She felt so confused, torn between wanting to cuddle back up next to him and trying to protect her heart from breaking."

"Let tonight be just about us. Tomorrow we let the complications back in."

"You make it sound so simple," she said with a sigh, sliding her fingers through her tangled hair.

"In some ways it is simple." His gaze was completely candid. "Do you know what I want to do right now?"

"We already did that twice," she retorted.

His charming grin took the lingering fight right out of her. "Well, you know the third time is a charm. But—"

"But?"

"What I really want to do is sleep with you tonight, Jess. I want to hold you in my arms all night long."

"Just sleep?" she said doubtfully.

"Until we don't want to sleep anymore," he said, the light of desire flickering in his eyes. "But until then, that's what I want for tonight. What do you want?"

Looking at him, she saw everything she'd ever wanted. It probably wouldn't last past the night, so maybe she should enjoy the time they had. At least she'd have the memories.

"I want you," she said, knowing she couldn't pretend anymore.

A pleased smile spread across his face, then he opened up his arms and she moved back into his embrace. As he wrapped his arms around her, he placed a tender kiss on her head. "Sleep, beautiful Jess."

And that's exactly what she did.

He ran around the corner and down the street, shocked at the orange flames licking the night sky like a monster. He stopped abruptly, the smoke making his eyes water. Small pops turned into loud bangs, the fire leaping toward the sky with each one. He heard sirens in the distance. They were too far away. He needed to get help. There were shadows on the street. There were people moving around, but why weren't they going to the house?

Someone was screaming. It was Stacy!

His heart stopped as she came running out of the house. At first he thought the fire was behind her, but as she ran, it stayed with her, the sparks in her hair, in her clothes. She turned and looked across the street.

Did she see him? Was she calling to him for help?

Then the fire engines raced down the street. His dad jumped off the truck, running to Stacy. He wrapped her in a blanket and rolled her on the ground.

It was going to be okay. His dad was here. His dad would save her.

He felt dizzy and sick. There were too many lights, too many shadows, too many noises. He had to get out of here.

But Stacy was calling to him.

"Don't you see, Sean? Tell them. You have to tell them."

She was grabbing his shoulders, shaking them, telling him to wake up.

Wait, that wasn't Stacy's voice.

"Sean, wake up."

His eyes flew open and he saw Jessica looking at him with concern. Her hands were on his shoulders. She'd been the one shaking him.

"You were having a nightmare," Jessica said.

He swallowed, his throat dry and scratchy as if he'd really been breathing smoke. He could feel sweat running down his face, and his hair clung to the back of his neck in damp clumps. He forced himself to breathe, to calm down, to remember it was just a dream.

"What was that about?" Jessica asked, curling her legs up under as she sat up in bed next to him.

"Same old dream," he muttered.

"The fire?"

"Yes. It's always pretty much the same until the end. I'm across the street. Stacy runs out. The fire engines arrive."

"What happens at the end?"

"Stacy says something to me. It changes with every dream, and it never makes sense."

"What did she say this time?"

He thought for a moment, not even sure he could remember, but then her words rang through his head. "She said,

'Don't you see, Sean? Tell them. You have to tell them.'"

"Tell them what?"

"I don't know, Jess."

"What has she said other times?"

"The other morning she said, *Look in the light*."

Jessica frowned. "I don't think it's Stacy talking to you, I think it's your subconscious."

"Great. That still doesn't tell me what I'm supposed to see or say."

"That's what you meant the other night when you said you feel like you know something, but you don't know what it is."

He nodded in agreement. "Yes."

"I wonder what's buried in your mind," she mused.

"Hell if I know. It's been twenty years and it hasn't come out yet. I'm not holding out a lot of hope that it suddenly will."

"And you've always had these dreams?"

"They went on hiatus for about ten years. After I moved out of my parents' house, they disappeared."

"Now you're back in your parents' house and the dreams have returned. I guess that makes sense."

"Does it? Hopefully, when I move out in two weeks, I'll leave them behind again."

"I have a feeling the dreams aren't just tied to your parents' house but also to Stacy's house." She tucked her hair behind her ears. "Changing the subject slightly…"

"Okay. What?"

"I don't know what I'm going to do about that house, Sean."

"What are you thinking?"

"That it might not be a safe place for Kyle and me to live. How can I bring my son home without knowing with one hundred percent certainty that he's going to be safe there?"

"Maybe he can stay at Nicole's for a few days."

"Do you really think we're going to solve this in a few

days?"

"I don't know," he said, hearing the frustration in her voice. "We can stop looking into the fire."

"It's too late for that. We've already rattled someone."

"Maybe the computer was all they wanted," he suggested.

"But we don't know that for sure. Until I go through every last item in the attic, there's still a possibility that there's something else in that house that's going to bother someone."

She was right. "We could clear out the attic in a big, public way," he said. "We can put everything on the front lawn and have a garage sale. Once everyone realizes that there are no more secrets in the house, you should be safe."

"That might work," she said slowly. "But what if there are still some secrets, Sean?"

"Then we need to find them."

"I'm not sure what I'm looking for. Will I know it even if I see it? I feel like we've learned a bunch of stuff, but we still don't know enough."

"I agree. I think we should talk to Lana again."

"She wasn't very helpful the first time."

"But we know more now than we did then. We can ask better questions. For example, we know about Sally's emails to Robert and also about Robert's business problems. Maybe if we present her with the information we've gathered, it will jog her memory, and she'll say something to lead us in the right direction." He could see the skepticism in Jessica's eyes. "I know it's a long shot."

"It really is, Sean, and I think I should focus on the attic. We should split up. You go see Lana, and I'll unpack boxes."

He frowned at her suggestion. "I don't want to leave you alone in the house."

"I have to go back there sometime, it might as well be today. I'll be okay. It seems doubtful the burglar would come back, especially not in the daylight. I'll keep the doors locked.

It will be fine."

Despite her strong words, there was a hint of worry in her eyes. "I can postpone talking to Lana and help you out."

"No, I think you're right about speaking to Lana again. You're also right about cleaning out the attic."

"I'm on a roll," he said dryly.

"You appear to be. We can accomplish things faster if we split up. And speed is important, because I can't leave Kyle at Nicole's house forever. Nor do I want to have to explain to him or Nicole why he can't come home yet."

"Sounds like a plan."

"Yes." She let out a breath. "Mind if I take a shower?"

"Mind if I join you?"

She hesitated. "I think I should make this a solo shower."

Her guard walls were already going back up. He'd had a feeling that would happen once the morning came, but he was still disappointed.

She slid off the bed, grabbed her clothes and headed into the bathroom, giving him one last glimpse of her beautiful body. He wondered if he would see it ever again.

While Jessica was showering, he put on his boxers, jeans and pulled a t-shirt over his head. Then he started the coffeemaker. As the coffee brewed, he checked the fridge, wondering if he might be able to pull a miracle breakfast out of it, but quickly realized that would indeed be a miracle considering he had a six-pack of beer, a carton of milk, and a block of cheese that was starting to mold. He tossed the cheese in the trash and closed the fridge. Breakfast would have to be found elsewhere.

Jessica came out of the bathroom a few minutes later. Her hair was still a little damp and falling in soft waves around her shoulders. Her face was pink, her skin glowing, her mouth soft and inviting. He moved without even thinking, needing to kiss her as much as he needed to take his next breath. He slid his hands on her hips as he stole a quick kiss from her minty fresh mouth. "You taste good," he murmured.

She gently pushed him away with a somewhat breathless smile. "Do I smell coffee?"

"Freshly made."

"Great." She walked past him and opened the cupboard, pulling out a mug.

He could see the tension in her body, the nervousness in her eyes, and when their eyes met, there was an intimate awareness of just how close they'd been the night before.

He wanted to make love to her again, hear her delighted cries of passion, feel her body against his, as they took each other higher than they'd ever been before. He'd loved watching her let go of the control she always had over her life, her emotions. She'd been free and wild and incredibly beautiful.

She cleared her throat. "You're staring at me, Sean."

"I can't seem to take my eyes off of you," he admitted.

She caught her breath. "You musicians always know the right thing to say to a woman. You know the words we want to hear."

"I wasn't thinking about what you wanted to hear; I was just speaking the truth." He paused. "I'm sorry that my nightmare changed the tone of this morning. I had a lot of plans before shower time."

A wash of red colored her cheeks. "You are bad."

"You liked that last night."

"I did, but it's morning now, and we have to face reality. Nothing has really changed. You're still you, and I'm still me, and there are still all those reasons we don't work as a couple."

"I'm having a hard time remembering what those reasons are."

"They'll come back to you once we leave this apartment, once you're back in the band making music with your friends, signing autographs for the groupies, hitting a club at midnight on a Tuesday, and signing up for a tour that will take you to seven cities in seven weeks."

"Nice of you to wrap up my life in a jaded, cynical bow," he said, unable to hide his annoyance.

"Am I wrong?" she challenged.

He couldn't say that she was, at least not about the life he'd led, but he'd changed. Things were different now and not just because of her, but also because of him, because he wanted more than what she described. But she didn't want to hear that, because she was looking for reasons to split them apart.

"That's what I thought," she said when he didn't answer.

"It's not that simple," he protested.

"Why are you arguing? You don't want me either. I'm tied to your family, and my life doesn't mesh with yours. We don't need to rehash everything. Let's just move on before we hurt each other."

"The last thing I want to do is hurt you."

"I feel the same way. So I'm going home now." She grabbed her keys. "Call me when you get back from Lana's."

"Let me walk you to the house so I can check things out."

"No," she said decisively. "I'm okay. If anything looks out of place, I'll call the police."

He shook his head in bewilderment. "How did everything change so fast, Jess?"

She shrugged and gave him a sad smile. "The sun came up."

Twenty-One

After returning to the house, Jessica did a quick check of all the rooms, feeling only marginally better when she was done, but breakfast and coffee put her in a better, more determined mood. The break-in had made her feel like a victim, but today she was back in control. She was going to attack the day, starting with the attic.

As she climbed the stairs, she felt some pretty wonderful aches that reminded her of the night she'd shared with Sean, a night she'd been trying to put out of her head since she'd gotten out of Sean's bed and into a cold shower. But now the memories refused to be shut out.

Sean had been so passionate, demanding and yet also generous. Her body tingled with a longing that she didn't think was going away any time soon. How on earth would they go back to being just friends? How could she see him and not want him? It was going to be impossible.

She was in love with him. She wanted him in her life and in her bed. But she had Kyle to consider. She couldn't love someone who wouldn't be good for Kyle, too, and all those memories of men walking in and out of her childhood made her scared that Kyle would see the back of those same doors.

On the other hand, she knew that Sean was not like those

men. He would never hurt Kyle or her if he could help it. But could he help it?

She couldn't ask him to be someone he wasn't or to give up a career that made him happy.

So where did that leave them? Exactly where they'd been before. Only now she was going to have to deal with not just her imagination of how great they would be together but also with her memories.

She was in trouble, big trouble.

But she couldn't think about all that now. She had to focus on the attic, on making sure her house would be safe for Kyle when he eventually came home.

For the next two hours, she went through boxes. She started at one end and worked her way toward the middle. An hour later, she had filled three bags with trash and set up two piles, one to discuss with Helen and the other to go to charity.

Ready for a break, she took the trash downstairs and out to the driveway. As she tossed the bags in the can, she saw Sally watering the plants along the driveway.

Sally saw her and froze, her hand shaking so much on the hose that she started to spray the sidewalk instead of the greenery. Jessica knew in that moment that she'd found her burglar. Anger ran through her. Sally had violated her privacy and made her afraid to be in her own house. Jessica was not going to let her get away with it.

"I'm glad I ran into you, Sally," she said briskly, walking down the driveway until they were only a few feet apart.

"Why is that?" Sally's gaze darted around as if she were looking for an escape route.

"Someone broke into my house last night and stole Robert's computer."

"Who—who would do that?" Sally stuttered.

"You," she said bluntly.

"I don't know what you're talking about."

"Then let me explain. I found emails on Robert's computer from you to him, suggesting that you might have information he'd be willing to pay for. I'm guessing you don't want those emails to come to light and that's why you practically passed out when you saw we'd found the computer."

"You're crazy," Sally said, paling at Jessica's words.

"What information did you have, Sally? Something about his business? His family? What?"

"You must have misunderstood what you read."

"I don't think so. I also found photos of you and Robert together. You looked quite cozy. Were you two having an affair? Were you threatening to tell Lana? Was that the information you wanted Robert to buy?"

Sally's jaw dropped in shock. She put her hand to her heart. "Why—why are you asking me these things?"

"Because I'm tired of being in the dark. The first night I moved in here I heard you on the phone. You were worried about what I was going to find in the house. Now I know why you were worried. So it's time to come clean."

Sally drew in a breath, her lips tightening as she thrust her chin into the air. "You don't know what you're talking about. There was nothing between Robert and me but friendship. I can't say the same for some people."

"What does that mean?"

"You should mind your own business, Jessica."

"It's my business to clean out Helen's attic and to protect my home. I have a six-year-old, Sally. I will not allow anyone to put him in danger. I need to know what's going on, and I need to know now. What did you have on Robert?"

"Nothing."

"Then why did you steal the computer?"

"I didn't do that," she protested.

"I don't believe you. Maybe I should talk to Brett. Maybe he can tell me why you'd want that computer. You mentioned his name in your email to Robert. It sounds like Brett knows whatever secret you're hiding."

Sally stiffened. "Brett is the biggest liar of all. He's always had an agenda."

"That's what he said about you. I'm done playing nice, Sally. Did you know that Sean's brother-in-law is a police detective? He can pull prints off any surface—a window frame, a doorknob, a table," she said, mentioning all the places where Sally's hand might have come in contact with a piece of furniture. "I'm pretty sure he can figure out that you were the one who broke into my house and stole that computer."

"Robert's secrets were his," Sally hissed. "You had no business going through his computer."

"Is that a confession?"

Sally's husband's car pulled up out front, and panic flashed through Sally's eyes. "You need to leave, Jessica."

"Maybe I should meet your husband." Jessica realized she'd just found Sally's weak spot. "I can ask him about the computer, the emails, the photos of you and Robert. I'm sure it would be an interesting conversation."

"You will not speak to him. You have no idea what went on back then."

"I know what's going on now. So talk to me. Tell me the truth, and maybe I'll decide to keep your secret."

"I can't talk to you right now." Sally glanced at the car. Her husband was pulling his briefcase out of the back seat. "But he has a meeting later. I'll come over then."

"If you don't come by, I will find you," Jessica promised.

"I'll come. I'll tell you everything. Just don't talk to the police." Sally dropped the hose and moved down the driveway to turn off the faucet. Then she greeted her husband with a kiss. They walked across the lawn to the front door.

Sally's husband was a tall, thin man dressed in an expensive suit. He didn't give Jessica even a glance.

Apparently, he was less interested in the neighbors than his wife was.

As she returned to her house, Jessica hoped she hadn't made a mistake in confronting Sally, but it was too late to take it back. And it seemed like the direct approach had worked. Sally had come very close to admitting she'd taken the computer. Now that she knew Sally was worried about anything getting back to her husband, Jessica had some ammunition to fight with.

She returned to the house, grabbed a water out of the fridge, and headed back to the attic to see what other secrets might still be lurking.

→⇒⇐←

Sean knocked on Lana's door just before noon. He'd hit a lot of traffic on the way to Seascape and each minute that passed had made him wonder if he'd made the right move. But he was finally here. Hopefully his instinct was right, and Lana had more to tell him.

When Lana opened the door, she gave him an unhappy and unwelcoming look. "What are you doing here, Sean?"

"I need to talk to you."

"I thought we'd said everything there was to say."

"I'm afraid not. Can you give me a few minutes?"

"I have a lunch in an hour."

"It won't take that long," he promised.

She shook her head in bewilderment. "Why are you suddenly so caught up in the past, Sean?"

He hesitated and then gave her the truth. "Stacy talks to me in my dreams."

Her face went white. "I don't understand. What do you mean? What does she say?"

"A lot of things that don't make sense." He paused for a

moment. "The dreams started right after the fire and went on for years. They came back when Jessica moved into your house. They're even more vivid, more demanding. I feel like Stacy wants me to do something, and yes, I know that sounds crazy. But that's why I can't let go of the past. Not until I've asked every question and had it answered."

"Stacy never comes to me in my dreams," she said, pain in her eyes. "Do you know how much I want to see her? Even if it's only in my subconscious?"

"I think I have an idea."

"All right. Come in."

They settled once again in the living room where they'd spoken two days earlier.

"So what do you want to know, Sean?"

He searched for a way to ease into the conversation, but he couldn't find anything that would make the question easier to hear. It was past time for bluntness. "Is it possible that your husband was being blackmailed by Sally Watson?"

Lana sucked in a quick breath of air, her hands gripping the arms of the chair she was sitting in. "Why would you ask me that?"

"I found Robert's computer, and there was an email on it from Sally to Robert. She wanted to meet him. She had something to tell him, and she didn't want you to know."

"Sally wrote that to him?"

He nodded, watching her reaction closely. Lana appeared surprised and yet she wasn't. Now there was anger filling her gaze.

"What kind of information did Sally have? Was it about his business dealings?"

Lana slowly shook her head. "No, it was personal. Do you remember the date of that email?"

"It was the day before the fire."

"Really? I thought she was bluffing." Lana got up and

paced around the room.

"What was she going to tell him?"

"I don't want to get into this."

"You have to. This is no longer just about Stacy or the past; it's also about the present. Last night your old house was broken into, and the computer was stolen. It was the only thing taken."

She stared at him in confusion. "I don't understand."

"Obviously someone felt there was something on that computer that could hurt them. My guess is that it was Sally. I think she had an affair with your husband and was threatening to tell you if he didn't pay up."

Lana stared back at him, not giving anything away.

He had to convince her to help him. "Here's the thing, Lana. Jessica has a six-year-old son. If they're in danger, I need to know why so that I can protect her. And if there is anything else in that house that someone is going to want, I need to find it before they do. I believe you know more than you're telling me. Please let the secrets go. Don't let anyone else get hurt."

She sat back down on the edge of her chair. "All right. Sally was blackmailing Robert, but they weren't having an affair. Brett and I were having the affair." Lana shook her head in bemusement. "I can't believe I just said that out loud. I've never said it out loud to anyone."

"How long did it go on?" he asked, shocked by her revelation. He hadn't guessed that Lana was the one who was cheating. He'd had the whole thing wrong.

"About nine months. I was very unhappy in my marriage, Sean. Robert loved his job more than me. He'd go to work at seven in the morning and come home at ten o'clock at night. We rarely had a family dinner. We'd go months without making love. I was so lonely. And I was bored, too. Robert didn't want me to work. He liked me to be available for whatever he needed and for the kids. I was fine with that in the beginning. I liked having a man to take care of me. But as I got older, I realized my life was always about Robert—his dreams, his goals. I got tired of that."

"How did the affair start?"

"Brett was rehabbing his shoulder from his last surgery. He was home a lot during the day. His wife, Natasha, was an interior designer for very high-end clients, and she traveled two weeks out of every month. Brett and I would run into each other during the day. Brett liked to play with the kids. He'd see us out front, and he'd come outside to throw Blake baseballs or kick soccer balls to Stacy. We became friends, good friends, and one thing led to another. It just happened, Sean. I didn't plan it. I felt horribly guilty when we were together, but I couldn't stop, because I was happy. Brett gave me attention, and he was there for me."

"How did Sally find out?"

"She saw us kissing one day. She was a sneaky, meddling woman, who also had too much time on her hands. I think she liked Brett as more than a friend. Maybe she sensed that he was into me and not her and decided to pay us both back. Anyway, she took some photos of us, and she sent them to me with a threat to tell my husband if I didn't pay her to be quiet."

"Sally was married to a successful man. She had money. Was it about revenge?"

"It was about both revenge and money. Sally's husband was rigid and controlling. He kept her on a budget. She was always complaining that she had to ask for permission to spend ten dollars."

"How much did you pay her?"

"The first time it was five hundred dollars. Then it went up to a thousand, and I had to pay her in cash. After the third payoff, I started getting angry. It was difficult for me to get the money after Robert quit his job. So I told Sally I was done. She said she was going to tell Robert that if he didn't continue paying her, she would tell everyone about my affair, including his business partners, friends, neighbors, anyone who would listen. She felt sure he would pay to keep her quiet. I guess she followed through on her threat. Did Robert answer the email?"

"No, but that doesn't mean he didn't talk to her. He didn't say anything to you about it?"

"Not that night. The next day, the day of the fire, Robert was working in his office at home. He had the door closed. When I opened it to tell him I was going on the field trip, he practically bit my head off. He asked me why I couldn't see that he was busy." Her mouth trembled. "That was the last thing he said to me. Maybe Sally did tell him about my betrayal. Perhaps that's why he was so angry with me."

"You could ask her."

Lana uttered a cynical laugh. "Like she'd tell me the truth. She'd use my uncertainty against me. I'd rather not know."

Lana certainly had an odd way of running her life, Sean thought. She was an expert at hiding from the truth and locking away anything that might hurt her.

"You said Robert was working that day at home, but he'd quit his job. What was he so busy doing?" Sean asked.

"I assume he was looking for another job, and I think some of his clients might have left Clark to come with him. I don't really know. He didn't talk about his work with me."

"I spoke to Clark Hamilton. He told me that Robert stole from the company, and that because of their long friendship, he agreed to let Robert resign rather than be arrested."

Surprise filled Lana's eyes once again. "I can't believe that's true. Robert was a lot of things, but he wasn't a thief."

"Clark was very convincing, and Robert did quit his job without another one in place, a job that you told me he loved more than you."

"That's true," she said slowly. "I don't know. I wish now that I'd pressed him for more information but at the time we weren't really talking. I felt guilty about the affair. Robert was unsettled having nowhere to be every day. We were in a bad place."

"Why didn't you go to Sally's husband after Robert died and tell him what she'd done to you? Robert was dead. There was no secret left to protect. You must have wanted to take revenge on Sally."

She shook her head. "After the fire I just wanted to crawl into a hole and die, but I had Blake to take care of. I knew I couldn't do that and stay in San Francisco. I couldn't go back into that neighborhood, see Brett standing on his porch or Sally spying on me through her curtains. That part of my life was over. I didn't care about Sally and her blackmail anymore. Nor did I want to talk to Brett and hear his apologies. I just wanted to be somewhere else, where maybe I could one day find some peace."

"What do you mean—Brett's apologies?" he asked, latching on to the latter part of her statement.

"He was sorry for the affair."

"And..." He sensed she was still holding back.

"A few weeks before the fire, Brett started asking me to leave Robert. He said he would leave his wife, and the two of us would start a new family. He wanted to be a father. He loved my kids and he loved me. It was tempting; I'll be honest about that. But it was a huge step, and I wasn't ready to take it. The kids loved their dad, especially Stacy. She was a daddy's girl. So I stalled, until..." Her voice trailed away.

"Until what?" he asked impatiently.

"Brett ran out of patience. The day of the fire, Brett told me he couldn't live without me. He couldn't keep pretending to his wife. He begged me to tell Robert it was over, but I refused. I said I wasn't ready to leave. Brett was furious. He had a short fuse anyway, but that day he was beside himself. He told me that if I wasn't going to tell Robert, he would. I pleaded with him not to do that. He said if I wanted to stay married, it was going to have to be with the truth, everything out in the open."

"What happened? Did he talk to Robert?" Sean asked.

"He told me he spoke to Robert an hour or so before the fire. Brett said that Robert wasn't surprised, that he'd known for a long time that I was cheating on him. Robert said he would let me go, but I had to ask him for a divorce."

"Hang on. That doesn't sound like the way a man would react upon hearing from his wife's lover that his wife wants to leave him. It's way too calm. If some guy said that to me, I'd punch him in the face."

"Robert wasn't a physical man. And I'm not sure he cared all that much," she said. "Anyway, I never had a chance to ask Robert about any of it. When I got home, the house was on fire, Stacy was on her way to the hospital and Robert was dead."

"You didn't find it to be a huge coincidence that your husband dies in a fire an hour or so after he hears about your affair?"

She stiffened. "Actually, I did think about that."

"But you didn't tell anyone. It's not in any of the investigation reports."

"I was distraught when I spoke to the investigator. I didn't know which way was up; the world was spinning."

"It stopped spinning eventually. You had time to think, to speak, if you'd wanted to."

"Fine. I didn't tell anyone, because I was afraid that Robert had set the fire to kill himself, that he was despondent about not having a job and about me wanting to leave him."

"And you wanted the insurance money, didn't you?"

"Yes. Maybe that sounds mercenary, but I didn't have a job and I had a child to raise, and I wasn't sure it was a suicide, Sean. The fire investigator didn't go in that direction, so I decided to keep my mouth shut. And there was another reason to stay quiet. I didn't want Blake to have to grow up thinking his father killed himself."

He gave her a long look. "Do you think Robert killed himself, Lana?"

She stared back at him, uncertainty in her eyes. "I really don't know, Sean."

"Even with Stacy in the house?"

"I don't believe he knew she was there. He had a rule that no one was to disturb him in his office when the door was closed."

"Why didn't Brett tell the police or the fire investigator about his conversation with Robert?"

"I don't think he wanted to get involved. He didn't want to get blamed for the fire or for Robert killing himself. The only person he told was me."

"And you protected him. Maybe Brett started the fire, Lana. Maybe he killed Robert in a fit of passion. Did you ever think about that?"

She gave a definitive shake of her head. "I know Brett didn't do that, because he drove across town to talk to me while I was supervising the kids at the zoo. He was with me when the fire started. He only beat me back to the house by a few minutes."

Sean sighed. He thought he'd been on to something, but her story took Brett out of the equation.

"Why didn't you get together with Brett after Robert died?" he asked.

"I couldn't look at him without seeing my baby's casket, without wondering if Robert had killed himself because of my affair, which meant Stacy had died because of me, too. Once I left San Francisco, I never spoke to him again."

"He didn't try to find you? I thought he was in love with you."

"I threw my phone away. I told my sister not to tell anyone where I was. If he looked for me, he didn't find me."

That made sense. "Is that all of it?" he asked.

"Yes. Jessica doesn't need to be worried. There's nothing else to find in that house. I destroyed the pictures Sally sent me, and if Sally already took the computer, then she has everything she needs to protect herself."

"Unless Sally sent photos and a blackmail demand to Robert that weren't on the computer," he said.

Lana's eyes widened. "I—I guess that's possible. But Sally isn't dangerous. She's conniving and sneaky and obviously likes money and blackmail, but she wouldn't hurt someone, especially someone like Jessica, who is not involved in the past."

He hoped she was right. "What about Brett? Is there anything in the house he might be worried about?"

"I can't imagine what. I heard his first wife left him. Who else would care about our old affair?" She glanced at her watch and then got to her feet. "I really have to go, Sean."

He stood up. "There's one last thing that puzzles me. The other day Jessica and I ran into Brett at Helen's new apartment. How could Brett be friends with Helen, knowing that he had an affair with you? She obviously adored her son."

"I assume that they became close because they were living across the street from each other. Since Helen didn't know about our affair, she was probably friendly to him."

"It just seems a little odd that Brett wouldn't keep his distance from Helen after everything that happened."

"I don't know what to tell you. It's been a long time since Brett and I were together. Maybe it just didn't matter anymore."

It was hard to believe that.

"I don't mean to be rude, Sean," she added. "But I hope I don't see you again."

"I can't promise that. There are still some things that don't add up for me."

She sighed. "You need to let Robert and Stacy rest in

peace. Whether Robert set the fire or it was an accident, the result was the same." She walked him to the door.

"Does your husband know about any of this?" he asked.

"He knows I lost my husband and my daughter in a fire. That's all he needs to know."

Sean stared back at her, seeing the defiance in her eyes. "You really haven't learned anything about keeping secrets, have you?"

Twenty-Two

As Sean drove back to San Francisco, he went over everything he'd learned from Lana. While she had told him a lot, not all of her story made sense, especially the part about Brett and Robert's allegedly civil conversation. But then, that was Brett's story. Since Robert was dead, only Brett knew what had really gone on between them. He doubted he was going to get a different story out of Brett than the one he'd already told Lana.

So Sean knew everything now about the neighbors and the affairs. But there was still something missing.

He heard Stacy's voice in his head again—*look in the light*.

What the hell did that mean? Where was the light? What was he supposed to see?

Had Stacy seen her father start the fire? Had she known he was trying to kill himself? Maybe she'd thought he was trying to kill her, too.

Frowning, he tapped his fingers on the steering wheel as traffic slowed to a crawl. He felt foolish for even thinking his dream had some meaning. Stacy wasn't a ghost. She wasn't coming to him in the night. It was just his subconscious trying to make sense out of what didn't make sense.

Or did things make sense? Robert had lost his job, learned his wife was having an affair and was being blackmailed by the neighbor. That was enough to drive anyone over the edge. It was a trifecta of pain.

As he thought about the first part of that trifecta, his mind turned back to Robert's job, and Lana's refusal to believe that Robert had betrayed his friend or turned into a thief.

Maybe that was his next move, another conversation with Clark Hamilton. His second conversation with Lana had yielded results. Perhaps the same thing would happen with Clark.

He pressed his foot down harder on the gas and changed lanes, eager to get back to San Francisco.

⎯⎯⎯►►◄◄◄⎯

An hour later, Sean walked into Clark's office.

"I'm sorry, Mr. Hamilton left for lunch," the receptionist told him. "If you'd like to leave him a message or make an appointment for tomorrow or later in the week, I'd be happy to take care of that for you."

"Do you know when he'll be back?" He wanted to speak to Clark today so that when he saw Jessica again, he'd be able to assure her that he'd covered all the bases and that the only person who could have taken the computer was Sally. Once they neutralized Sally, Jessica and Kyle would be safe.

"He has appointments out of the office this afternoon. It could be a while," she said.

"All right," he said, feeling frustrated. "What time does he have open tomorrow?"

She pulled up a new screen on her computer. "He can see you at three. Can I ask what this is about?"

"It's a personal matter."

"Your name is Callaway, right?"

"Yes. Sean Callaway."

"And a number where I can reach you?"

He gave her his number and told her he would see her tomorrow.

As he went down to his car, he considered his next move. It was probably time to check in with Jessica, maybe confront Sally and also speak to Brett. Maybe if they took what each person knew and put it all together, the whole picture would finally become clear.

He stepped off the elevator on the first level of the parking garage. As he walked towards his van, his gaze caught on the shiny silver bumper of a vintage Corvette. The license plate read TOPVG8M. His heart began to beat faster as he pieced out the letters TOP-OF-GAME. Hadn't Clark used that expression in their first conversation? He'd said that Robert had been at the top of his game until he got too greedy.

His head spun, memories suddenly colliding in his brain. The images that usually waited for his dreams flashed in front of his eyes.

Here in the dark garage, with the light bouncing off the bumper and the license plate, he felt like he was back in his nightmare.

Orange flames licked the night sky like a monster. Small pops turned into loud bangs, the fire leaping toward the sky with each one. Sirens in the distance. People moving around. Stacy screaming. Then she was in front of him, pleading with him as fire swirled around her.

He looked away. He was blinded by light.

"Look to the light, Sean."

He turned his head. A car was going down the street very slowly. The driver was looking at the fire. As the vehicle came under the light, he saw the license plate—TOPVG8M.

Sean's breathing came hard and fast. That license plate was right in front of him.

He moved his gaze toward the front of the parking space and saw the sign: *Reserved for Clark Hamilton.*

The truth slammed into him.

Clark Hamilton had driven by Robert's house the night of the fire. He hadn't stopped or tried to rescue Robert. And there could only be one reason why he hadn't done either of those things.

Clark had wanted the house to burn down. He'd wanted Robert to die. Why?

To pay Robert back for stealing from him? Or to protect his own secrets?

Robert had to have had something on Clark. It was the only answer that made sense. So who was the bad guy? Was it Robert or was it Clark? Or had they both been doing something shady?

He'd sort that out later. Right now he needed to warn Jessica. Clark wasn't in his office. He could be anywhere. He could be on his way to Jessica's house.

God!

What if Sally hadn't been the one to break into the house? What if it was Clark? What if there was something in that house that hadn't been destroyed in the fire?

Sean ran to his van and jumped inside, speeding through the parking garage, anxious to get outside so he could get a signal on his phone. As soon as he hit daylight, he called Jessica. It went straight to voicemail. "Jess, get out of the house, go to Nicole's. It's important. Call me as soon as you get this," he said.

He called Emma next, but she didn't answer either. He left her an urgent message to call back, then tossed the phone on to the console and prayed he was wrong about Clark.

He was only ten minutes away. They were going to be the longest ten minutes of his life.

-→»«←-

Jessica was deep into the back of the attic when she found a box full of file folders that appeared to be related to Robert's business. Her heart sped up. Maybe she'd be able to find evidence of Robert's alleged swindling. They'd been looking for proof of something. Hopefully, she'd just found it.

She sat cross-legged on the floor and pulled out the first file. She flipped through the papers seeing charts and diagrams and a breakdown of investments, but not knowing what the client wanted to invest in, she had no idea if anything was wrong. She moved on to the next file and the next, reading notes Robert had made in the margins of some reports. His words always had to do with making a move, changing over to a different stock or bond or mutual fund. He seemed to be meticulous in his notes and very thoughtful. But he was also working with big money. Some of the accounts were in the millions. Had he seen all those zeroes and decided he wanted a bigger cut? Had he suddenly realized how much control he had over the money and how much trust his clients had placed in him? Most people probably wouldn't know what Robert was doing with their money and as long as they were making money, they wouldn't care.

But what if they stopped making money? What if they suddenly wanted their money back and Robert couldn't deliver? That had to be when things had fallen apart.

That was certainly what Clark had implied. But there were usually two sides to every story. What was Robert's side?

It took her a half hour to work her way through the files, and she came up with nothing. Maybe there was nothing to find.

She shoved the box to the side and reached for a long cylinder lying on the floor. It was labeled *Blueprints for House*. That was curious. Had Robert been planning to remodel the house? She opened the lid and pulled out what she expected to be architectural drawings. But the envelope inside the cylinder had nothing to do with a home remodel. There was one word written across the front, *Clark*.

The word gave her a jolt.

She opened the file and saw a list of financial transactions, copies of checks, bank statements, and then a small notebook. It was some sort of a journal, she realized as she began to read. Robert had jotted down a chronology of events, beginning with what he'd titled *The Hook*.

She read the following paragraphs with fascination, a sense of shock growing within her as she realized that Robert was revealing exactly what had happened in his company, how it had started, and then how it had grown. She moved on to *The Swindle*.

That's where Clark's name began to figure prominently.

Robert had been putting together a case against Clark, she realized.

Robert hadn't stolen the money, taken the clients for a ride; it had been Clark.

Her chest tightened as she read on. The evidence was damning. Clark could go to jail for what he'd done.

Had Clark known that Robert was building a case against him? Had he thrown Robert out of the business too late, not realizing that Robert already knew everything?

The last part of the journal was titled *The End*. Robert listed a series of steps he intended to take, including talking to the Security Exchange Commission and the district attorney's office.

But the end hadn't come because Robert had died.

Maybe the fire hadn't been an accident or suicide but rather murder?

Her mouth went dry. Fear ran through her as she realized what she had in her hand—everything she needed to destroy Clark Hamilton.

She slowly got to her feet. She needed to call Sean. She

patted the pocket of her jeans and realized she'd left her phone in the kitchen.

The sound of footsteps made her jump. She whirled around, expecting to see Sean or maybe Sally, but the man facing her stole the breath right out of her chest. It was too late to run. Clark Hamilton was blocking her way to the door, and he had a gun in his hand.

She'd never seen a real gun up close, and the sight of it sent terror through every inch of her body.

"You know," Clark said, his gaze landing on the file in her hand.

"You said Robert stole from the company, from the clients, but it was you," she said, desperately trying to stall until help could arrive. Not that anyone was on their way. Sean was down in Seascape talking to Lana. But Sally had promised to come by after her husband left. There was still hope that her nosy neighbor might barge in.

"I made a mistake," Clark said with a dismissive shrug.

She was shocked by his casual disregard for what he'd done. The man had no conscience. "That's what you call cheating people who trusted you with their money—a mistake?"

He gave her a small, evil smile. "No. My mistake was making sure this whole house didn't burn down. I thought the papers were in Robert's office next to the garage. Apparently, I was wrong."

She swallowed back a growing knot in her throat. "You set the fire? You killed Robert and his daughter?"

His expression changed for a split second, a glittering glimpse of regret that vanished quickly. "I didn't know Stacy was here. I didn't see her."

"But she was here, and she died. How could you kill a child?"

His jaw tightened. "I told you I didn't know she was home.

I never meant to hurt her. But Robert backed me up against the wall. He was going to turn me in. All he had to do was look the other way. He owed me that. I was the one who made us all the money. It was me! My brilliant mind! Her death is on him, not me."

She couldn't believe how Clark had turned the story around in his head. "How did it happen? Did you argue, fight? Was it planned? Or did you just get the idea when you got here?"

"I came over to talk to Robert, but when I arrived, he was unconscious."

"What? That doesn't make sense."

"I don't know what happened to him. The garage door was open, so I walked right into the house. Robert was on the floor of the kitchen. He was out cold. He must have fallen and hit his head on something." Clark shrugged. "I didn't know. I didn't care. I looked through his office, but he had tons of files in there. I didn't have time to go through everything, so I decided to set a fire. It was remarkably easy. It was almost as if Robert had set it up for me."

A smile crossed his disgusting mouth, then he continued. "I shut the garage door and dragged his body over to the car. I opened up the hood. Then I knocked over everything that could burn, kerosene, gasoline—it was all right there for me. All I needed was a match, a spark and then boom. Robert went out in a blaze of glory. I was only sad that he would never know who killed him. I would have liked him to see my face one last time."

"You were friends," she said in bewilderment.

"He betrayed me."

"You betrayed him."

"No, I made him. And then he wanted to take me down."

"He threatened to go to the police," she guessed.

"Of course he did. It was a pointless threat. I always knew

there was a possibility he would find out what I was doing, so I took care to make sure he was involved. His signature was on many of the transfers of money. He couldn't take me down without taking himself down."

"But he was still going to try," she said. "That's why he kept this file."

"No one takes me down. No one." There was no apology in his voice, no hint of remorse, no effort to pretend he was anything other than a murderer, which made Jessica realize that there was no way he was letting her out of this attic.

Her stomach turned over at the realization. Clark was going to kill her. He had to; she knew too much.

Her heart ripped in two as she thought about her son. She couldn't leave Kyle alone. He'd already lost his father. He couldn't lose her, too. She had to find a way out of this. She had to fight so she could live, so she could be a mother to her son.

Her gaze darted around the attic. Clark was standing between her and the stairs. He was a big, square man, who probably had at least eighty pounds on her and he had a gun. She wasn't going to be able to rush him or get past him. But there had to be a way. She couldn't just give up.

"I would have preferred to kill Helen," Clark said in a voice that seemed almost hazy, as if he was losing all touch with reality. "After the fire, I wondered if Robert had confided in his beloved mother, but it quickly became clear that she knew nothing. She never liked me, you know. She tried to talk Robert out of going into business with me. She said she didn't trust me."

"I guess she was right," Jessica said.

His lips tightened. "She was a bitch. Maybe you are, too."

"I have a child," she said desperately. "A son. I'm all he has. Whatever you're thinking, you need to reconsider. I don't care about what you did. You can have these papers. They don't mean anything to me. I just want to go on with my life. I won't tell anyone. I don't feel compelled to share your crimes with the world."

"People always say that, but it's never true. As soon as you're safe, you'll tell someone, maybe the man you were with the other day."

She shook her head. "I can keep a secret. This has nothing to do with me. I'm just a renter. I don't care about the Emery family."

"You cared enough to come and talk to me."

She had no answer for that.

"Hand me that file," he ordered.

She hesitated for one second, afraid she was going to lose the only leverage she had. Then again, maybe if she complied, he'd let her go. She extended her hand, and he grabbed the file with greedy fingers.

"Now your cell phone."

"It's downstairs," she said, holding up her hands. "You can see it's not in my pockets."

"I wish it hadn't come to this," Clark said. "But I've protected my secrets for twenty years, I can't let you destroy everything now."

"I promise I won't tell," she repeated.

"I know you won't tell, because I'm going to make sure of that."

"If you shoot me, they'll know it was murder. They'll figure it out. Sean won't stop looking for answers. He'll find you. It's better if you just let me go."

"I don't need to shoot you. I'm going to burn down the whole house, not just the downstairs. And you're going to be nothing but a pile of ashes, just like Robert."

It was now or never. She tried to rush past him, but he flung her aside like a rag doll. She landed in a pile of boxes. She struggled to get up, to fight. Then the gun came down on the back of her head, and pain exploded in her brain. As she sunk into unconsciousness, all she could hear was the sound of the stairs coming up and the attic door closing.

Twenty-Three

Sean had only felt this kind of panic and terror once before—when he was eight years old, when he looked out of his bedroom window and saw smoke coming from around the corner, and he knew, somehow he knew. The memories hit him again, but this time things were going to be different. This time no one was going to die.

He tried to tell himself that it was possible Clark wasn't at the house, that he didn't know they were on to him, that he still felt confident that his secrets were safely hidden away.

But someone had stolen the computer. Was that Clark? Or was that Sally?

His mind spun. Did they have two people to deal with? Were they connected? Or did Clark and Sally have different interests?

He needed fewer questions and more answers.

He pounded on the steering wheel in frustration as the car in front of him stopped for a red light. Why hadn't he realized he'd seen the Corvette twenty years ago? Why had he blocked it out of his mind? He'd known all along who burned down the house, who killed Stacy, and he couldn't see it. That knowledge poured more guilt on the already huge pile that he carried.

"*It's in the light.*" He heard the voice again, but this time it sounded like his subconscious and not like Stacy.

His eight-year-old brain had locked away the pain and everything that went with it. But he knew the truth now. He floored the van with gas as the light changed.

Five more minutes, he told himself. That's all he needed. He picked up his phone and called Jessica again. Still no answer. He tried his parents' house. No answer there either. Where the hell was everyone?

"Hang on Jessica," he muttered. "I'm coming."

—➤➤◄◄—

Jessica fought her way back to consciousness. Her head throbbed with intense pain, and her chest felt incredibly tight. She tried to breathe, but she couldn't suck in any air. Coughing, she forced her eyes open. The attic was dark now, the only light coming through the one small window. The air was thick, smoky…

Fire!

The realization propelled her to her feet. Clark had said he was going to burn the whole house down this time. How long had she been unconscious? Judging by the amount of smoke— too long!

She moved toward the door, but she couldn't release the steps. Clark must have locked the door from below. She jumped up and down, hoping to jog something loose. She'd rather fall through the floor then suffocate or burn to death in this attic.

A wave of fear ran through her with that thought. She looked around the attic for something she could use to break the glass window. Maybe she could get enough air in to keep her alive until help came.

Someone would see the smoke and call the fire department. Sally and her husband were right next door.

But would Sally rush to her aid? Or did she also want to see the house burn down along with everything and everyone in it? Would she let someone die to protect her blackmail?

Jessica grabbed an old umbrella and swung it at the window. The umbrella broke but the window remained intact.

Her eyes were running now, and she was having trouble breathing. Was this how Stacy had felt? Her heart went out to the little girl who hadn't made it out of this house. She didn't want the same thing to happen to her.

Her mind turned to Sean. He'd be destroyed if she died in the fire. He might not love her the way she loved him, but he cared about her, and for her to die like Stacy…she didn't know how he would handle it.

She wished now that she'd told him she loved him. She wished she'd called Kyle before he went to school and told him she loved him, too. But it was too late for any of that.

Coughing, she sank to the floor, and prayed that help would come in time.

Sean turned the last corner and raced down the street. As he pulled up in front of the house, he saw the smoke, and the flames. Every bad feeling he'd had was coming true. It was just like the last time.

No, it wasn't!

Because he wasn't going to stand by and do nothing.

Jumping out of the car, he ran toward the house, ignoring the fear rushing through his body. The front door was locked. He picked up a brick and tossed it through the living room window. The glass shattered, and he hauled himself inside, not caring about the shards of glass that cut his arms and clothes. He tumbled into the living room and scrambled to his feet. As he ran toward the stairs, he barreled into a man coming down.

The older man stumbled back against the wall, a gasoline can in his hand, and a wild, crazy light in his eyes. Clark had gone over the edge. Sean could see the trail of gas in the hallway, and there was smoke rushing down from the upstairs. Clark must have started the fire on the second floor.

"Where's Jessica?" he demanded.

Clark didn't reply. He threw the gas can at him and pulled out a book of matches.

Sean dodged the can. Then he rushed forward and tackled Clark to the ground.

The older man fought back with ferocity.

"Not going to lose everything now," Clark ground out, swinging his fist at Sean.

The blow barely grazed his jaw. He hadn't grown up with four brothers without learning how to dodge a punch.

Now it was his turn. He slugged Clark in the face, and blood spurted from Clark's nose as he howled in pain.

Sean hit him again. While Clark was trying to recover, Sean opened the front door, grabbed Clark and threw him outside as sirens blazed in the distance.

Then he ran up the stairs. The second floor was engulfed in flames. He glanced quickly in Jessica's room but didn't see anyone. The attic stairs were up, which told him exactly what he needed to know. The switch didn't work, so he ran into Kyle's room, grabbed a chair and used it to release the latch. The trap door opened, and he pulled down the stairs.

"Jessica," he yelled, racing up the steps.

There was no answer.

He found her lying in a crumpled heap on the attic floor. She was barely breathing. He gathered her into his arms and ran back down the stairs.

She stirred. "Sean?"

"You're okay," he said, relieved to hear her voice, to see her eyes open.

But when he saw the wall of flames in front of him, he wasn't sure they were going to be okay at all. The only way out was directly in front of them. He tightened his arms around Jessica and said, "Close your eyes and hang on."

Then he ran through the flames, feeling the heat licking at his arms and the back of his neck.

Had Stacy run through fire just like this? Had she also thought she could outrun the fire?

He forced her image out of his mind.

He made it down the hall, and the stairs appeared in front of him. As he hit the first step, he saw firefighters coming through the door. The first man to reach him was his brother, Burke.

Burke looked at him in shock, then said, "Give her to me."

He shook his head. He wasn't letting go of Jessica until she was safely out of the house.

He ran down the stairs, dodging more firefighters on their way in. When he got outside, he raced to the edge of the grass and then set Jessica down, relieved to see no sparks in her hair or clothes, no burns on her beautiful face. She was breathing, but she had slipped into unconsciousness again.

"Move aside, sir," a paramedic said to him.

He didn't want to leave her, but she needed help. He got up and stood back.

Burke came to his side, putting his hand on his arm. "She's going to be okay, Sean."

"She has to be."

"Your face is bleeding."

He wiped blood from his nose and whirled around, suddenly realizing that they were missing a body. "Where is he? Where's Clark?"

"If you're talking about an older man who was beaten into unconsciousness, he's over there," Burke said, tipping his head toward the far side of the yard where a man on a stretcher was being loaded into an ambulance.

He started forward, but Burke held him back. "Let him go. Let the police handle it," he ordered.

"He set the house on fire. He tried to murder Jessica, the same way he killed Robert and Stacy."

Surprise flashed through his brother's eyes. "It was murder?"

"I should have left him inside. I should have let him die. Why the hell did I save his life?"

"Because you're not a murderer," Burke said. "And this time he didn't kill anyone." He tipped his head toward Jessica, who was sitting up now, an oxygen mask over her nose and mouth.

Sean dropped to the ground, putting his arms around Jessica. He needed to feel her body next to his, to really believe that she was going to be all right.

After a moment, she pulled back slightly and lifted the mask. "Thanks for saving me. I knew you would."

His jaw tightened, and his heart filled with emotion. She didn't know how close he'd come to not getting there in time.

"Clark killed Robert," she said. "He set the fire."

He nodded. "I know. Don't talk now. Just breathe."

"We can't let him get away with it."

"We won't. He's on his way to the hospital and then to jail. I'll make sure of that. Put the mask back on." He tried to do it for her, but she grabbed his arm.

"Wait." She gazed into his eyes. "When I thought I was going to die, I was really sorry that I never told you I loved you. I do love you. You don't have to say it back. You don't have to do anything about it. I just need you to know."

"I love you, too," he said, the words coming from deep in his heart. "Now put the damn mask back on."

She smiled and did as she was told. As he got to his feet, he saw Emma running down the street. "I couldn't believe it when I heard there was a fire here again," she said when she reached them. "Are you all right, Jessica?"

Jessica nodded, her hand dropping from the mask at Sean's warning look.

"She's going to be fine," he told Emma. "It was Clark Hamilton who set both fires, this one, and the last one. It's a long story, but I need the police to arrest him. I don't want him getting out of the hospital and disappearing."

"Don't worry. I'll take care of that. It would be nice if you had some proof though."

Jessica pulled her mask down. "I found papers in the attic. I gave them to Clark."

"Then he still has them, or they're in the house," Sean said with a sinking feeling, realizing their proof might be going up in smoke again. "Dammit."

"No way," Emma said. "Clark would have put the papers somewhere safe before he started the fire."

"His car," Sean said, looking around the street. The Corvette was at Clark's office but one of the other cars on the street had to be his. There was an SUV two doors down and a black Mercedes at the end of the block. "The Mercedes," he said. "I bet that's his car."

Emma put a hand on his arm, stopping him from taking off. "I will find his car. I will talk to the police, and I'll make sure that his office and his home are secured. Even without proof of the first fire, we've got him on this one. He's not getting away with this, Sean."

He looked into the determined blue eyes of his sister and knew he could believe her. "Thank you."

"Don't thank me. I never should have suggested you and Jessica go talk to him," she said, guilt in her eyes.

He immediately shook his head. "No, don't go there. We've all had far too many regrets where this damn house is concerned. I asked you to help. You had no way of knowing what we were getting into."

"I should have guessed. Whenever there's a question of suicide, there's usually a question of murder. I'm going to talk to the police."

As Emma left, the paramedic came back to Jessica and said, "We'd like to take you to the hospital and get you checked out."

"I don't need the hospital," Jessica protested.

"She's going," he told the medic. "You're going," he repeated, looking into her eyes.

"Kyle—"

"I'll call Nicole. She'll take care of Kyle."

"I thought I was going to leave him without a mother." Tears blurred her eyes.

He took her hand and pulled her to her feet. "Kyle is going to be fine, and so are you. I'll meet you at the hospital." He pulled the mask back over her face and said to the medic, "Take care of her. She's very important to me."

"She's very important to me."

Sean's words rang through Jessica's head on the way to the hospital, as she got thoroughly checked out and spent a good hour breathing in some really fine oxygen.

She'd told him that she loved him, and he'd said he loved her, too. It was amazing and wonderful, but as time passed, and her heart settled down to its normal beat, she wondered if they hadn't got caught up in the moment. Not that she hadn't meant what she'd said, because she had. She loved him with every ounce of her being. And if he even loved her a tenth as much, she would be okay with that.

Finally, the doctors released her, and when the nurse wheeled her into the waiting room, she almost started crying.

The room was filled with Callaways—Sean's parents, his grandparents, Emma and Max, Aiden, Drew and Ria and seventeen-year-old Megan, Shayla and Colton. She couldn't believe so many people cared enough about her to come to the hospital. Although, it was probably Sean they cared about most.

Sean crossed the room and gave her a loving smile. "It's about time."

"You're the one who insisted I get a checkup. By the way, I'm fine."

"And I am really happy to hear that. I'm taking you home."

She suddenly realized she didn't know where that was anymore.

"My home," Sean said quietly. "Actually, my parents are insisting that you come to their house, so they can feed you and watch over you and generally drive you crazy."

She gave him a watery smile. "That sounds good."

He smiled back at her. "Tell me if you feel the same way in an hour."

⇢⇥⇤⇠

Jessica did feel the same way in an hour. After settling her in on the living room couch in Jack and Lynda's house, the family had done everything they could to make her comfortable. They'd brought her a blanket, fed her an incredible dinner, made sure her tea never went cold, and were now offering her freshly baked cookies out of the oven. As she looked around the room, at all the people who'd taken her into their family, she felt incredibly blessed.

She turned to Sean, who hadn't left her side. "Your family is wonderful."

"They're your family, too," he said.

She didn't know if he meant because of Kyle or because of

him, but she didn't really care.

"I just got off the phone with Nicole," Emma said, entering the room with Max at her side. "She wanted to rush over here, and make sure you're all right, but I told her that you wanted her to stay with Kyle. She promised to keep everything perfectly normal for him until you know what you want to tell him tomorrow."

"I really appreciate that," she said, not sure yet what she wanted to share with her six-year-old.

"What happened with Clark?" Sean asked as Max sat down in the chair next to the couch.

"He's been booked for arson and attempted murder, to start," Max replied. "In conjunction with the fire department, we'll be reopening the investigation into the first fire."

"I found the file you were talking about in Clark's car," Emma said. "The evidence did not burn. He's going to pay for all of his crimes."

Jessica was more than happy to hear that. After everything they'd been through, she did not want Clark to go free. "He told me the whole story before he knocked me out. He was the one who stole from the company he owned with Robert. Robert caught him and threatened him, but Clark had been smart enough to use Robert's name on transactions. Clark framed Robert to take whatever fall was coming."

"But Robert didn't go quietly," Emma said. "He was also building a case against Clark as evidenced by the file I just read through."

"Clark thought that file had burned in the first fire," Jessica said. "But when Sean and I went to see him and told him that we'd found pictures of him and Robert in India, he worried that there was more to be found."

"I set you up," Emma said with a frown. "I should have done that interview myself."

"It still would have set Clark off," Jessica said. "Please

don't blame yourself, Emma."

"She's right," Sean put in. "I'm the one who asked you to get involved. This is on me."

"It's not on any of you," Jack interjected. "The original investigation was poorly handled."

Sean's father hadn't said much up until now. In fact, he'd been quietly watching them for the past few hours. Now he strode forward. "I was at the scene first. I should have realized it was arson. There was a clue I missed. I still don't know what it was, but it was there. And the fire investigator should have looked into the financial records and interviewed Robert's business partner as well as the neighbors. I don't know what happened to the attachments to the original report, if they were misfiled, or if there was some specific reason why the investigation was stalled. Since the investigator is deceased, it will be difficult to get answers, but I intend to look into it." He paused, looking straight at Sean. "I yelled at an eight-year-old kid for letting his friend go home when I didn't do my job as well as I could have. I'm sorry about that."

Jessica was stunned by Jack's admission, knowing that this apology meant more to Sean than he could ever say.

"Clark was clever," Sean said slowly. "He obviously hid his tracks."

Jack's expression was still grim. "That doesn't let me off the hook."

"I don't want you on the hook," Sean said. "I want this to be over. Clark pays for his crimes and the rest of us go on with our lives."

A long look passed between father and son, and then Jack slowly nodded. "All right."

"All right," Sean echoed.

"One thing I missed," Jessica said. "How did Clark get knocked out?"

"That was me," Sean told her, a proud light in his eyes. "I

ran into him when I came into the house. I should have left him in there to burn. That's what he deserved."

"I'm glad you didn't." Sean would have carried that guilt with him for the rest of his life, and she didn't want that for him.

"Well, I'm glad I got there in time," Sean said. "I wasn't sure I would."

She frowned. "What do you mean? Weren't you just coming back from Lana's? Wasn't it just great timing?"

"No. There's a lot I haven't told you, and most of it can wait. But after I left Lana's, I went to Clark's office. He wasn't there, but his Corvette was in his parking space. There was something about the way the light hit the bumper that made me pause. I found myself back in my nightmare."

"The light," she murmured. "Stacy said, *Look in the light.* Wow."

"Yeah, wow is right. I read that license plate TOPVG8M and I knew I'd seen it before. I'd seen it the night of the fire when Clark drove away from Stacy's house. He was there, watching the house burn down. It suddenly all clicked into place. I tried to call you, but you didn't answer."

"My phone was downstairs."

"I wasn't sure if Clark was at the house, but I had a bad feeling." He shook his head, his eyes still showing the fear he experienced. He brushed her hair away from her face with a tender gesture. "It was the longest ten minutes of my life."

"There's something I don't understand," Emma said, drawing Jessica's attention back to her. "And if you want to wait on all this, Jessica, we can, but I am curious if Clark told you how he started the first fire."

"It was weird," Jessica said, remembering their conversation. "Clark said he came to the house to confront Robert, but when he got there, Robert was lying unconscious in the kitchen. Apparently, he took that as a sign from the universe that he should kill him and set the house on fire."

"Who knocked out Robert if Clark didn't do it?" Emma asked in confusion.

"That was probably Brett Murphy," Sean interjected.

Jessica turned to him in surprise. "What do you mean?"

"Lana told me that she and Brett had an affair. It went on for almost a year. Sally started out blackmailing Lana, then she eventually moved on to Robert."

"We thought the affair was between and Sally and Robert."

"But it was between Lana and Brett," Sean reiterated. "Lana told me that Brett wanted her to leave her husband, but she wasn't sure she could do that. Brett got fed up with her stalling and decided to walk across the street and tell Robert his wife was cheating on him. This was about an hour before the fire broke out. Brett claimed that they had an amicable discussion. But I'm guessing now that there was a fight. Brett must have knocked Robert out and run. After the fire, when Robert's body was discovered, he probably thought he'd killed him. And when Stacy also died, there was no way Brett could tell anyone what happened. Lana's child was dead, and while Brett didn't start the fire, he may have contributed to the result."

Jessica nodded. "Because if Robert had been alert and conscious when Clark came inside, maybe Clark couldn't have done what he did. Clark did say that he never saw Stacy in the house. It's not any consolation I know."

Sean shook his head, his expression grim. "No, it's not. Stacy paid the price for everything her parents did wrong."

"I had no idea there was so much drama going on around the corner," Emma said. "Affairs, blackmail, murder. Who would have guessed?"

"I certainly didn't," Lynda said, bewilderment in her eyes. "I was friends with both Sally and Lana. I had no idea they had so many secrets."

"Speaking of Sally," Jessica said. "I confronted her earlier. I told her that I knew she broke into my house and stole Robert's computer. She didn't admit it, but I could see the truth in her eyes. Then her husband came home, and she clammed up. She promised she would talk to me later, but obviously that didn't happen."

"You shouldn't have confronted Sally on your own."

"I couldn't help myself. I was tired of being a victim." She paused, looking into his eyes. "Do you have all the answers you need now, Sean?"

"I do. Thanks for helping me, Jess."

"Thanks for saving my life."

"I can't believe you ran into a house on fire," Jack said, drawing his son's gaze back to him.

"I didn't know I had it in me," Sean said.

"I did," Jack said, surprising them all. "I know we haven't gotten along, Sean. What I've learned in the past few days has made me realize where some of your attitudes came from. I wish you would have been up front with me a long time ago. But I want you to know that I'm proud of you, son. You faced your biggest fear to save someone else's life. It's the greatest act of heroism anyone can do."

"I had to save her." Sean turned away from his father and gave her a tender smile. "Because I love her."

Emma gasped. "You what?"

"I love her," Sean repeated, his gaze holding hers. "And I think she loves me back."

"You know I do," she said.

Sean looked back at his family. "So even though it will probably drive Nicole out of her mind with worry, Jessica and I are going to be together. And whoever has a problem with that is just going to have to deal with it."

Emma laughed. "Now you sound like a Callaway, Sean."

Sean grinned. "The apple didn't fall as far from the tree as

I'd hoped. Now, Jessica and I are going upstairs to the apartment and have the rest of this conversation in private." He stood up and pulled her to her feet.

"Thanks for everything," she said, seeing nothing but smiles and love coming her way. "I can't tell you how much it means to me to have so much support. I never knew what family was really about until I met you all. I feel incredibly blessed." She blinked away a tear, feeling the emotions of the past few hours beginning to well up.

"We're blessed to have you and Kyle in our lives," Lynda said, getting to her feet. "And I'm also delighted that you and Sean have found each other."

"I'm thrilled, too," Emma declared. "Of course, I knew all along that Sean was in love with you. I was just waiting for you two to stop playing the friend game. Max, are you ready to go, too?"

Her husband got to his feet. "I'll keep in touch regarding the follow-up investigations."

"Just make sure Clark goes to jail," Sean said.

"I don't think there's any doubt that will happen," Max said.

With a few more hugs and goodbyes, Jessica and Sean made their way out of the house and up to Sean's apartment. The studio was warm, cozy and quiet, just what Jessica needed. She sat down on the foot of the bed and let out a weary sigh. She could hardly believe so much had happened since she'd gotten out of this very bed about twelve hours ago. "It's been quite a day and night," she said. "I liked hearing what your dad had to say. It's about time he realized what an incredible son he has. You two had a breakthrough."

"I think we did." He paused to run his hand through his hair, and she could tell there was something on his mind.

"What is it, Sean? What's still troubling you?"

"I had that license plate and that car in my head for twenty years. Why did it take me so long to see it?"

"It didn't mean anything until you started looking into the fire. And it was buried behind a lot of pain and guilt. Your mind would take you back to that place in your dreams, but in the daylight you forced it out of your head. You had to do that to cope with the grief. I think it's completely understandable. When you had to remember, you did. You looked in the light and you found the answer. Then you saved my life."

"You could have been killed because of me. I started the investigation. I got everyone worked up about the past and protecting their secrets."

"Hey, I'm the one who moved into the house. Even if you'd done none of those things, I would have still been cleaning out that attic. And I would have found the same information and probably started asking the same questions. But it's all over now. It's done. Stacy can rest in peace and hopefully you can as well."

"I hope so," he said. "I don't know if you've thought about this, Jess, and I hate to bring it up, but the house and probably all your stuff is gone."

"I know. I'm going to have to find somewhere new to live—again. I wonder if anyone has told Helen."

"I'm sure the police will get in touch with her. You don't need to worry about that."

"I'll think about it all tomorrow."

"Good idea." He walked across the room and dropped to his knees in front of her. Then he took her hands in his.

Her heart skipped a beat and a nervous tingle ran through her body. "Uh, Sean, what are you doing? You're not going to…" She couldn't bring herself to say the word. It seemed unimaginable but also more than a little exciting.

"Propose?" he asked with a grin. "Now that's an idea."

"Don't you think we should go on a date first?"

"A lot of dates," he agreed. "And you can relax. I'm not

proposing. Not tonight anyway." His gaze met hers, and his expression turned serious. "I know you need time to trust me, Jess, to believe that I'm not going to be like all those other musicians who came in and out of your life."

"I don't think you're like any of them. I already trust you, Sean."

"Good, because I intend to be in your life and also Kyle's."

She was relieved to hear Kyle's name cross his lips so easily. "Kyle and I are a package deal."

"Of course you are, and he's a great kid. I would be very lucky and honored to be part of his life."

She drew in an emotional breath. "That's a really nice thing to say."

"It's the truth."

"Here's another truth, Sean. I know how hard it is to step into a family, because I did that with Travis and Kyle. And I know how difficult it is to go from being a creative artist to doing average, every day boring kind of stuff. Because I did that, too. I still do. I'm not sure that's what you really want, Sean."

"There's no way in hell that being with you will be boring. Look at the past few days."

"Well, hopefully, our lives would be a little less exciting than today."

"We don't have to decide anything right now, Jess. I just want you to know that while I might have told you I loved you in the heat of the moment, I've known how I felt since the first day I met you. That's why I tried so hard to stay away from you. I knew you were going to shake things up in a big way, and I didn't know if I was ready, but I am ready." He squeezed her hands. "You're a special woman, Jess. You're very important to me, and I don't want to let you down. I want to be the man you need, the man you deserve. I want you to have the family life you pictured when you were growing up. I want the rest of your life to be everything you ever dreamed."

Tears blurred her eyes. "That's the most incredible thing anyone has ever said to me."

"I mean every word," he said, passion in his voice.

"I want you to have your dreams, too, Sean, even if they take you away from me. When I saw you on the stage at Drake's, I knew you belonged there."

"Maybe occasionally on a Friday night," he conceded. "I'm always going to want to make music, but my dream is you. It always has been; I just didn't know it. You're my Moonlight Girl, Jess. That girl never had a face until I met you. Then I knew who she was."

Her heart swelled with emotion. "It's not fair. You're a songwriter. You're much better at words than I am."

He smiled and used his thumb to wipe a tear off her cheek. "Just tell me how you feel."

She thought for a moment, wanting to get the words exactly right. "I feel happy, somewhat amazed, a little scared but mostly excited about the future."

"That sounds about right," he said with a loving smile.

"Okay. So I have one more question," she said.

"What's that?"

"Are you ever going to kiss me?"

He grinned. "I was just getting to that." He cupped her face with his hands, gave her a long, adoring look, and then gave her a kiss that promised everything she'd ever wanted and more.

Epilogue

One month later

Ashbury Studios was packed with people for the grand opening party, many of them Callaways. Jessica walked through the long hallway from the parking lot, exchanging hellos and hugs with Sean's cousins, aunts and uncles, and grandparents. She was thrilled to see so much family support. But the two people she hadn't seen yet were Sean's parents, Lynda and Jack.

While Jack and Sean had made some repairs to their relationship, they still had a long way to go, and Jessica knew that Sean really wanted his dad to show up for the party, to see what he'd been working on and saving for the past few years.

When she reached the main studio, she found more Callaways, including Sean. He was standing with Kyle and Brandon, Nicole, Ryan, and Emma.

When he saw her, a happy smile spread across his face as he said, "That took awhile."

"I know. The realtor was late. What have I missed?"

"You missed nothing, but I missed you." He gave her a quick kiss.

Emma rolled her eyes. "It's true what they say. The most stubborn bachelors fall the hardest."

Sean laughed. "I can't deny that I've fallen hard."

"So did you get the house?" Nicole asked.

Jessica nodded. "Yes, no more renting for me. I now officially own a two-bedroom townhouse. And the best part is that it's brand new. There are no secrets within the walls, no old mystery to be solved. I am going to be the very first owner. I am very excited about it."

"Mom is going to put shark wallpaper up in my room," Kyle announced to the group. "I got to pick it out already. And bunk beds, too, because Brandon likes the bottom, and I like the top."

"It's going to be awesome," Sean said, patting Kyle's shoulder.

"Well, if it isn't the Callaway clan out in full force," Hunter said, joining the group. He gave them all a broad smile. "What do you think?"

"Amazing," Emma said. "And I think I speak for all of us. But we can't believe that you and Sean kept this a secret for so long."

"Your brother's choice, not mine," Hunter replied. "Now who wants to see the control room?"

"Me," Kyle said immediately. "And Brandon wants to see it, too."

Brandon didn't add his voice but he did look excited at the thought of going into a room with a lot of shiny buttons and switches.

"Just be careful, Kyle," Jessica warned. "Listen to Hunter, and don't touch anything."

"Don't worry. I'll watch them," Hunter said.

"I'll help you," Ryan added, following Hunter and the boys into the control room.

"So how did you get enough money to do this, Sean?" Nicole asked curiously.

"I saved my pennies."

"Must have been a lot of pennies. And here I thought you were just a free spirited rock and roller."

"I'll always be that," he said with a grin.

"Yeah, but now you're a businessman, too," Nicole said. "It's going to take some getting used to."

"I'm still the same guy." Sean paused as one of his band members called his name, then excused himself. "I'll be right back."

As Sean left, Nicole turned to her and said, "Emma and I want to see your space, too."

"It's not my space yet," she replied. "I'm still in the very early stages of figuring out if I can really run a dance studio all by myself. And whether or not I can make the numbers add up. I spent a lot of money on the townhouse. But I can show you what it looks like."

"I have a feeling you'll be able to make it work," Nicole said.

"I hope so." She led them up to the second floor. As they stepped into the open space, she said, "We'll eventually divide this area into two studios. There will be lots of mirrors and a good floor. Down the hall, there will be a small office and two dressing rooms."

"I love the light," Nicole said as they walked toward the middle of the room.

"It's what I noticed first," Jessica admitted. "The big windows and the high ceilings make you feel like you're dancing in a very special place."

"Are you going to teach adults?" Emma asked. "I wouldn't mind taking a class. Nicole would love it, too, wouldn't you, Nic?"

Nicole immediately shook her head. "I have two left feet. I was never good at dancing and the only thing I liked about ballet class was the pink tutu."

"I'm sure Jessica will let you wear one," Emma teased.

"I'd love for you to take a class," Jessica said. "I want to offer as much variety as I can for adults and kids."

"So much for not having a plan," Nicole said with a pointed look. "You've thought about this a lot."

"I haven't been able to stop thinking about it."

"Then do it, unless you're worried about spending so much time with Sean," Emma teased.

"Not a chance. I'm crazy about that man, and I'm glad you're both okay with Sean and me being together. You're my best friends here in the city, and you're both really important to me."

"Aw," Emma said, coming over to give her a hug. "We feel the same way about you."

"We do," Nicole agreed, also giving her a hug. "We're all family now."

"We are," Jessica said with a nod. "When I was a little girl, all I wanted was a family. That was my real dream. It wasn't to dance on Broadway or be in a ballet company. Sure, I wanted those, too, but in my heart, all I really needed was love. I had it once with Travis but that didn't last. And his family couldn't stand me, so I never belonged with them. But now I have you both and the whole crazy Callaway clan. I have sisters and brothers, nieces and nephews, and grandparents. I'm overwhelmed with how wonderful and accepting everyone is."

"I think you left someone out."

She turned at the sound of Sean's deep voice.

"What about me?" he asked. "Don't you have me, too?"

"Yes, but you are in your own category."

"That's what I like to hear." He turned to his sisters. "What do you guys think of this space?"

"It's great," Nicole answered. "I can picture a bunch of little girls in ballet clothes running around. I think Jessica is going to create a fantastic dance studio, and you, my brother, are going to have a really successful music studio. The two of you are on your way. I'm thrilled for both of you."

"I am, too," Emma added. "You should be proud, Sean."

"I'm feeling good I have to say, and my life is even better, because I have Jessica." He gave her a loving smile. "Did you tell them we're going to live together?"

"I didn't know if you wanted everyone to know," she said.

"I have no more secrets," Sean said. He smiled at Emma and Nicole. "Jess and I are going to share her new place until we get married."

Emma's jaw dropped. "You're getting married? When? And where's the ring?"

"We haven't gotten that far yet," Sean said.

"Sean, dear brother, you don't propose without a ring," Nicole said.

Jessica smiled as both of Sean's sisters exchanged an exasperated look. "Don't blame him," she said. "I told Sean I wanted us to pick out a ring together."

"Make sure it's a big one," Emma said. "Apparently, my younger brother is good at saving money."

Sean laughed. "Good point."

"Do you have a date in mind?" Nicole asked.

"We're thinking this summer," Jessica said. "But it's not going to be a big fancy deal. It will just be family."

"With our family, that will be a big deal," Emma said. "I'm so happy for you both. I can't wait to have another sister. When are you going to tell the family?"

"In about five minutes," Sean said, checking his watch. He smiled at Jessica. "Are you ready?"

"Absolutely."

Emma and Nicole led the way down the stairs. As they reached the first floor, they ran into Jack and Lynda.

Everyone seemed to drop back as Sean faced his father, the man who had never heard him play live. Jessica could feel the sudden tension in the air, and silently wished for one of them to speak, preferably Jack. This was Sean's night. And he deserved a night that was wonderful and perfect.

Jack slowly extended his hand. "This is an incredible studio, Sean. You've impressed the hell out of me."

"That must be a first," Sean said as he shook his father's hand.

"I'm looking forward to hearing you play," Jack added.

"I'm glad you came. I think you're going to enjoy the show." Sean turned to Jessica. "Shall we kick things off?"

As they left his parents and walked through the crowd of Callaways, she whispered, "Are you sure you don't want this night to just be about you and the studio?"

"Not a chance. My life would be nothing without you." He motioned for Kyle to come over and join them. Then he swung the little boy up in his arms and the three of them stepped up to the microphone.

"I want to thank you all for coming," Sean said. "Before we get into the music, I have a special announcement to make. This beautiful woman has agreed to be my wife, and this amazing kid is going to let me be his stepdad."

The crowd erupted into applause and shouts of congratulations.

Sean gazed down to Jessica. "I love you so much."

"I love you back," she said softly.

"When are we getting married?" Kyle asked with an excited grin.

She laughed. "Very soon."

Sean set Kyle back on his feet and then pulled her into his arms. "I'm the luckiest man on earth."

"And I'm the luckiest woman. Now it's time for you to sing me a song."

"I wrote a new one just for you."

"What's it called?"

"*All A Heart Needs*. Because all I need is you, Jess."

"Right back at you." She pulled his head down and gave him a kiss. Then she walked back to her family and her friends as the man she loved sang his heart out—just for her.

THE END

Keep reading for an excerpt from

the next book in the Callaway series

THAT SUMMER NIGHT
(Coming September 2015!)

ONE

Shayla Callaway woke up in a sweat, her heart racing, her mind spinning with horrible and disturbing images that came both from her imagination and her memories. It took a moment for her to remember that she wasn't in a remote village in Colombia, but in the San Francisco apartment she shared with another medical resident. She'd been home for five days, but she had yet to fully process what had happened when her residency in South America had been cut short by a terrible night of violence.

A persistent ring finally broke through the haze of her nightmare. She hoped it wasn't the hospital, asking her to come in and cover a shift. She wasn't ready to go back to work yet. Her hands needed to stop shaking first. She had two weeks before her next rotation started, and she hoped by then she'd be ready to return to the career she'd been pursuing for the past eight years.

But there was no familiar hospital number flashing across her phone, just the word *blocked*.

Adrenaline ran through her already hyperaware body. She drew in a breath and told herself there was nothing to be afraid of. The phone stopped ringing. She waited for the voicemail to light up. Instead, the phone began to ring again. Whoever was calling was persistent. It could be a wrong number, but she didn't think so. She grabbed the phone and answered with a breathless, "Hello?"

"Shayla?"

The male voice crackling on the other end of the line was the same one that had been haunting her dreams. It belonged to Dr. Robert Becker, her friend, her mentor, and the brilliant doctor who had led her research team in Colombia. He'd been missing since a trio of armed gunmen had broken into the clinic killing two people and leaving a trail of injuries and trauma behind. But Robert had not been one of the dead or the injured; he'd been unaccounted for—until now.

Her hand tightened around the phone. "Robert? Where are you? Are you all right? I've been so worried about you."

"I need your help Shayla."

She frowned as static filled the line, cutting off the rest of his sentence. "I can't hear you." She got out of bed and walked around, hoping to improve the line between them.

"Can you hear me now?" he asked.

"It's better, but you're still breaking up."

"Listen Shayla, I don't have much time. I need you to go to the lab and get the gift you gave me for my last birthday. You remember what that was, don't you?"

"Uh—you mean—"

"Don't say it out loud," Robert said quickly. "I don't know who's listening."

"What are you talking about? Who would be listening?"

"I can't tell you over the phone. I'm in trouble, Shayla. I need you to give the present to my brother, Reid, and ask him to bring it to me on Sunday."

"Your brother? Isn't he in the Army somewhere?"

"He's out now, and he's my only hope of getting out of this

alive."

She didn't like the sound of that. "Robert, what is going on?"

"It's complicated. I can't explain now. I just need you to do what I'm asking."

The urgency in his voice heightened her worry. "Why don't I talk to the police, to my brother-in-law, Max? He can help you with whatever trouble you're in."

"No. This is bigger than the local cops. I can't trust anyone right now but you and my brother. You need to find Reid and tell him to meet me."

"Where?"

Robert hesitated. "I want you to tell him something, and you have to say it exactly this way. Are you ready?"

"Go ahead."

"It is not the mountain we conquer but ourselves. Say it, Shayla."

"It is not the mountain we conquer but ourselves. What does that mean?" she asked, her bewilderment growing with each cryptic word.

"My brother will know. Tell him Sunday afternoon, four o'clock."

"Wait. Sunday is three days from now. Why so long?"

"I'm not sure how long it will take me to get there or for you to convince my brother to help me."

"Why wouldn't he help you?"

"I'm sure he'll tell you. I also need that present, Shayla. Has anyone gone through the lab since you got back, anyone you didn't recognize?"

"Yes. The day after I returned, I went into the lab, and there were two men in the lab. They said they were from the FBI and that they were looking for information that might be helpful in locating you, Robert."

"What were their names?"

She had to think for a moment. "I think one was Special Agent Frost. I don't remember the other one's name. Do you know them?"

"No. I have to go, Shayla."

More static came across the line. "Wait, where am I going to find your brother? Do you have his number?"

"No, but his best friend, Jared Stone, owns the Cadillac Lounge. He'll know where to find Reid. Don't tell anyone about this call but him, Shayla. Do you understand? No one at the hospital. No one in the police department. No one at Abbott."

"What about your ex-wife? Lisa came to see me yesterday, asking if I'd heard from you."

"Shit!" he swore, adding, "Definitely not Lisa. As far as anyone knows, you haven't seen me or heard from me in a week. Got it? And don't remove the present from the lab if there is anyone else there. This is very important Shayla. I need to be able to trust you. My life might depend on it."

"Of course you can trust—" The connection broke before she could get the last word out.

She stared at the phone, a dozen questions running around in her head. She tried to call Robert back, but the call wouldn't go through. She set her phone down on the bed and glanced at the clock. It was almost eight a.m., and early morning light filtered through the part in the curtains. At least, the sun was coming up. She didn't have to think about trying to force herself to go back to sleep for another few hours.

She walked across the room and stood in front of the noisy fan that was doing little more than moving the warm air around. Normally, San Francisco in the summer was cool and foggy, but an unusual July heat wave had hit the day before, and it was hot even now. Today would be a scorcher.

As the cool air hit her body, she thought about Robert's call. He had been agitated, nervous, fearful, which were not emotions that she normally associated with him. He was usually calm, purposeful, analytical, methodical—all the things a good scientist should be. But the man on the phone had sounded desperate and out of control. What on earth was he involved in?

She thought about his two requests. One would be easy. The other might be more difficult. She'd known for Robert for almost ten years, and he had only mentioned his brother to her one time and that was when his brother had won some prestigious Army medal for saving the lives of several men in his unit. Other than that, she knew nothing about Reid Becker. But she would do what Robert had asked her to do, because Robert had had her trust and respect since she was sixteen years old.

She'd met Robert during her first week of college. Having skipped two grades, she'd been an awkward sixteen-year-old freshman year, able to compete academically but completely out of her depth when it came to social relationships. Eight years older than, Robert had been a third year medical resident who'd come to speak to her chemistry class about a career in medicine.

After that lecture, he'd taken her under his wing, telling her he'd hit college when he was fifteen and knew exactly what it felt like to be isolated by a brilliant mind and social immaturity. Over the years they'd kept in touch as she made her way through medical school, and Robert gained a reputation as a brilliant medical researcher. When she'd had a chance to take a ten-week residency under Robert's lead in Columbia, she had jumped at the chance, never imagining how it would all end.

Turning away from the fan, she walked into the bathroom and stripped off her damp tank top and pajama bottoms and then stepped into the shower. She let the steady cool spray beat down on the tight muscles in her neck and shoulders, hoping it would chase away the tension created by her nightmare and intensified by Robert's call.

After her shower, she dressed and went into the small kitchen to make breakfast. While the coffee was brewing, she popped a piece of bread into the toaster and then glanced around the kitchen, finding comfort and reassurance in the comfortable and somewhat familiar mess; not that she'd been in the apartment long enough for anything to feel that familiar. She'd been living at her parents' house up until three months ago, saving her money to pay off her enormous medical school debt.

As one of eight kids, she'd known from a very young age that getting herself through school was going to be up to her. Her parents had told each of her five brothers and two sisters that they would help with the first two years of college tuition but after that they were on their own. While she still had plenty of debt to handle, when her friend, Kari, had asked her to move into her apartment so she and her roommate could split the rent three ways, she'd said yes, eager to be on her own and also closer to the hospital. She was no longer a student. She was a doctor, and she needed to make her way in the world. Unfortunately, that world seemed a lot scarier now than it had a few weeks ago.

She stiffened, hearing a key in the lock. Kari, a petite brunette, who usually looked cheerful and energized, entered the room with a decidedly weary step. She'd been on duty the last twelve hours.

"You're up early," Kari said in surprise. "Too hot to sleep?"

She nodded, happy to have the heat as an excuse. She hadn't told anyone what had happened in Colombia, not even her family. While the Callaways were wonderfully supportive, she couldn't bring herself to talk to them about that night of terror. Maybe later, when it felt less new. Maybe then it would be easier to talk about.

"The E.R. was hopping all night," Kari continued. "People sure get trigger happy when the temperature rises."

Kari had no idea that her casual words set off another wave of panic within Shayla. She was supposed to work in the E.R. on her next rotation. How was she going to handle gunshot wounds and stabbings and more violence? She'd always thought of herself as a strong person, until now…

Shayla tried to drive the anxiety away by changing the subject. "Do you want some coffee? I just made a fresh pot."

"No thanks. The last thing I need is more caffeine. I'm going to try to get at least three hours of sleep before I go back to the hospital. Dr. Emery is going to let me watch a hysterectomy this afternoon."

"That's great," she said, knowing that Kari's goal every day was to get into as many surgeries as possible.

"What are you doing today?"

"I'm not sure. I may go in to the lab."

Kari nodded approval. "Maybe it will be good for you to get back to work. You haven't been yourself since you got back from Colombia. Has there been any news about Dr. Becker?"

"No," she lied.

"Well, I hope he's all right and that he shows up soon." Kari stifled a yawn. "I'm going to hit the sack. See you later."

As Kari left the room, the front door buzzer rang. Shayla almost jumped out of her skin. It was too early for visitors. She walked over to the intercom and warily said, "Yes?"

"It's Emma. Can I come up for a quick second?"

Shayla inwardly groaned. She'd been avoiding Emma's calls for the last five days; she should have guessed her big sister wouldn't give up that easily. "Kari is sleeping. I'll come down." Maybe if she didn't let Emma into the apartment, she could get rid of her more quickly.

That Summer Night releases September 2015!

About The Author

Barbara Freethy is a #1 New York Times Bestselling Author of 42 novels ranging from contemporary romance to romantic suspense and women's fiction. Traditionally published for many years, Barbara opened her own publishing company in 2011 and has since sold over 5 million books! Nineteen of her titles have appeared on the New York Times and USA Today Bestseller Lists.

Known for her emotional and compelling stories of love, family, mystery and romance, Barbara enjoys writing about ordinary people caught up in extraordinary adventures. Barbara's books have won numerous awards. She is a six-time finalist for the RITA for best contemporary romance from Romance Writers of America and a two-time winner for DANIEL'S GIFT and THE WAY BACK HOME.

Barbara has lived all over the state of California and currently resides in Northern California where she draws much of her inspiration from the beautiful bay area.

For a complete listing of books, as well as excerpts and contests, and to connect with Barbara:

Visit Barbara's Website:
www.barbarafreethy.com

Join Barbara on Facebook:
www.facebook.com/barbarafreethybooks

Follow Barbara on Twitter:
www.twitter.com/barbarafreethy